WILD HUNT

THE GATEKEEPER'S FATE: BOOK TWO

EMMA L. ADAMS

1

Never turn down an invitation from a faerie.

I'd learned that lesson earlier than most people did, but *accepting* an invitation from a faerie is often as likely to be fatal as the alternative. Really, it was better to hope not to be contacted by a faerie at all. Not that everyone has a choice in the matter. I should know.

I'd been waiting for the Sidhe to knock on the door of my brand-new rental house for almost two weeks when that day finally came one cold October morning. When I heard a light tapping on the front door, I peered through the gap in the living room curtains to see the outline of a tall, male Sidhe standing outside. From the blue-and-silver attire he wore, he must have been a delegate from the Winter Court, which meant he'd come to drag me before his Queen in order to explain why I'd been avoiding her for the past few weeks. Or however much time had passed in Faerie since my last visit.

Drawing in a deep breath, I opened the door. "Can I help you?"

"I hope you can." The Sidhe's bright blue eyes were undoubtedly Winter fae, but his phrasing didn't sound like a noble's. Up close, his clothes were a little *too* shiny. A glamour, and not a great one. He must be half-fae, not full Sidhe, which meant he hadn't come from the Winter Court after all.

A momentary rush of relief warred with a buzz of irritation at the universe for dragging out my fate as long as humanly possible. I *knew* the Unseelie Queen would raise hell when she finally learned why I'd been avoiding her, but sometimes I wished she'd get it over with.

"Well?" I said, with a little more impatience than necessary. "What is it you want my help with, then?"

"I'm Leyton, and I'd like to hire you," he said.

"Hire me?" I echoed. "If you're looking for the Goodfellow Detective Agency, their office isn't far from here. I've worked with them before, but I'm not an employee."

"I would prefer the help of someone who has experience with Unseelie fae," he said.

Alarm bells rung in my skull. "You mean with the Court? Or with Winter magic itself?"

"Neither."

"Then it shouldn't be a problem for you to ask the Goodfellow Detectives," I said. "I'm still on call if they need my expertise, but it's bad for my reputation to show biases in favour of Winter over Summer or vice versa."

Puck might not be a certified detective as far as the mortal realm's standards applied, but most half-faeries cared little for qualifications, and he had the paperwork to back up his status. He also didn't have the threat of the

Unseelie Court hovering over his shoulder like an axe waiting to strike.

"If you're sure," he said doubtfully.

"I am," I said. "I'll go wake my assistant, and we'll head to the office."

How he'd got hold of my address was a question I'd have to ask later, once I'd persuaded Roseanne to vacate her room. I didn't blame her for spending all her free time in what was likely the nicest bedroom she'd ever had in her fifteen years, though if I were her parent and not her entirely unqualified guardian, I might have had concerns about her not getting outside more.

As far as I was concerned, though, a teenage death faerie with some major trauma deserved every luxury I could give her.

I rapped on her bedroom door with my knuckles. "Roseanne?"

"Come in," came the sleepy reply.

I pushed the door inward, revealing Roseanne sprawling on the narrow single bed in her cupboard-sized room. Since she'd moved in, she'd arranged the furniture so that the wardrobe blocked the window and gave the room a cave-like appearance, while random bits of junk like stones and leaves were strewn on the floor, along with a couple of books Ilsa had loaned her. When I'd found Roseanne, she'd hardly had any possessions to call her own. I didn't have much of my own either, so I'd spent the last couple of weeks helping her with the essentials while trying not to burn through all the money I'd earned as a result of stopping the Wild Hunt from overrunning the city.

"We have a client," I told her. "He came to us first, but I

suggested we'd get Puck and Hawk involved, since they're the experts."

Roseanne yawned. "What's he want?"

"Not sure yet," I said. "Something that requires an expert on the Unseelie, supposedly. Maybe he's got a nest of redcaps in his house."

"Fun." Roseanne sprang off the bed and fetched a pair of serrated knives from a pile in the corner before sheathing them at her belt. Her clothes were as battered as mine, but she made her secondhand outfits look good, while I looked more like I'd raided a jumble sale. At one time, I'd been able to use glamour to make myself the best-dressed person in the room. But these days, I had to do my best with the limited options on offer. I didn't have the natural stunning beauty of a half-faerie, either, unlike Roseanne, with her glossy hair, blemish-free skin, and long lanky frame. She shrugged into her tattered coat. "Hope he's offering a bunch of money."

So did I, considering how much I'd already spent on both the deposit on our new house and on my unexpected teenage charge. Still, I was the one who'd had the smart idea of taking the Morrigan's daughter under my wing— in almost a literal sense, since her mother's magic was still rattling around in my veins.

Hence the inevitable upcoming visit from the Unseelie Court. When I'd taken out a magical loan from the Morrigan in order to stop some defectors from the Wild Hunt from enacting a ritual to summon a death god, I hadn't expected to *keep* that magic. Weeks later, though, it had yet to abate, while the goddess herself had vanished from the chains that bound her to her throne without leaving a single trace behind. I didn't doubt for a second that I'd be the one the Sidhe blamed when they found her gone, despite preventing the Wild Hunt from using said death god as a sacrifice in exchange for gaining their immortality back, with the Courts as potential collateral damage. When in doubt, blaming the human was a reliable go-to strategy.

Especially when I'd denied the Unseelie Queen the chance to snag Roseanne as her own.

I headed back downstairs, hoping our client wouldn't run screaming when he realised who my assistant actually was. Helping stop the Wild Hunt's rampage had gone a long way towards repairing my reputation in the local half-faeries' eyes, as well as towards their gradual acceptance of my teenage death faerie housemate, but that didn't mean we hadn't hit a few bumps along the way. The Morrigan was a source of terror both inside and outside Faerie, since even most Sidhe found the giant crow-shifter unnerving, while death fae in general were considered untrustworthy. As a result, I did my best to act as a shield between Roseanne and anyone who might judge her for her parentage. Given my own chequered family history, I had entirely too much experience in that area.

I entered the living room with Roseanne on my heels. "Leyton, this is my assistant, Roseanne."

"Oh," said Leyton. "It's… a pleasure to meet you."

His tone was a little wary but not overtly hostile. Being Unseelie, he'd be aware of the Death Kingdom as an entity within the Winter Court, but I doubted he'd ever ventured there in person. Few did, if they had a choice in the matter.

After leaving the house, we walked out of half-blood territory and made our way down the cobbled street to the nondescript office standing on the corner, marked simply with a sign that read Goodfellow Detectives. I didn't bother knocking before pushing the door inward, revealing a sizeable office whose wood-panelled walls were decorated with paintings depicting landscapes reminiscent of the Summer Court. Puck and Hawk had added a couple more since my last visit, with images of vibrant flowers and trees surrounding grassy clearings and wildlife which actually moved in and out of the picture frames. The Aes Sidhe's glamour was capable of creating images which looked realistic enough to be mistaken for the real thing—even by other fae.

Puck sat behind the desk when I walked in, idly twirling a pen in his hand. The half-Sidhe descendent of the notorious trickster Robin Goodfellow wore a smart-casual getup of a white shirt and a pair of dark trousers, while his hair gleamed in the shifting colours of autumn leaves with gold and red tints mingling with flaming orange and dark brown. Gold flecked his Summer-green eyes, too, while his brows rose at the sight of the tacky glamour our visitor wore.

"Hey, Holly." He dropped the pen and rose smoothly to his feet. "Who's this?"

"Leyton here says he wants to hire a detective," I said. "I figured that description applies more to you and Hawk than to me."

Leyton's gaze travelled from Puck over to Hawk, who'd just walked out of the back room. "Aes Sidhe? You didn't mention they were Aes Sidhe."

"Should I have?" It wasn't a big secret, or so I thought, but Puck frowned at Leyton, and so did Hawk. The second Aes Sidhe had medium-brown skin and wore his dark hair cut short, while he dressed in the same smart-casual clothing as Puck did.

Hawk's Summer-green eyes studied the newcomer. "Is there a problem?"

"Depends if you're glamouring me or not," said Leyton. His own glamour was glaring enough to be seen across the room, but he hovered near the door as if contemplating fleeing the office.

"We're not glamouring you," Puck said. "We're running a business here, and we don't make a habit of putting spells on our clients. Tell me what you want to hire us for, and I'll let you know if we can help you."

"All right." Leyton kept one eye on the moving paintings as he walked towards the desk. I hadn't expected working with Aes Sidhe to be a deal-breaker, though they did have a varied reputation among the other fae. Most had believed them to have died out after their Court had split away from Summer when their leader had a falling out with the Erlking and gone into hiding underground. It made sense that their sudden reappearance would conjure a flurry of rumours. "There's a fae in my house who's causing trouble. I hoped you could get rid of it."

"What kind of fae?" I asked.

Leyton's attention fixated on me. "A dead one."

"Death fae?" Oh boy. Beasts like the sluagh and death stealers weren't exactly uncommon in this realm, post-faerie invasion, but that didn't mean I was particularly keen to see another one after the Wild Hunt's attack a few weeks ago. Unseelie magic in general was fuelled by death and decay, as opposed to the life energy which powered Seelie magic, but the death fae were considered unpleasant even by Winter's standards.

Leyton shook his head. "Not a death fae. A ghost."

Oh. "Have you asked the necromancer guild?"

"I didn't think they could see faerie ghosts."

"Some can." Though very few people had both the spirit sight *and* the ability to see through faerie glamour, since the latter was almost exclusively possessed by half-faeries. The sole human exceptions I knew about were my cousins, Ilsa and Morgan. "Can you tell me more about this ghost?"

"It won't leave my house," he said. "It froze all my water pipes and then took up refuge in the bathroom and won't come out."

Oh boy. If he'd been unlucky enough to end up with an Unseelie poltergeist in his house, I understood why he'd wanted my help, but there was nothing a non-necromancer could do to get rid of a ghost in a permanent manner.

"We can't banish it," I said, "but I might be able to convince the spirit to leave the house."

Banishing the ghost permanently was beyond my capabilities, but if we drove Leyton's spiritual squatter out of half-blood territory, then at least we wouldn't have to deal with the other fae bitching at me for inviting my necromancer cousins into their homes. Roseanne had the ability to see the dead whether they were fae or not, but she wasn't old enough to apply to join the guild herself, while Puck and Hawk would only be able to see the spirit if it chose to make itself visible to them. No, this was definitely a job for the necromancer guild, not us.

"All right," said Leyton. "Are you free to come over now, or do you need more time to prepare?"

"You guys can go ahead," said Hawk. "I'll stay behind and watch the office."

Hawk usually opted to stay behind when the rest of us ran dangers, since his own magical skills were limited to healing and glamour and he freely admitted that fighting wasn't his forte. Puck, meanwhile, had the ability to transform into animals, flames, and piles of leaves, among other things—a by-product of his trickster fae heritage. A ghost ought to be easy enough for him to scare off if my powers of persuasion didn't work.

I fell into step with him as we walked, letting Leyton overtake us and lowering my voice. "Why'd he think you were glamouring him?"

"Some Aes Sidhe can cast a glamour the instant they set eyes on you," he replied. "The strongest can cast a powerful influence over others' emotions and weave illusions so real that they're indistinguishable from the magic of the faerie realm itself. I'm guessing he picked up on some of the rumours."

"Does that mean your animal forms are glamour?"

"Not exactly. My animal forms are more than a regular illusion, though with the Aes Sidhe, there's a more fluid division between glamour and reality than most fae are familiar with. The strongest can make illusions become real, and our Queen's skill was so vast that she was even able to use her glamour to create an army of living, breathing soldiers."

"Damn." I vaguely recalled Hazel mentioning Queen Etaina's army of creepy, perfectly obedient clones, but it'd somehow slipped my mind that she'd *created* them like some kind of mad scientist in a lab. The battle in the Summer Court had ended with most of the Queen's forces laying their lives down for her in a literal sense, but the knowledge that they might never have had anything resembling free will made goose bumps trail down my spine. "No wonder the Courts felt threatened when the Aes Sidhe resurfaced."

Faerie itself was formed of layer upon layer of illusions so deep that even the Sidhe didn't know all its secrets, though that knowledge had likely died out along with their predecessors. The era of the Ancients had been centuries, if not millennia, before most of the current Sidhe had been born, and few had encountered the gods who'd once walked their lands.

Roseanne skipped over to join us. "We're going ghost-hunting, are we? Need me to get some salt?"

"If you didn't eat it all," I said, earning a grin from Puck. "Salt's more useful for getting rid of zombies than ghosts, though. If we can't scare it into leaving, we'll ask a necromancer to bring some candles for a proper banishment."

"I thought Ilsa didn't need to use candles," said Roseanne.

"She doesn't, but the guild likes things to be done the proper way," I said. "I bet the other half-faeries will be less than thrilled at me for bringing anyone from the guild into their territory as it is."

My cousin Ilsa wielded the talisman of the Gatekeeper of Death, which gave her a permanent link to the gates of the afterlife and the ability simply to shove any wayward spirit through if need be. Wraiths were trickier, being the spirits of long-deceased Sidhe, but even they weren't a match for her. In hindsight, it shouldn't have surprised me that Roseanne had taken a shine to Ilsa after she'd got over her nerves and introduced herself. I'd already known that Ilsa wouldn't have any issues with her parentage, but Roseanne was naturally wary of meeting anyone new after being burned so many times in the past.

All the same, even Ilsa didn't know I'd retained the Morrigan's power long after it was supposed to have returned to its owner. Nor did she know the goddess of death had vanished and that I had a private suspicion that I might have played a part when I'd pushed her magic to its limits during the fight with the Wild Hunt. Specifically, when I'd thrown aside the usual laws on raising the dead and used her power to heal Puck from a fatal wound.

In fairness, the Morrigan's magic wasn't subject to the usual laws in this realm *or* Faerie, but even I hadn't expected that forcing her formidable healing magic upon Puck's bleeding, dying body would actually bring him back from the brink of death. Her regenerative magic was so immense that iron chains had little effect on her, but I'd never seen her use that power on another person. I'd acted entirely on instinct, out of desperation, and it wasn't until I'd seen the empty throne where the Morrigan had once sat in chains that it occurred to me that the formidable queen of the death fae might have had a limit to her abilities after all.

She'd *told* me that the powers she'd loaned me had been a temporary favour, and she was as incapable of lying as any Sidhe of the Courts. I'd thought her invincible, one of the last true immortals in Faerie, and if the Sidhe found me guilty of her absence, I'd envy the humans whose rotting corpses filled the moat around the Morrigan's empty lair.

I did my level best to shake off all thoughts of the

Morrigan as Leyton opened the gate to half-blood territory and led us to a plain brick cottage with a neat garden. A familiar chill hit me the instant he opened the front door, the unmistakable cold aura of Winter magic coupled with the emptiness of the grave. Suppressing a shiver, I followed Leyton into the hall and up a staircase on the right.

At the top of the stairs, he gestured through an open door. A layer of ice covered the entire inside of the bathroom, thickening around the bath and sink as the taps flowed with water which turned to ice when it hit the floor. A ghost hovered on the ceiling, his silvery hair transparent, blue eyes indicating his nature as a Winter fae. If the ice wasn't enough of a clue, that was. He looked about the same age as Leyton, which meant nothing, because it was hard to tell with faeries. He might have been in his teens or his thirties for all I knew.

Then he spotted us, and a spark ignited in his blue eyes. "Get out, intruders!"

2

I rolled my eyes at the ghost. "You're the one intruding on someone else's property. Bugger off and move on."

Necromancers usually had a few stock speeches to convince ghosts to move on to the afterlife, ranging from the calm and reassuring words they used to break the news to the ones who didn't know they were dead to the threats they employed against the stubborn spirits who were happy to use their new incorporeal status to cause mischief for the living. From the gleam in this one's eyes, he belonged to the latter category.

"I prefer it here, thanks." The ghost fired off a handful of vibrant blue Winter magic, which brushed my shoulder as I hopped down the single step into the bathroom to avoid being hit. My feet skidded on the icy floor, and the ghost laughed in a childlike manner when I grabbed the wall for balance. "Besides, I live here."

"*Did* he live here?" With one palm resting against the

wall, I addressed Leyton over my shoulder. "Before you moved in?"

"Maybe," he said. "I've only lived here about a month."

I returned my attention to the ghost. "How did you die?"

"What kind of question is that to ask someone?" He put on a wounded expression. "I'm hurt."

I gave him a flat stare. "If you're looking for sympathy, go ask a necromancer. Granted, I don't think you'd get any lenience from them either, but at least you'd be out of my hair."

He gave a short, humourless laugh. "Charming, aren't you?"

"Speak for yourself," I said. "If you're this lucid, you must remember how you died."

In answer, the ghost raised his hands. I ducked, the bolt of bright blue energy soaring over my head and striking the opposite wall. Ice formed where the light struck, while Leyton retreated downstairs to avoid being hit.

Unimpressed, I drew my iron knife and waved it at the ghost. "Want to find out if you can get iron poisoning from beyond the grave?"

The ghost stuck his tongue out at me. I swung the knife, took aim, and threw it straight through the centre of the ghost's forehead. He swayed and let out an indignant noise, but he didn't fall back. "You'll pay for that."

Three short blasts of bright blue light shot from his hands—not at us, but at the frozen taps. The ice shattered, sending several jets of icy water into the air like geysers. While Puck and Roseanne turned into birds and flew out of range, a torrent of ice-cold water crashed into my chest and knocked me flat onto my rear. Winded, I struggled upright against the step while Puck and Roseanne flew above the ghost and let out bird-shrieks of warning. Silently cursing Leyton for leaving us to face the ghost alone, I abandoned all pretence of getting out of this without tapping into the Morrigan's powers. I didn't like using her magic in front of strangers, but Leyton seemed to have no intention of coming back upstairs and helping, despite the sodden wreck the ghost had made of his bathroom.

So be it, then.

Shadows unfurled below the backs of my hands, which shifted into the claws of a large bird. Webs of darkness spread up my sleeves, and I dropped my voice. "I warned you. You didn't listen."

The ghost's bright blue eyes paled. "You can't be her. It's impossible."

"Believe me, it's not." More darkness spread across my torso, wrapping me in dark feathers. "Go beyond the Gates of Death."

I didn't have a powerful talisman to give him a shove into the afterlife, but I didn't need one. I raised a claw and blasted shadowy magic into his chest, and he flew backwards, straight through the wall of the house and out of sight.

Puck and Roseanne both landed, shifting back into their human forms. Both were soaking wet—shifting hadn't spared them from being hit by the jets of icy water —and Puck's hair looked endearingly rumpled.

"Can your flames melt the rest of the ice?" I asked.

"No need," Puck replied. "It'll melt on its own now he's gone. Nicely done."

Footsteps sounded on the stairs as the house's owner returned to peer warily around the corner. "Did you banish him?"

"Not exactly, but I can't see the afterlife, so I can only assume he's not coming back," I said. "Roseanne, do you see him?"

She shoved a handful of sopping wet hair out of her face. "Not in here. I don't know how to look further."

Roseanne might have more potential as a necromancer than I did, but she had no training and she had yet to commit to joining the guild when she turned sixteen.

"Good," said Leyton, eyeing the water on the floor. "I'll clean that up—"

"Go to hell." The ghost reappeared in a flash of blue light. Magic blasted from his palms and knocked all of us backwards. When Leyton tripped over, fear etched on his face, his glamour collapsed, revealing he'd been wearing pyjamas the whole time. Awkward.

So much for scaring off the ghost. "I told you to get out of here."

"Your creepy magic won't work on me." He shot me a sneer. "I'm here to stay."

"You wish." Unfortunately, my dagger lay on the icy floor and getting it back would mean walking back in range of the ghost's icy assault. How had the Morrigan's magic failed to scare him into fleeing?

The ghost veered into my path as though he suspected I intended to grab my knife, blue light coalescing in his palms and forming an icy spear-like shape. Puck leapt forwards, transforming into a leaping flame that emitted an orange glow around the ghost's transparent form. The icy spear melted in his hands, while a sudden breeze propelled my knife back towards me.

"Thanks." I reached out and caught it in my hand, while Puck shifted back into human form to land at my side.

The ghost scowled. "You're no fun."

"This isn't your house, dickhead," I told him. "Why are you hanging out in a stranger's bathroom? Tell me the truth. How'd you die?"

The ghost pouted. "I was hit by a car."

"And is there a reason you stuck around?" I asked. "Unfinished business? Revenge?"

"I can't leave."

"Yes, you can," I said. "You just vanished. I saw you."

"I told you, I can't." He flew right up to me, his eyes blazing with annoyance as well as anger. "I can't move on. I'm stuck here."

"Look, just float out of the room and towards the Gates of Death," I told him in the most patient tone I could muster. "It's not rocket science. You can see the afterlife better than I can."

"I don't see any gates."

"That's because you're looking at me. I'm not a necromancer, but if it comes down to it, I *will* give you a shove in the right direction, and I won't be gentle next time."

"I tried to leave," he protested. "There's nothing on the other side but grey."

"That's the afterlife." What kind of ghost didn't know what Death looked like? "Did you expect a vibrant technicolour forest like the Summer Court? Because if so, you're going to be even more disappointed with what's on the other side of the gates."

"Fuck you," he said. "I thought you weren't a necromancer. How would you know what it's supposed to look like over there?"

"I have friends in the guild."

His face set. "Then ask *them* to help me. Otherwise, I'm going nowhere."

Puck took a step forwards. "Why should we believe you?"

"Because you won't be rid of me any other way." The ghost held a hand over the puddle of water on the floor, which began to freeze again. "I can do this all day."

"You're lying," I said. "You're perfectly capable of leaving if you want to."

A lot of ghosts lost most of their common sense upon departing the land of the living, but this guy seemed pretty lucid despite his stubborn insistence that Death shouldn't be a dreary grey landscape. Given my own lack of spirit sight, Ilsa would have to set him right on that one.

Leyton cleared his throat from behind us. "Isn't the ghost gone?"

"He says he's stuck," I said. "I'll need to bring in a necromancer."

He gave me a dubious look. "You know a necromancer?"

"I'm related to two of them." I should by rights have ended up as one myself, given that the spirit sight ran in my family, but I'd been left with zero magic at all once I'd lost the title of Winter Gatekeeper. "I'll send them a message, *if* our ghost agrees to put the theatrics on pause for a bit."

The ghost shot a rude gesture in my direction, but he

obligingly refrained from unleashing another flood while I reached into my pocket for my phone to fire off a text to Ilsa.

My cousin's reply came promptly: *Busy on a mission. Will be free in an hour. That okay?*

I repeated her response to Leyton. "Does that work for you?"

"I guess." He eyed the melted ice all over the bathroom. "How do I stop the ghost from wrecking my house in the meantime?"

"Put a line of salt by the door," I said. "It'll keep him confined to the room, but it won't stop him from flooding the rest of the house if he wants to, so I'd make preparations to deal with the insurance company if I were you."

There ought to be a procedure for damage caused by ghosts, given the sheer volume of spirits on the loose in Edinburgh, but you couldn't count on anything. As we headed downstairs, Ilsa sent me another message—*make it two hours.*

"Must be a long mission," I remarked. "Maybe she's dealing with a poltergeist."

I almost texted Morgan instead, except he was often on the same missions as Ilsa and had a habit of losing or breaking his phone on a frequent basis anyway. I passed on the new time frame to Leyton, who went to the kitchen to fetch some salt. While salt didn't harm ghosts the way it did undead, it was generally a deterrent to spirits and would at least give him some peace until Ilsa came to evict his unwanted guest.

"We'll come back later," Puck told him. "With a guild necromancer."

"If you're sure." Leyton didn't look particularly happy

at the idea of being left in here with the ghost, but while the Morrigan's magic hadn't driven the spirit away, the Gatekeeper of Death would be more than a match for him.

"I'm sure," I said. "Put the salt in a line near the door. We'll be back before you know it."

Leyton didn't look convinced, but he didn't raise any objections when we left the house, still dripping wet from our earlier soaking.

"I swear that ghost disappeared when you used the Morrigan's powers on it," said Roseanne. "Are you sure it's a normal spirit?"

"I wouldn't know," I said. "Ilsa's never mentioned dealing with one who claimed not to be able to find *Death* before, but that sounds more like an excuse to me. If he's having trouble finding the gates, then the Gatekeeper of Death will be more than happy to point him in the right direction."

3

While we waited for Ilsa to escape her mission at the guild, Roseanne and I went to Puck's office to dry off from our impromptu soaking. You'd think no longer working for the Winter Court would mean I spent less time covered in ice, but no such luck.

"I'm intrigued," said Hawk, after Puck had finished explaining the situation. "You got rid of the ghost and it came straight back?"

"I pushed him through the wall, but he materialised inside the house again," I explained. "I thought I gave him a good scare, but he came back and started complaining about not being able to find his way through Death."

"That's inconvenient," he said. "That why you're calling in a necromancer?"

"Yeah, since necromancers can actually see what they're doing when it comes to the afterlife," I said. "Otherwise, it's like trying to walk through Faerie without the

Sight. You *think* you can see where you're going, but it's just as likely that you're being led astray."

"That can happen even *with* the Sight," Puck added. "Depending on which part of Faerie you're in."

"True." Hawk studied me. "I don't think you ever told us why you have it, even though you're human."

"The Sight?" I'd assumed my ability to see the fae was self-explanatory, but then again, he and Puck hadn't known I was a former Gatekeeper until I'd told them directly. As half-faeries, they hadn't lived for centuries like most Aes Sidhe had, and their experience of the rest of Faerie was limited. "It's an aftereffect of spending so much time in Faerie. When someone travels between the two realms on a regular basis, the regular blinders which normal humans have on are lifted."

Half-faeries naturally inhabited the gap between worlds, but humans had mostly been oblivious to the fae prior to the invasion. Except for the Gatekeepers, of course. Our eyes had been opened to Faerie from birth, while the very ground we walked on had been a creation of glamour. I'd never had the words to describe how it felt when the breaking of the Gatekeeper's Curse had shattered those foundations beneath my feet. Perhaps Puck and Hawk had felt something similar when they'd walked away from their own Court. I didn't know.

"Makes sense," said Hawk. "It becomes ingrained eventually, I imagine."

Puck nodded from across the room. "I've heard the same is true for humans who've spent a lot of time in Faerie."

"You mean the ones who get kidnapped by them," I said. "Assuming they survive, of course."

"You had to bring down the mood, didn't you?" Hawk said.

"It's true." I'd be dead a hundred times over if not for my Gatekeeper's training and the Sidhe's reluctance to let me perish and leave themselves with the hassle of finding a replacement. Since there was no backup available, it'd been in their own interests to stop me from getting trampled by a troll or eaten by an ogre before my mother had passed the title on.

My phone buzzed with a message from Ilsa. About time. "Ready to go?"

"You bet," said Roseanne. "Hawk, are you coming?"

"Ah, no thanks," he said. "I'll stay here in case we get any calls."

"I thought you wanted to see the Gatekeeper in action," Roseanne said. "You said you did, didn't you?"

Hawk gave a shrug. "Nah, I'm good."

"You did, though." Roseanne tilted her head to one side. "Ilsa will get rid of the ghost. It's pretty much harmless, anyway."

"You're scared of ghosts?" I asked.

Hawk's face reddened a little. "No, I just have a healthy wariness around things that ought to be six feet underground."

"Uh-huh." Fearing the dead wasn't uncommon among half-faeries, but the guy had faked his own death in front of the Wild Hunt, so it surprised me that he'd be afraid of a relatively harmless ghost. Roseanne snickered, while Puck shot me a grin.

Hawk glowered at us. "Fine, I'll come. Happy?"

The four of us retraced our steps to half-blood territory, where my cousin Ilsa waited near the gates. Her foot-length dark necromancer cloak left a trail of dirt and cobwebs behind her, while more sticky webs clung to her long, dark hair.

"Sorry I'm late," said Ilsa. "You wouldn't believe the day I've had."

"Did it involve zombies?" Judging by the smell lingering around her cloak, I'd guess so.

"Among other things," she said. "What kind of ghost do you need my help with?"

"One who thinks he can't find the way through to Death." I led the way back down the road to Leyton's house. "He won't leave, even when I tried my creepy Morrigan trick. Obviously, I can't see the Gates of Death myself, so it's not like I could give him directions."

"I can help him," she said. "How violent is he?"

"He's flooded this poor guy's bathroom and then froze the place, but he said he was trying to get a necromancer's attention in the hopes of moving on. I can't imagine you'll have too much trouble."

"Don't speak too soon." Puck reached Leyton's house first and knocked on the door.

The dishevelled half-faerie answered a moment later. He hadn't bothered putting his glamour back on, though he'd at least changed into actual clothes rather than the pyjamas he'd been wearing earlier. Judging by the way his damp hair clung to his face, the ghost had given him another soaking at least once since we'd left.

"Good, you're back," he said. "It's even worse than before."

"In what way?" I entered the hallway behind Puck, beckoning Ilsa to follow me. "This is Ilsa. She's a guild necromancer who can get rid of your ghost."

"And him?" He caught sight of Hawk, who stood at the back of our group next to Roseanne.

"I'm the backup," he said. "Whereabouts is the ghost?"

"Stuck in the bathroom surrounded by a salt barrier, the last time we checked," said Puck. "Unless it got out?"

"No… he's still up there," Leyton said. "And he's trying to take the barrier down."

"How?" The icy water trickling down the stairs answered for him, and when I reached the top, I found the water had climbed to the same level as the single step leading out of the bathroom and soaked the landing carpet.

Ilsa took the lead, her footsteps squelching against the sodden carpet. "Is anyone there?"

The ghost appeared in front of her. "Boo."

Ilsa didn't so much as flinch, which came as no surprise. Necromancers wouldn't get very far if simple jump scares bothered them. "So you're the ghost. Got some unfinished business?"

"No. I'm happy here." The ghost folded his arms across his chest. "Who are you?"

"Ilsa Lynn. Necromancer."

"You're with the guild?" The ghost's manner changed, and he straightened upright, his feet nearly touching the ground. "I'm trapped over here. I can't get out."

"I doubt it." Ilsa pulled a book out of her pocket and flipped it open, bathing the ghost in glimmering blue-white light. "Go beyond the Gates of Death."

Magic blasted into the ghost, knocking him through the wall of the house. All of us watched for a tense few seconds in case he reappeared again, but nothing remained but water, ice, and the lingering deeper chill of the magic Ilsa had used.

"Is that it?" Roseanne sounded disappointed. "I thought it would be flashier."

"Sorry to disappoint." Ilsa lowered her hand, closing the book. "I didn't see him go through the gates…"

"Wait, you didn't?" I hadn't seen the gates either, but her book's power was worth ten sets of necromancer candles or more. Surely that had been enough to blast him into the afterlife.

"Let's see if he's outside." She ran downstairs, and the rest of us followed her down into the hallway.

Leyton greeted us with a hopeful look on his face. "Is he gone?"

"I'm going to check," Ilsa said. "I knocked him out of the house, straight through the wall."

"She did the same earlier." He jerked his head in my direction. "Didn't work."

"She isn't a—" Ilsa broke off as Puck pushed open the front door, revealing the ghost standing on the doorstep, his arms folded across his chest.

"You threw me out of my house!" he said accusingly.

"You don't live here anymore," I pointed out. "Also, you should have gone beyond the gates."

"Wait, he used to live here?" asked Hawk. "Really?"

"Months ago," Leyton said irritably. "I live here now, and this is ridiculous. I thought you necromancers were professionals."

"We are." Ilsa stepped up to the ghost and held up her talisman. "Go beyond the gates. I command you."

Light suffused her palms, spreading from the book to

the ghost, but he remained locked to the spot, and no gates appeared to draw him in.

"I think he might be right about being stuck," Hawk muttered. "That or someone switched out her magical book for an algebra textbook."

"This isn't funny," I said out of the corner of my mouth. "Also, that's a talisman, not a regular book. Have a little respect."

Puck's smirk disappeared. "What could possibly stop a ghost going through the gates?"

"Spiritual superglue, maybe." Despite his light tone, Hawk kept his distance from the hovering spirit.

"I've had enough!" Blue light blasted from the ghost's hands, and we all ducked as it spiralled into the sky above our heads. "I want to leave."

"You're not helping the situation," Ilsa said. "Wait there for a second. I'll send you where you belong."

"Maybe Death doesn't want me." His hands brightened again. "Or maybe you're not a real necromancer."

"Don't be absurd." Ilsa was no usual necromancer, true, but that didn't mean she wasn't one of the most badass ghost-hunters I'd met in my life. One of her first banishments had been the wraith of my deceased mother, for crying out loud. This pesky spirit should have been long gone after the first hit from Ilsa's talisman.

Ilsa raised her talisman once again and shouted, "I banish you beyond the Gates of Death!"

A bolt of bright blue energy shot from the book and crashed into the ghost, while a murky grey fog rose to surround him. The afterlife. *Took long enough.*

The ghost let out a wail of relief at the sight of the swirling grey, and the shadow of a pair of enormous gates appeared at his back. Ilsa's talisman illuminated the gates so even we non-necromancers could see the grey pallor of Death beckoning the ghost into its depths.

"I banish you, ghost," said Ilsa. "Go in peace."

The light of her book engulfed the ghost once more, and this time, he flew backwards and vanished amid the tide of transparent figures drifting through the huge shadowy gates. With a shaky exhale, Ilsa lowered the book, its light dimming. The gates vanished, while the fog died down until nothing remained.

"Is he definitely gone this time?" I asked.

"I think so," she said. "I *hope* so. This is the fifth time today where a banishment hasn't stuck."

"Wait, you've had four other ghosts get stuck as well?" That couldn't be right. "What's going on with them? The ghosts are having trouble accessing the gate, is that it?"

"Yeah, it's taking about ten times the usual effort for us to push them through," said Ilsa. "Even the weakest ghosts. I swear it was like pushing against the force of a giant magnet to get this one poltergeist to go to the other side. I'm not sure if the issue is with them or with us, to tell you the truth."

"Has anything like this ever happened before?"

"Not in my experience," she said. "I've not been Gatekeeper for that long, comparatively speaking, so maybe the book can give me more information. Not that it's given me any help yet."

"That sounds... inconvenient." The book was inhabited by the consciousness of a dead god with a mind of its own, and while its magic answered to Ilsa's command, it didn't always cooperate when it came to answering her questions. Despite that, Ilsa always acted so competent that it slipped my mind that she'd become Gatekeeper less than a year and a half ago and had joined the necromancer guild months after that. Morgan too.

As for me, I'd lived in the mortal realm permanently for months, and yet, I might as well have moved to a foreign country. Faerie's illogical rules were so locked into my mind that it sometimes tripped me up that the same roads led to the same places and time passed in a linear fashion. It didn't help that the invasion had caused fae beasts to move into this realm, too, but I'd been a toddler at the time of the faerie invasion, and by now, most people hardly remembered the world before, where all the supernaturals had hidden in the shadows and the Gatekeepers alone had been privy to the fae's secrets.

I couldn't even picture that world now. The invasion had ended with millions dead and the realm flooded with destabilising magic which had permanently screwed up the spirit lines so the undead frequently rose of their own accord. I didn't envy anyone who had to help clean up the aftermath, that was for sure.

Leyton poked his head out of the doorway. "Is it safe?"

"Yes," Ilsa said. "I'm afraid I won't be able to get rid of the ice…'

"That's fine," he said, resigned. "I'll deal with the water. Thanks anyway."

While he and Puck arranged payment for dealing with the unruly spirit, Hawk remained at a safe distance from the lawn as if worried the ghost would come back. Even Roseanne looked unnerved, while Ilsa kept a close grip on her talisman as we left Leyton's house and walked to the gate leading out of half-blood territory.

"Hope that's the last we see of that ghost," said Ilsa. "I'll refrain from mentioning this one to the guild, considering Lady Montgomery is as stressed out as the rest of us."

"You should at least take some of the profit." Puck handed her a bundle of notes. "Since you did most of the work."

"It's nothing," she insisted. "Really, you should have been able to scare off the ghost on a regular day."

Unease flowed down my spine. This wasn't the first stubborn ghost I'd encountered. My own mother had managed to hang on even after being banished behind the gates, tenaciously clinging to existence, but she'd been the former Winter Gatekeeper and stronger than the average spirit. Besides, Leyton's ghost hadn't *wanted* to stay here.

"Does Lady Montgomery have any theories about what might have caused this?" I asked. "It's not linked to the incident with the Wild Hunt a few weeks ago, is it?"

"Not if they're still in jail," she said.

"I'm pretty sure I'd know if they weren't."

I think. The Unseelie Queen had been ominously quiet since the battle, though I hadn't exactly been falling over myself to show my face in front of her. Not when the instant she looked into my eyes, she'd see the Morrigan's magic staring back at her.

Shit. It couldn't be the Morrigan's magic which had somehow screwed up Death, could it? She lived in Faerie and not the mortal realm, and she didn't carry human souls to the afterlife, but I couldn't help but think there might be a connection to the night of the Wild Hunt's ride.

The night I'd taken magic that wasn't mine.

4

———

Our reprieve didn't last for long. Puck called me the following day when Roseanne and I were eating breakfast. When the buzzing didn't cease, I put down my cereal bowl and answered the phone. "Hey."

"The ghost is back."

"What ghost?" I asked. "Not Leyton's?"

"Unfortunately," said Puck.

"Damn." So much for yesterday's banishment being a simple job. Yet how could the ghost have possibly returned from the Gates of Death, especially when Ilsa's Gatekeeper's talisman had pushed him through to the other side? "Are you sure Leyton isn't mistaken?"

"Given that I could hear the ghost in the background when he called us, I'd say not."

I groaned. "Hang on. I'll message Ilsa and see if she's free."

"Let me know if she is." He hung up the phone, while I fired off a message to Ilsa asking if she was free to help.

Roseanne, meanwhile, helped herself to the rest of my cereal while I waited for a reply. "The ghost's back? Same one as yesterday?"

"So it seems." My phone buzzed with a message. "Ilsa's already out on a mission. This same crap might be happening all over the city, for all we know."

Ghosts being unable to go through the gates was bad enough on its own, but the gates spitting them back out into the first layer of the veil was another issue entirely.

Roseanne dropped her spoon back into the cereal bowl. "Seriously? Do all the ghosts in the city want to stick around?"

"Not sure they *want* to." I messaged Ilsa asking when she'd be back, and she replied saying her brother Morgan was on archive duty and that I was welcome to wait with him in there until she finished her mission. "I'm gonna head to the necromancer guild to wait for Ilsa and see if she knows what's going on."

"Count me out," said Roseanne.

"You don't want to come?"

"Are you even allowed to keep wandering in and out of the guild when you aren't a member?"

"Since when did you care about obeying the rules?"

"I don't."

Roseanne had often talked of her interest in joining the guild after her sixteenth birthday, so I didn't blame her for not wanting to get on their bad side. As for me, my attempted trial at a ghost-hunting mission a few months ago had come to a decisive end when I'd manifested zero skill at necromancy whatsoever. The guild's members hardly lived in luxury, but a steady job was hard to come by. Until the substantial payment I'd gained from handling the Wild Hunt, I'd lived on the wildly fluctuating finances of a freelancer who dealt with troublemaking fae nobody else wanted to. If Roseanne could snag something more stable when she was old enough, then it'd only be a good thing.

"What do you want to do, then?" I asked Roseanne. "I don't know how long Ilsa will take to come back from her mission."

"I can entertain myself." She climbed to her feet. "Let me know when the action starts."

"All right." I rinsed out our cereal bowls before grabbing my coat and shoes and heading out into the crisply cold Edinburgh morning. Half-blood territory reflected the change in seasons in the form of shifting autumn colours, leaves littering the pavement, and a gradual transition from bright Summer flowers to leafless Winter bushes. A thick hedge surrounded the territory, while thorny vines grew into the shape of gates which separated the half-faeries' corner of the city from the world on the other side. As far as I was aware, the defences were more to keep the humans safe from the unpredictable magic of the fae than anything else, though they'd come in handy during the Wild Hunt's attempted siege.

I'd gained a temporary acceptance from the other half-faeries after dealing with the Hunt, and so had Roseanne, though their views might change if she chose to join the necromancer guild. The necromancers themselves wouldn't have any issue with her signing up. Most of them knew little about the Morrigan, and besides, Roseanne *looked* human, which was all that mattered to anyone who didn't have anything against half-faeries in general. The necromancers wouldn't get far with their ghost-hunting if they believed in every illogical superstition that crossed their path.

All the same, I'd never heard of the Gates of Death rejecting their ghosts before, and it sounded like Ilsa hadn't, either. I sent Puck a brief message telling him I was going wait at the guild for Ilsa, figuring that he and Hawk would prefer to stay at the office until she was free.

Located in Edinburgh's Old Town, the necromancer guild was housed within a large stone building with iron wards built into the walls to keep out both zombies and hostile fae. Since I was neither, I walked straight through the solid oak doors without being challenged. In the lobby, a number of cloaked necromancers milled around, none of them sparing me a glance. I headed for a staircase leading upstairs to the archive, a small room crammed with bookshelves where Morgan sat behind the desk. The oldest of the Lynn siblings glanced up from the book he was reading when I walked in.

"Hey, Holly," he said. "Joined the guild yet?"

"No." *Honestly.* He asked the same question every time I came here, as though he expected me to answer in the affirmative if he persisted for long enough. "Not a necromancer, remember?"

"Neither was I when I joined up."

"Yes, you were. You just didn't know it yet." From what Ilsa had told me, Morgan had somehow managed to keep his ability to detect ghosts a secret from his family since he was a teenager, and it wasn't until a particularly murderous ghost had targeted him last year that Ilsa had figured out what was really going on. "Is it true that the ghosts which have already been banished are returning through the gates?"

"Sounds like it," said Morgan. "Maybe they're getting lost. Not like the afterlife has signposts."

"Pretty sure that's not how it works," I said. "You'd think Ilsa of all people would have been able to stop them from coming back."

"Nah, it's supposed to be the necromancer guardians' job to handle that side of the gates."

"Because they're already dead." Being a ghost was the sole requirement to ascend to the highest rank of necromancer and to become one of the few permitted to stay on as consultants for the living guild members. Guardians could also travel back and forth between the other side of the gates and the part of the veil visible from this realm, which would surely mean they had some idea of why the banished ghosts had made an abrupt return to this realm.

The door opened, and Jas walked into the archive. The slight necromancer's cloak dragged on the floor behind her, while her under-five-foot frame made me feel like a giant.

"Hey, Holly," she said. "Waiting for Ilsa?"

"Thought you were with her."

"Nah, she and River went out alone," said Jas. "The Gatekeeper's pretty much the only person who can handle the ghosts at the moment. They're too sticky for the rest of us to banish. Kicking them out is like trying to swim through mud."

"Has anyone spoken to the guardians?" I asked. "They can travel to the other side of the gates at will, so they ought to know what's going on over there, right?"

"Fair point," said Jas. "In all honesty, I've never spoken to them directly. I've taken plenty of notes for Lady

Montgomery at meetings with them, but they don't really talk to the rest of us."

"Yeah, most of us don't get into their top-secret meetings," said Morgan. "Besides, they're prone to waffling about inane crap most of the time, aren't they?"

"Yeah." Jas perched on the edge of the desk. "They're dead. It's not like they're renowned for their conversational skills."

"They'd notice if there was an issue in Death, wouldn't they?" I asked.

"Yeah, they would," said Morgan. "If *they* got stuck on the wrong side of the gates, we'd never hear the end of it. Lady Montgomery would have to put up a ward on her office to keep them out."

I looked between them. "You don't think that's what's going on?"

"No," Jas answered. "Like Morgan said, we'd know pretty quickly if *they* got stuck in the land of the living. They'd come straight back to haunt the guild."

"You think Death is definitely where the problem lies?" That meant it couldn't be linked to Faerie, right? Human and half-faerie ghosts didn't travel to the same afterlife as the Sidhe, as far as I knew, but that didn't mean I could entirely rule out a connection to the Wild Hunt's attempted ritual—and the Morrigan's disappearance.

"Where else would it be?" Jas asked. "Ilsa certainly thinks the issue's somewhere in Death."

"She can't be expected to handle every ghost in the city on her own, can she?" If she tried, she'd burn out pretty quickly. Besides, there hadn't been a Gatekeeper of Death in at least one generation before her.

Once, I'd thought—or rather, hoped—the next Gatekeeper of Death might be me, but right now, I was kind of glad the responsibility had fallen on Ilsa's head instead.

"She seems to think so." Jas checked her phone and jumped to her feet. "Wait. I think she needs backup."

"I'm not allowed to leave this room," Morgan grumbled. "You'll have to grab Lloyd instead. He's training Mackie to throw knives around, so you might want to duck."

"Noted." Jas stepped towards the door. "Are you going to wait here, Holly?"

"I'll come along and see if I can help." Not that I'd been able to do much to the other ghost, but I was increasingly convinced that this situation was linked to the events of a few weeks ago, and Ilsa needed all the backup she could get if the guild wanted to keep their Gatekeeper in one piece.

"Sure." Jas led the way to the end of the corridor and pushed open another door, leading me through a cramped space filled with benches and lockers until we came to a pair of wooden doors inset with long windows that revealed a wide training room.

Shelves containing candles and various weapons lined the wall on one side, while mats had been set up on the polished wooden floor. On one of those mats, Jas's friend Lloyd and a slight Asian girl of maybe twenty were sparring with wooden sticks. Lloyd, a tall black guy with locs, glanced over at us when we walked in, while the girl seized the chance to give him a thwack on the shins.

"Ow." He dropped his stick. "Time out, Mackie. I think Jas has come with a mission. Right?"

"Ilsa needs our help," said Jas. "Want to come?"

"Sure." He grabbed his necromancer cloak from where

it lay discarded on the floor and shrugged it on over his T-shirt and jogging trousers. "Mackie, find someone else to practise with, okay?"

"Why can't I come?" Mackie said. "The fire was more Morgan's fault than mine. Anyway, you might need me there."

"Boss's orders," said Jas. "She told you to stay put, so you can either keep training in here or switch places with Morgan on archive duty."

"Exactly," said Lloyd. "Behave while we're gone, that clear?"

"Sure, whatever." Mackie twirled the stick in her hand and made for the group of sparring necromancers at the other end of the hall.

Lloyd, meanwhile, followed us out into the locker room. "You're coming, too, Holly?"

"I needed Ilsa to come and help with a ghost," I said. "Didn't count on her being tied up, but I figured she needs all the help she can get."

"No kidding," he said. "That was Mackie, by the way. The guild's second psychic, aside from Morgan."

"She's temporarily suspended from missions after her last solo mission with Morgan went slightly offtrack," added Jas. "Which anyone might have seen coming."

We headed back downstairs and left the guild's headquarters, before turning right down the cobbled street. The older stone buildings contrasted the modern facades of restaurants and bars which didn't quite mask the impression that we were walking through a place which had seen its fair share of ghosts, before and after the faerie invasion.

Jas took the lead, taking several sharp turns before

coming to a halt in a deserted street. Deserted, that is, except for the candles scattered around River and Ilsa, who stood in the centre of the street surrounded by several transparent spirits. No wonder they'd needed backup.

Ilsa gripped the book in both hands and shouted, 'Go beyond the Gates of Death!"

Neither gates nor grey smoke materialised. Instead, one of the ghosts veered towards River, while a second caught sight of our approaching group.

"Ooh, we have company," said the ghost. "Catch."

Magical energy shot from his palms, and our group scattered before it struck. Jas and Lloyd ran to pick up the discarded candles—which looked as though someone had started to set up a circle only for the ghost to knock it over—while the Morrigan's shadowy magic brought a shiver to my skin. Could I use it to take out several ghosts at once? I'd barely handled *one,* but I counted at least three spirits surrounding Ilsa and River.

A fourth ghost popped up directly in front of me. "Go away."

Light blasted me in the eyes, and I slammed into the wall, my breath whooshing out. Blinking the glare away, I caught my balance as another magical attack sent both Lloyd and Jas crashing into a heap. Necromantic energy didn't freeze like Winter magic, but it hit hard and left me struggling to catch my breath.

"I said, go beyond the Gates of Death!" Ilsa yelled at the ghost, to no effect. "Rest in peace and stop bothering us."

"Fix those candles!" Jas disentangled herself from Lloyd and gave a lunge for the nearest candle, which lay on its side. Flipping it upright, she moved towards the next one, only for one of the ghosts to get in the way.

"Hey, dickface!" Lloyd blasted the spirit in the back with a handful of bright necromantic magic, while Jas flipped the next candle the right way up.

Keeping an eye on the ghosts, I quickly counted the candles. We needed twelve to make a circle to trap the spirits. Eleven lay on the ground, so I moved in to help straighten up the ones which had fallen over.

A ghost—a half-Summer Sidhe judging by the green tint to the magic swirling around her hands—waylaid me. "Ooh. What are you?"

I ignored the ghost and flipped the nearest candle the right way up. Shadows stirred beneath my fingertips, and when the ghost's icy touch seared my shoulder, I raised a palm. "Go away."

The ghost stared at my hands, which flickered into claws without my conscious command.

"You're the one," said the ghost. "It's you."

"What do you mean by that?"

"Go in peace!" Ilsa yelled. "Holly, get out of the circle!"

Crap. While I'd been occupied with the ghost, she'd placed the remaining candle, and if I wasn't careful, I'd end up trapped in the circle with a bunch of angry ghosts.

When I leapt out of the circle, the ghost tried to follow me, but River snapped his fingers and all twelve candles lit up with vibrant blue light. An indignant screech escaped the ghost as it slammed into an invisible barrier, which stretched across the circle of candles and kept all the spirits trapped inside.

Ilsa raised her talisman, exhaustion etched on her features. "Go beyond the Gates of Death. All of you. *Now.*"

A vibrant blast of magic struck the ghosts at once, while the dark shape of the Gates of Death appeared above the circle, drawing the ghosts into their embrace.

"Go on." Ilsa held her talisman up with both hands, the current of energy continuing to push against the ghosts until they vanished from sight.

"They're gone." River approached the circle, his gaze scanning the grey fog swirling within. "Better wait a couple of minutes in case anything comes back."

"Good riddance," said Lloyd. "You okay, Ilsa?"

"That was harder than necessary." Ilsa slid the talisman back into the pocket of her cloak. "Holly, did you say Leyton's ghost is back again?"

"He said so," I said. "Haven't checked myself yet, but Puck could hear him on the phone."

"I pushed that bloody spirit through the gates with my own hands," said Ilsa. "I *saw* him travel to the other side. This makes zero sense."

"Has anyone spoken to the necromancer guardians?" I asked. "I know only top-tier necromancers have access to them, but they seem like the ones who'd know."

"Not that I'm aware of, but I'll ask Lady Montgomery," said Ilsa. "Last I checked, even she doesn't know why Death has suddenly started rejecting its dead."

My heart climbed into my throat. "Ilsa… you don't think this might be linked to the Wild Hunt, do you?"

"Why would it be?" she asked. "They're locked up in the Unseelie Court's jail. That's about as far from Death as it's possible to get."

"You know Faerie isn't entirely severed from this realm, though," I said. "The Grey Vale links directly to Death, in fact."

"It does?" said Jas. "Nobody told me that."

"I thought I mentioned it," said Ilsa. "Yes, the Vale and Death overlap in some areas, which is why some of us can see into the Vale when we use our spirit sight close to the Ley Line. It's also why monsters from the Vale sometimes wander into our realm."

"They get in via Death." Jas nodded. "Since the invasion screwed up both sides of the Line. Makes sense. Is something wrong in the Vale, then?"

"I hope not," Ilsa said. "The Vale is the Sidhe's responsibility. Or it should be."

I rolled my eyes. "Would they really fall over themselves to help out a bunch of human necromancers?"

Ilsa's gaze snapped onto mine. "Have you heard...?"

"From the Court?" *If I had, I wouldn't be here.* "Not a word. I gathered they have better things to do than to check in with the former Gatekeepers."

Like deal with the ghosts in *their* realm. I'd seen at least two of them drifting around the Morrigan's territory during my last visit, but I'd neglected to mention that development to Ilsa. She had enough to handle without adding Faerie on top of it, and besides, in Faerie, there *was* no banishment of the dead. The dead moved on of their own accord... or the Morrigan ate their souls.

At one time, the Wild Hunt had been tasked with ferrying the souls of departed fae to be reborn, but they'd been disbanded even before the source of immortality had been broken, which left the Morrigan as the sole death fae who might have some knowledge of what lay on the other side of immortality.

It's you, the ghost had said. What had it meant? An unknown spirit couldn't possibly know I'd taken the

Morrigan's magic, right? Yet even if there *was* a connection, I wouldn't know where to begin looking for her. She couldn't die. Her immortality wasn't conditional like the Sidhe, but it was anyone's guess as to how the term "dead" applied to a death goddess whose magic defied the usual rules of the Courts.

River moved in to collect the candles, while I turned back to Ilsa. "Want to come with me to see to Leyton's ghost?"

Ilsa gave a long-suffering sigh. "Is there any point? I doubt a second banishment would achieve much."

"Then what's the alternative?"

"Candles?" suggested Jas. "Can't we trap all the ghosts in summoning circles until we have a solution?"

"We'll run out of candles," said Lloyd.

"We will," agreed Ilsa. "That might work as a temporary solution for the ghosts who are causing the more serious issues, though."

"Like property damage," I said. "Tell you what, if I take some candles with me, you won't need to come and help. You can go back to the guild and take a nap."

"She's got you there," said Jas. "River, want to give her the candles?"

"Change of plans." He stopped picking up candles to check his phone. "We've been asked to come back to the guild to speak to the boss."

"Since when does Lady Montgomery send text messages?" Lloyd wanted to know. "Jas and I have never had one from her."

"That's because she's River's mother," said Ilsa. "He had to teach her how to use a mobile phone. Meaning I told *him* how to use it, and he passed on my instructions to her."

"Faerie doesn't tend to require that skill," said River mildly. "Anyway, you're welcome to take the candles, Holly. If you can get the ghost contained, then we can come back with a necromancer patrol to do the banishment if necessary."

"All right." I walked over to the pile of candles he'd gathered. "Got a bag I can borrow?"

"Nope," said Jas. "We carry everything in our cloak pockets. It's easier."

I gave an eye roll. "We don't all have pockets a mile deep, you know."

"There are downsides," said Lloyd. "Like when you leave a snack in there and forget about it."

Jas poked him in the arm. "Yeah, you figure out pretty quickly when you realise the smell isn't coming from the zombies."

Resigned, I scooped up all twelve candles and carried them bundled awkwardly in my arms. I'd grown used to putting everything in my pockets in Faerie, since bags and accessories had a tendency to disappear, but one of those cloaks would come in handy at the moment.

Despite my misgivings about joining forces with the guild, I'd better hope Lady Montgomery would be able to provide some answers. After all, in my experience, anything which affected the dead inevitably spelled bad news for the living.

5

Once I'd reached half-blood territory, laden with candles, I went to find Roseanne and enlist her help on our necromancer banishment. Instead, I found the house empty and a scribbled note on the kitchen table telling me that she'd met up with Puck and gone to see Leyton herself.

I dug out a plastic bag in the kitchen to put the candles in and picked up the mostly empty saltshaker in case I needed it. Then I retraced my route through half-blood territory until I came to the small brick cottage where Leyton lived.

When I knocked, Hawk, of all people, answered the door. "There you are, Holly. Where's your cousin?"

"She got called to an urgent necromancer meeting with her boss," I explained. "This ghost business is an ongoing issue for the guild, so they're hoping the head necromancer might be able to shed some light on the cause. Are Puck and Roseanne in there?"

I was surprised he'd shown up himself, given his attitude towards the ghost beforehand, but maybe he hadn't wanted to be left out this time around. Or maybe he was as curious as the rest of us as to why the reluctant spirit had found himself stranded in the land of the living again.

"Yeah." He stepped aside to let me into the hall. "I take it the necromancers have a game plan?"

"I hope they will, but until then, we're on our own." I walked after him into the cosy living room, where we found Puck and Roseanne with an irate-looking Leyton. "Has the ghost frozen the bathroom again?"

"No," said Leyton. "He's been hiding in cupboards instead, so I managed to get him into the cloakroom. I hoped you'd be bringing someone to banish him."

A rattling came from a closed door nearby, in front of which a layer of salt had been sprinkled in a line. I held up the bag of candles. "Can we set these up around him?"

"Not without opening the door," said Roseanne.

"Candles?" said Leyton. "That's not a permanent way to get rid of the ghost, is it?"

I shook the candles. "It's a more reliable way to keep him in the cloakroom rather than letting him into the bathroom again."

"Don't give him ideas." Hawk backed out of the living room. "I'll watch the front door."

"For what?" I gave Puck an incredulous look, but he just shrugged without offering an explanation for his friend's presence here despite his obvious fear of ghosts.

Roseanne, meanwhile, held out a hand for the bag of candles. I handed them over, and she yanked open the cloakroom door.

The ghost leered at me. "Back again, are you?"

"Speak for yourself," I said. "How'd you end up back on this side of the gates?"

"I never got through. Some necromancer your cousin turned out to be."

"Okay, that's bullshit." Fluttering sounded when Roseanne shifted into a crow and zipped over his head with the bag of candles dangling from her beak. I prepared to intervene, but she seemed to have it all figured out. Dropping the bag, she scattered candles over the cloakroom floor, below the cloaks hanging on hooks along the back wall, and then let Puck reach across the salt line to move the candles into a proper circle.

"Will that work?" Leyton asked me. "Doesn't seem much of a plan."

"It's the only one we have," I replied. "We can trap the ghost in the circle until the necromancers undo the problem. As long as the circle remains intact, the ghost shouldn't be able to get out. You'll have to give up your cloakroom for a bit, but it's a small price to pay."

"Why do you have a traffic cone in your cloakroom?" Hawk hovered on the far side of the room. "Not judging, mind."

"Drunken trophy," Leyton muttered. "Anyway, I'd rather trap that bloody ghost outside the house than listen to him whining at me until the necromancers fix their problem and come to get rid of him."

"Whining? You're one to talk." The ghost attempted to slide out of the circle of candles, but Roseanne's bird form flew directly through his transparent body and knocked another candle upright with her beak. "There's no privacy for you now. I've already seen you showering."

"Not helping." I moved in to help with the last of the

candles as Roseanne flew out of the cloakroom. "Once this circle is closed, don't open the door, and don't do anything which might knock the candles out of line. If you don't, then the ghost shouldn't be able to escape."

Each candle contained enough necromantic energy to fuel a barrier which prevented the ghost from escaping indefinitely. Unless, as happened in rare circumstances, the ghost's power grew too strong to be contained... as had happened to my mother. I'd kept her wraith contained within the house by borrowing some candles and hiring someone from the local necromancer guild to set up a secure circle, but her eventual escape had left the necromancers' deaths on my conscience, and if not for Ilsa's magic, the rest of us would have perished too.

I couldn't believe that same power had failed in the face of a few comparatively weak spirits. There must be more going on, but until then, we could at least spare Leyton from dealing with more ghostly shenanigans for a while. I flicked the switch on the nearest candle and moved to the next, until all twelve small flames had ignited. The ghost let out a noise of despair when the twelve lights connected, forming a barrier around his transparent form which covered the entire cloakroom.

"Job done." I high-fived Roseanne when she shifted back into her human form again.

Hawk cleared his throat from near the window. "There's a problem outside."

"That sounds like an understatement." I crossed the living room to his side and saw immediately what the problem was. Two more ghosts hovered above the lawn, looking up at the window with mournful eyes. "Who're they?"

"Did they live here too?" Hawk asked Leyton.

"What?" Leyton went pale at the sight of his new visitors. "Not that I'm aware of."

"Ghosts generally haunt the places where they died or where they spent a lot of time when they were alive." I grabbed the salt canister from the bag where I'd stashed the candles and headed for the front door. "So unless they died on your doorstep, they're here for a reason."

Roseanne popped up at my elbow. "I doubt he cares."

"What are you doing?" asked Hawk. "Don't *talk* to them. I doubt they're selling double glazing."

Ignoring him, Puck reached the door first and pulled it open, addressing the ghosts. "Are you lost?"

The ghosts drifted towards us, while I pointedly moved to bar the way into the hall. By the brightness of their eyes, both of them appeared to be half-faeries, one Winter and one Summer.

"There's only room for one ghost in here," I told the spirits. "He doesn't want company. Go on, shoo."

The Summer half-faerie ghost looked sadly at the door. "But it looks so warm in there…"

"If you have questions about housing, take it up with Brook," said Puck. "On second thought, don't. I bet he's having a bad day too."

I gave him a sideways look. "You don't think there are more ghosts near his house as well?"

Given that Brook was the person to go to when a half-faerie needed help, there was a fair chance he'd been approached by a lost spirit or three.

"I'd say yes," said Puck. "He does have a few spare rooms, last I heard. Granted, they're usually donated to *living* faeries who need assistance. I suppose ghosts don't take up much space, at least."

"I'm sure he'll be thrilled," said Hawk. "I'll stay here and watch the candles."

"They don't need watching," said Roseanne. "Those two ghosts aren't scary. Look at them."

"No, thanks." Hawk shuffled back in the hallway. "Go on, send them packing."

"You're scared of ghosts?" Leyton asked. "Didn't you live in *Faerie?*"

Hawk went brick red. "I am *not* scared of—"

"Calm down, children," said Puck. "Roseanne, I didn't mean you. Don't give me that look."

Roseanne sidestepped and beckoned to the ghosts. "Come on, get out of here."

When the ghosts didn't move, I said, "Look, nobody else will help you. Until the necromancer guild gets here, anyway."

"Or until we get more candles," Puck added in an undertone. "Does the guild have any going spare, Holly?"

"Hey, it's a miracle I got *one* set." Maybe Brook would be able to help, though I doubted he had any more experience with ghosts than anyone else here.

Brook lived near the front gate to half-blood territory, having moved into his mentor's house after Blaine had died at the hands of the Wild Hunt and taken over his position in helping any half-faeries who'd fallen on hard times. He was also the reason I had a roof over my head, though he might not have been as charitable if he knew I might in any way be responsible for this current ghost infestation. Not that I'd be telling anyone my suspicions until I knew for sure.

When I knocked on Brook's door, the green-eyed Summer half-Sidhe looked as dishevelled as Leyton when he answered, suggesting my assumption that he wasn't having a pleasant day had been dead right. He gave a groan when he saw the ghosts hovering behind me. "Not again."

"Seen these guys before?" I indicated the ghosts, who drifted behind me to peer into the hallway.

"I already have five spirits sheltering in my house," said Brook. "Honestly, I hoped your necromancer friends might have a solution, Holly."

"The guild is looking into the situation," I said, "but even Ilsa is at a loss to explain why ghosts which were already banished are returning."

"Ghosts which were *already* banished?" Brook echoed. "That's not possible."

"The necromancers would agree, except the ghosts say otherwise." I suppressed a shudder when one of the ghosts reached *through* me towards the warm hallway. Stepping aside, I let the ghosts drift towards the house, sincerely hoping the problem in Death was limited to Edinburgh and didn't extend farther afield.

Brook's shoulders slumped. "Send them in, then."

The ghosts entered the house with murmurs of gratitude, disappearing through an open door on the right. Brook, meanwhile, ran a hand through his dishevelled hair. "I would appreciate it if one of you would send me an update when the guild has a solution."

"We don't know how long that'll take," I warned him. "If you want to ghost-proof half-blood territory to stop any more from getting in, then that's an easier short-term solution."

"With what, salt?" Roseanne asked. "Or candles?"

"Salt is less effective," I explained for Brook's benefit. "You can use it to deter a spirit from entering a room, but some of them might be angry enough to ignore a temporary barrier. Candles, though, are more or less impenetrable unless they're knocked over."

"I can see if I have any candles," Brook said uncertainly. "Maybe Blaine left a few in the house somewhere."

"Regular candles won't do much," I added. "The necromantic ones are made out of a sturdy material and can be lit by flicking a switch. It's harder to trap a ghost in a circle if you have to keep stopping to strike matches and relight candles after the ghost blows them out."

"How do you know all this?" His gaze flickered across our group. "Your cousin?"

"No, I thought it was common knowledge." Had he paid no attention to the necromancer guild in recent years? Given his location and the fact that he was half-Aes Sidhe, who'd literally lived underground until recently… possibly. Puck and Hawk had similar gaps in their knowledge, which made *me* the expert. Not ideal for any of us. "Anyway, you'll never get hold of enough candles to bar the ghosts from getting into every single house, but if you put one up around the entire territory, it'll stop any more from entering."

"But they'll keep showing up in people's houses?" he asked. "We don't have *any* necromantic candles on our territory."

"I thought the guild hands them out in emergencies," said Puck. "Or so I heard."

"No, that's the mages," I said. "*They* have their own sets

of custom-made candles, but they're rich enough to afford them."

That was the problem. Half-blood territory was a space carved out of the city for people who had nothing, as most half-faeries were abandoned in this realm without any connections. While their magic had given them advantages in finding ways to survive, there were huge gaps in resources between them and other supernaturals, which became obvious in situations like this.

"The mages don't exactly have us on a priority list," said Brook. "But I'll make a call and see if they're willing to help."

"Or I can obtain them by other means," Puck said.

"You mean by going into trickster mode and stealing from them?" I raised a brow. "Only if you have a death wish."

"I wouldn't bet on them having dealt with a trickster before." His gaze went to the partly open doorway to a nearby room, where several ghosts had gathered to listen to our conversation. "I'll see if they're open to persuasion first. Hawk will help. He needs something useful to do."

"Doubt he'll want to get that close to those ghosts." I indicated the door. "It's worth asking, but if the mages have any unwanted hauntings of their own, they'll want to keep the candles for themselves."

"What's going on?" A strident voice rang down the street, and several half-satyrs clip-clopped into view of Brook's doorstep. "Why are there ghosts everywhere? Did your pet death faerie set them loose?"

Roseanne bristled. "*What* did you call me?"

"They showed up of their own accord," I told them.

"But I can set them loose on *you* if you don't stop insulting my housemate."

"There's ghosts all over the place," said a blond satyr in a leather jacket. "I only know one death faerie who's allowed to live here, and she's looking right at me."

"There'll be at least one extra ghost in here if you don't knock it off." Seeing the furious look on Roseanne's face, I hastened to hurry her away from them before her claws came out and proved their point.

Puck stepped in, addressing the satyrs. "We're going to stop any more ghosts entering half-blood territory. If you don't want them confined to your houses, I'd suggest you leave."

"Ignore them," I whispered to Roseanne. "They're talking crap."

Roseanne said nothing as we walked, but she hunched her shoulders, her mouth set in anger. I'd thought we were making progress with the other half-faeries, but one unexplained event had brought out their old prejudices again. The worst part was that if my "gift" from the Morrigan *was* responsible for the ghostly invasion, then the backlash would likely land on Roseanne as well.

"It's not fair," she muttered when we neared our house. "Why do they always blame me for this bullshit?"

I shook my head. "If anything, it's more *my* fault than yours."

She frowned. "Why?"

"Because… you know." I dropped my voice. "I did tell you the Morrigan disappeared, right? Her disappearance started all this."

Roseanne shook her head. "No, it didn't. She decided to loan you her magic, didn't she?"

"Yes, but I don't think she intended for me to use it the way I did."

Namely, bringing Puck back from the dead. River had been the only other person present at the time, though I was pretty sure he hadn't even told Ilsa what I'd done.

"She can't die, though," said Roseanne. "She's reborn into a new body every single time."

"Does that usually happen right away?"

"I have no idea," she said. "It's not as if I've spent that much time around her."

"I know." I didn't want to offload my problems on Roseanne, but there were so few people who knew anything about the Morrigan which wasn't limited to superstition. "I used to deliver letters between her and the Unseelie Queen all the time and I have no idea how her magic works."

I sure as hell hadn't known she had any kids, least of all half-human ones. Not that she seemed to particularly care for Roseanne, but she'd always struck me as calculating in her every action. Handing her magic to a human and then disappearing seemed out of character for the enigmatic death goddess.

"Time is always acting weird in Faerie," said Roseanne. "She'll be back."

I was supposed to be reassuring her, not the other way around, but how could I keep carrying this secret balanced on my shoulders? No... I had to come clean to Ilsa. Not only was she more familiar with Faerie than most necromancers, but her talisman contained knowledge inaccessible to anyone else in this realm. Granted, it wouldn't share that knowledge with *me*, but Ilsa ought to be able to wrangle answers from it if the state of the entire afterlife was at stake. Right?

I pulled out my phone and sent her a message before I second-guessed my decision. *I need to talk to you when you're free.*

I'm free now, came her reply.

"I'm going to see Ilsa," I told Roseanne. "I hope she learned something conclusive from her meeting with her boss."

6

I arranged to meet Ilsa outside the guild, not wanting to have such a delicate conversation in front of potential eavesdroppers. She was already waiting on the cobbled street when I showed up, her eyes underscored with shadows. "Hey, Holly. Any new developments?"

"More ghosts in half-blood territory and more annoyed faeries," I said. "Did you get any answers from the boss?"

"Nothing except that the guardians haven't checked in with the guild in a while," she said. "My boss is irked, to say the least. All the ghosts we've banished in the last week have come straight back again."

"Does she know when it started, exactly?" I asked. "Because that might help you figure out the cause."

"I have no idea," said Ilsa. "There's no obvious culprit to blame. I know you mentioned the Wild Hunt, but they're in jail."

"Yeah... about that." I drew in a breath. "Hypothetically, what would you do if I suggested *I* might be responsible for this?"

"In what way?" Her eyes rounded. "Seriously, Holly? You think *you* did this?"

I'd assumed she'd be angry, but not surprised. Then again, she'd seen me at my worst, and she'd forgiven me anyway, so maybe she'd be willing to work with me to fix this as well.

The words clogged my throat like a heavy brick until I forced them out. "The Morrigan is missing, and I think it's my fault."

Ilsa's hand dropped to the pocket containing her talisman. "She escaped?"

"She vanished from her cave without leaving a trace behind," I told her. "When I checked, there wasn't a single crow to be found. Her chains were completely intact, so she couldn't have torn herself free. Last time I set eyes on her, she loaned me her magic to fight the Wild Hunt. I think I did something in the fight which caused her to disappear, because I still have her magic, and I shouldn't." Breathless, I waited for her judgement to fall.

Her lips pursed. "That's why you've been avoiding Faerie."

"The Unseelie Queen herself ordered me to check in with the Morrigan, but she didn't give me any other instructions, so I came straight home right after I found out," I admitted. "I didn't want to be the one to break the news."

"Probably a wise idea," she said. "I would have thought she had enough magic that loaning some to you wouldn't have had an impact. Besides, she chose to give you her power."

I shrugged. "I don't have any other theories as to why Death is screwed up on both sides of the Vale."

Ilsa's brow furrowed. "You think the Morrigan's disappearance is causing human ghosts to get stuck in Death?"

"I don't know what else to think," I murmured. "I saw some ghosts hanging around in Faerie right after she vanished too. In the Death Kingdom. Not exactly a common sight."

"The Morrigan didn't do much when she was in chains," said Ilsa. "The ghosts might have popped up anyway. Her disappearance is Faerie's problem, not yours. I think you're right to avoid the Sidhe, though. They can figure it out."

"They won't be willing to talk when they find out I have this." I summoned a shadow to my palm in demonstration. "I've been trying not to use her magic, but it's not going anywhere."

Regardless, the Unseelie Sidhe might be the only people who'd be able to give me answers on the Morrigan's current location, dead or alive. Before they stuck my head on a pike, anyway.

Ilsa shook her head. "I'm sure it's not you. Chances are the guild will find a solution before anyone else does."

"Does your talisman have any answers?" My gaze dropped to the square-shaped outline in her pocket. "I mean, if the Gatekeeper's book can banish ghosts, it ought to know what's blocking them from getting into Death."

"I asked, but there's a dozen different possible causes," she said. "Until we get an update from a guardian, we're out of luck."

"Can't you summon one?"

"Trust me, the guardians don't like being stuck in

summoning circles any more than you or I would," she said. "As for the book, it can't see the other side of the gates any more than I can. I'd need to take it with me to the other side in person, and I can't say I'm that keen on the idea."

"Best avoid that." The Ancient who resided in the book had been bound there at our ancestor's hands, after it'd leapt to her defence in order to prevent her untimely death, and while it was a powerful repository of knowledge, it was also no more mobile than your average paperback. "Does it know anything about the Wild Hunt?"

"It doesn't seem to know about their link with the Aes Sidhe, at any rate," said Ilsa. "Given how many centuries they spent hiding underground, it's no surprise that my talisman didn't know they were the ones who took Thomas Lynn captive, and not the Courts. The other Lynns at the time didn't know any better themselves."

"Tell me about it." It made me feel marginally better to know that Ilsa had been as clueless as I was as to the true nature of the curse on our family before Hazel had—in her typical bull-in-a-china-shop fashion—crashed straight into the realm of the Aes Sidhe and unearthed their existence, which even most of the Summer Court had been unaware of. She'd then discovered that Etaina, their Queen, was the one who'd captured Thomas Lynn and locked his descendants into a vow. Since Etaina had then met her end at the jaws of the god of death she'd summoned herself, it was only when Puck had admitted to being Aes Sidhe himself that I'd learned Queen Etaina had once held an alliance with the Wild Hunt.

I didn't yet know the extent of that relationship, but I

gathered that it had involved exchanging information on dark rituals conducted using the blood of the Ancients.

When a group of cloaked necromancers walked past the two of us, Ilsa shifted on the balls of her feet. "I should head back in. I promised Jas and Morgan I'd tell them the details of the meeting, even if it wasn't all that exciting."

"Better than nothing," I said. "The half-faeries are having to appeal to the mages for emergency candles, by the way. Have you got any going spare?"

"I'll check," she said. "I'll let you know, okay?"

"Sure."

Ilsa re-entered the guild's headquarters, while I hovered on the doorstep, fighting the sudden desire to consult her talisman myself. If it would deign to speak to me, of course, which was about as likely as the ghosts calmly departing of their own accord.

I turned away and made my way back to half-blood territory, lost so deeply in thought that I didn't spot the Sidhe standing on the doorstep to my house until I'd already got out my key. My feet stopped mid-step as my other senses caught up to me, my gaze snapping to the messenger from the Unseelie Court.

"Lord Lyle." I kept my tone even to hide my thumping heart. "To what do I owe the pleasure?"

"I have been sent to escort you to my Queen."

Of all the timing. "For what reason?"

Not the Morrigan. Please not the Morrigan.

"She'll tell you herself," he said.

"Look, you remember the incident where she froze me solid, don't you? I'm not coming with you without a guarantee that I won't end up in the same condition again."

Admittedly, this time I wouldn't blame her for

turning me into a life-sized ice statue, but that didn't mean I could afford to waste time in Faerie when Earth had its own problems. I peered at Roseanne's window to see if she was in, but she'd likely holed up in her room until the coast was clear. Before Lord Lyle could say another word, though, Puck and Hawk walked into view, heading towards the gate out of half-blood territory. Both came to a stop when they saw the Unseelie knight.

"What's he doing here?" Puck asked me.

"He wants me to come with him to see the Unseelie Queen," I explained. "I said I wouldn't unless he told me *why* she wants to see me."

Lord Lyle's jaw locked. "You dare to reveal her request to the Unseelie Court's enemies?"

"Enemies?" Hawk sounded insulted. "I don't have enemies. Life's too short to waste on grudges. Even for the likes of you."

Lord Lyle looked as if he wouldn't mind hauling Hawk into Faerie, too, but Puck spoke up first. "What Hawk means is that we've never done anything to merit being called enemies of the Winter Court. *He* hasn't, anyway."

"You, however, have a reputation, trickster," Lord Lyle said. "The Unseelie Queen will not have me repeat her reasons for inviting the former Gatekeeper into the Court. Come with me and she will tell you herself, Holly Lynn."

"I'm not her Gatekeeper any longer." I didn't care who else might hear my raised voice, because if I followed him into Faerie, I wouldn't walk out again. Regardless of the many mistakes I'd made, I didn't want to die. I had a teenager dependent on me and a city full of ghosts to help deal with, and I wouldn't be able to help with either if I was frozen into an ice block until the end of time.

Lord Lyle's expression turned flinty. "This is not a request, mortal. I have been instructed to remove you by force if necessary."

"You mean abduct me," I said. "Look, there's nothing I can do for the Unseelie Queen in my current position. I know she's used to pushing me around, but is she truly desperate enough to have you kidnap a *human* instead of asking for the assistance of someone in her own Court?"

Despite my efforts to suppress it, I could feel the Morrigan's magic creeping under my skin, preparing for a fight. Perhaps it was that which caused Lord Lyle to take a wary step back, his gaze raking over me.

"You insult my Queen needlessly," he said. "It's an honour for you to continue to be allowed to enter the Court after losing your title, mortal."

"Honour is not a word I'd use." It wasn't his fault the Sidhe were incapable of perceiving of a universe which didn't revolve around them, but damn was it inconvenient to deal with. "The only way I'd consider going into the Winter Court is with a guarantee that I'll walk out of there under your protection no matter what comes out of my conversation with the Unseelie Queen."

"You speak as though you expect to be executed for treason."

"As you implied yourself, I'm not protected by my Gatekeeper's title any longer," I said. "And I know perfectly well what your Court thinks of mortals who don't do as they're told. Even you. Do you *enjoy* being sent to fetch me? I doubt you volunteered to babysit the human."

His jaw twitched. "I will not swear a vow to you, mortal, but I cannot lie, and I will give you my word that you will not be harmed while you are in the Winter Court."

Not outside of it? Well, it wasn't like he could do much to stop me from meeting an unfortunate end in the *mortal* realm. Besides, sometimes it was a good idea just to lance the blister and get it over with. "Fine."

"I'll go with you," said Puck. "As insurance."

"Seriously?" Hawk asked. "What do you mean by 'insurance'?"

"He raises a good point." I gave Lord Lyle an expectant look, my heart thumping. Did Puck not recall the last time the pair of us had been to Faerie? Maybe he did and that's why he insisted on inviting himself along.

"To make sure he doesn't find a loophole and leave you to die, for one," Puck said. "Or that there isn't an ambush waiting on the other side."

"You're being ridiculous, mortals," said Lord Lyle. "I have no intention of murdering either of you."

"Good, because if you did, you'd have to deal with our cranky ghosts until the end of time." Maybe I shouldn't have said that, but it wasn't like ghosts were non-existent in Faerie.

Lord Lyle's mouth tightened with disapproval. "You may come, trickster, but not to the Winter Court."

"Didn't plan to," Puck said.

"I want your word that you'll escort *both* of us out of Faerie again after we're done, then," I said. "No detours. No funny business. And if I end up turned into an ice block, then you'll do what you did the last time and get me out."

His pit-like eyes glittered as he dipped his head. "Fine. Come with me. There's no time to waste."

"Faerie is alarmingly good at wasting time *I* don't have," I said. "Let me tell my housemate where I'm going first."

Roseanne would definitely *not* be coming with me, not when the Unseelie Queen had almost forced me to hand her over as payment for her mother's perceived betrayal when she'd been under the spell of the former Huntsman a couple of years ago. Come to think of it… had the Morrigan actually died during that battle and then been reborn? If so, then that was her most recent return from Death, but I'd need to ask someone who'd been there at the time for the details. Definitely not the Unseelie Queen.

Lord Lyle stepped aside to let me enter my house, where I went looking for Roseanne. Rapping on her door with my knuckles, I whispered, "It's me. Don't worry, the Sidhe isn't going to come in the house, but I have to go to the Winter Court for a couple of days."

"What?" she squeaked from the other side of the door. "You can't go there."

"It's not really an invitation I can refuse," I said. "I have Lord Lyle's word that he'll do his best to get me back here in one piece, and besides, Puck is coming with me."

Why, I didn't have time to examine too closely. He'd expressed romantic interest in me once before, yet I couldn't seem to help pushing him away, intentionally or not. Whatever my thoughts on his motives, though, perhaps I did need an independent third party with me in case I ran into any trouble. I doubted Lord Lyle would go with me into the Death Kingdom.

"Please don't get stuck in Faerie," Roseanne whispered through the door.

"I'll only be a couple of days," I reassured her. "There should be enough food in the kitchen. I'll ask Hawk to check up on you, okay?"

She sniffed. Then: "Okay."

After leaving the house, I returned to Lord Lyle, who was currently locked in an intense glare-off with Hawk and Puck. "I'm ready, but I have another request."

"Another request?" he said. "What is it this time?"

"I want to visit the Death Kingdom first," I told him. "Then I'll come to the Court without any further detours."

"Accepted, provided you don't attempt to flee afterwards," he said. "Come with me… and you, too, trickster."

"Hawk, can you check in on my housemate?" I opted not to mention Roseanne's name, though Lord Lyle wouldn't necessarily know who she was. "She's pretty independent, but those half-faeries were being dicks again earlier because of the ghost situation."

"On it," he said. "Don't get eaten."

And on that encouraging note, Puck and I followed the Unseelie knight out of half-blood territory and towards the invisible line which divided this realm from Faerie. While I couldn't see the Ley Line unless I squinted hard enough to give myself a headache, Lord Lyle wasted no time in carrying us through. A dazzling flash of light caused me to screw up my eyes, and when I opened them, I found myself on a familiar leaf-strewn path.

"Meet me here when you're ready to see the Queen," said Lord Lyle.

Puck and I walked away from him, veering off the path towards the Death Kingdom. Finding that distant corner of Winter was somewhat difficult, given that Faerie didn't obey the usual laws of physics and nothing stayed in the same place. Even as Gatekeeper, I hadn't been immune to being led astray, so I kept both eyes open for redcaps and banshees. With each step, the air grew colder, tinged with the smell of decay. I quickened my pace past trees which had twisted into contorted shapes and prickly bushes eager to ensnare passing prey.

"Do you and that Sidhe know one another well?" Puck asked.

"Lord Lyle helped train me as Gatekeeper," I said. "He had a brief spell of convenient amnesia after I lost my title, but I guess he's accepted he can't pretend I don't exist when his Queen insists on inviting me to the Court whenever she wants to taunt her favourite mortal."

"And he won't tell you what she wants with you?"

"Nope." I smothered a sigh. "She doesn't know about... well. You'll see for yourself."

Puzzlement underlaid his reply. "I'll see what?"

I'd told Ilsa, so there was no reason I couldn't tell Puck too. If the Unseelie Queen knew about the Morrigan's disappearance, then the whole of Faerie would soon, I didn't doubt.

"It's easier to show you," I said vaguely. "Did you and Hawk have any luck convincing the mages to send an emergency pack of candles to Brook, by the way?"

"We left a message for them," said Puck. "Hawk is more optimistic than I am, but I can't say either of us has had much experience dealing with the Mage Lords. From what I gather, they think the necromancers ought to be solely responsible for anything involving ghosts."

"That's pretty standard. It'd be fine except that the regular necromancers can't get rid of those ghosts."

"They really don't know the cause of the trouble?" he said.

"Nope, and now they don't have either of us to help them," I said. "Because Faerie's problems are supposed to take precedence even when I live in the mortal realm now."

Movement stirred in the bushes ahead of us. I reached for my iron weapon, but the silent figure of a ghost appeared instead of a solid being, blinking at us with sad blue eyes.

"Ah." I halted. "Yeah… that's what I wanted to show you. Part of it, anyway."

"You know that ghost?" Puck asked.

"No." I waved the knife at the spirit. "Shoo."

If the spirit could be banished, it was beyond me to figure out how. Necromancer candles didn't exist over here, and besides, in Faerie, death was a dirty little secret that few acknowledged, despite the absence of the source of immortality and the fact that the Wild Hunt—who'd once escorted the dead to the next world—was no more.

Maybe death in Faerie had been broken for a while and my own actions had simply exposed the problem that had already been there. That wouldn't prevent me from taking the blame, so I led Puck through the Death Kingdom until we reached the top of the hill from which we could see the blood-drenched moat surrounding the large mound of earth that comprised the Morrigan's home. I walked over the bridge and held my breath at the stench from the rotting bodies beneath. Puck followed, his sharp gaze noting the absence of any guards on the other side. "Where's her security?"

"No idea, but you're about to notice an even more glaring absence." I beckoned him after me into the cave itself.

His brows rose. "You want me to come with you *into* her home?"

"Trust me, it won't be an issue."

I walked into the wide cave, which lay empty except for the unoccupied throne in the centre. No traces remained of the Morrigan except for the iron chains which had once held her captive.

Puck stared at the throne in silence for a moment. "She's free? She broke her chains?"

"Nope, she vanished," I said. "Into thin air, according to her security ogre."

His gaze left the throne and fixed on me instead. "Wait... do you still have her magic?"

"As of right now, yes."

"So you're saying that the Morrigan... she never took her magic back from you?"

"No, but it should have run out of its own accord," I said. "Instead, when I came back here, this was what I found. Needless to say, I got out pretty quickly, so the Unseelie Queen doesn't know."

"I imagine she wouldn't be happy to learn her prisoner escaped," he said.

"She didn't escape, trust me." I walked over to the throne and picked up a handful of thick iron chains. "They aren't broken. She vanished while she was still chained up."

Puck kept his distance from the iron, pacing around the throne. "There's something sparkling under there…"

I reached under the throne and pulled the glittering object into the light. "That's her crown. Guess it fell off when she vanished. Her birds have all gone too."

"Damn." He whistled. "Are you sure you want to see the Unseelie Queen after this?"

"Of course I don't *want* to," I said. "Lord Lyle didn't mention the Morrigan at all, so I'm wondering if Her Majesty actually knows."

"How can she not?" he said. "Doesn't she exchange correspondence with the Morrigan?"

"Occasionally," I said. "Nobody wants to give her bad news to her face, though. Even for a Sidhe, being turned into an ice statue isn't exactly pleasant."

"She did that to you last time." He spoke in a low, measured voice. "This is why I didn't want you to come here alone."

His words slid under my skin like the magic I was doing my level best to suppress. Whatever his intentions, this was not the time for me to get distracted.

I kept my tone free of emotion and didn't meet Puck's gaze. "Let's get this done."

We retraced our steps to the path linking the entrances to both Courts, where Lord Lyle waited for me. I spotted several ghosts on the way, but they gave us a wide berth for the most part. Sensible of them, really. Puck didn't say much, not giving anything away as to whether he agreed with my assessment of the connection between the Morrigan's disappearance and the necromancers' ongoing troubles in the mortal realm.

I walked up to Lord Lyle. "I'm ready to see the Queen."

The Sidhe lord turned right, and a path appeared which hadn't been there before, winding past snowy meadows and crooked, leafless trees. If you were important enough in Faerie, you could make the realm itself obey your commands, as opposed to constantly ending up in traps or meeting dead ends. I gave Puck a brief nod of goodbye and then marched down the path after Lord Lyle into the centre of the Unseelie Court.

He'd led us straight to the heart of his territory. Snow blanketed the large mound of earth in front of us, while two ogres guarded the tunnel leading inside. At the sight of Lord Lyle, they shuffled out of the way without an objection. They must have known I was coming.

Dread trickled down my spine like melting ice. The cave's interior looked much the same as ever, with glittering stalagmites, a star-studded ceiling glamoured to look like the night sky, and groups of redcaps serving refreshments. A band, comprised of several humans plucking at harps and similar instruments, played in the corner. I didn't look too closely to see what their instruments were made of, given the Unseelie Queen's fondness for detaching the body parts from anyone who didn't play fast enough.

In the centre of the cave, the Unseelie Queen lounged on her throne, her glittering white dress reflecting the night sky, gems sparkling in her ears and around her neck, and her glossy dark hair spilling over her shoulders. The air around her wavered as my human senses struggled to take in her sheer majesty, and I avoided meeting her gaze directly so as not to burn my eyes out.

Her red-painted lips pursed in disdain when she saw me, and her bright blue eyes narrowed. "So there you are, mortal. Have you come to keep up your end of our bargain?"

7

"I'm afraid I don't know what you mean, your majesty." I spoke in careful tones, all too aware of the Unseelie Queen's likelihood to leap from languid and indifferent to murderous in the time it took to blink. "We didn't make a bargain, did we?"

This had better not be about Roseanne. When she'd learned of my friendship with the Morrigan's daughter, the Unseelie Queen had ordered me to bring her in as penance for her mother's crimes, despite the fact that they'd both been forced to obey the former leader of the Wild Hunt against their will. I'd sent her a banshee as a replacement harbinger after one had attempted to murder me on my way out of Faerie and hoped that would cause her to put the matter aside, but the Unseelie Queen was as unpredictable as any Sidhe and just as prone to holding grudges—with unmatched magical prowess to back it up.

"You were once sworn to me," she said. "I once trusted you, mortal, so why did you not tell me of the Morrigan's passing?"

My heart leapt into my throat. "She's dead?"

"Do *not* lie, mortal." Her words brought an ice-cold breeze which struck me like a slap and made me take a step backwards.

"I'm not lying." I silently cursed the tremor in my voice. "I thought she disappeared, but she's reborn whenever her body dies, isn't she?"

"I have my pet death faerie to thank for letting me know," she said. "You knew, but you slipped away to the mortal realm without informing me, didn't you?"

So she *had* taken in the banshee I'd sent to her as a pet harbinger. Why she'd wanted one in the first place was a mystery to me, but it should mean that Roseanne was safe from her for the time being. I, however, wouldn't be so lucky.

"You didn't tell me to come back." I knew I was treading on dangerous ground, since the Sidhe hated when we mortals turned their own deceptive tendencies against them, but nothing I said would be satisfying when she'd already chosen where to lay the blame. "I assumed you'd want to learn of her disappearance from one of your own people, not from me."

"That wasn't your decision to make, mortal."

No doubt I'd have been screwed either way, given her mercurial nature—and that was without considering how I'd taken possession of some of the Morrigan's magic.

"I have no knowledge of where the Morrigan is," I said carefully. "If that's why you asked me to come here, there's nothing I can do to bring her back."

"That is not why I asked you to come."

"Then why?"

"There is a ghost here in my Court," she said. "I want you to get rid of it."

She wanted *me* to banish a ghost... from Faerie? "I don't know how."

"Your sister does," said the Unseelie Queen. "Bring her here."

"I don't have a sister." My heart gave an uncomfortable flip. "Do you mean one of my cousins?"

"It makes no difference to me," she said. "I want the one who has the power of an Ancient talisman at her disposal."

"You mean... Ilsa?" She had to be out of her mind. Ilsa had never *been* to the Winter Court before, as far as I was aware. Even Hazel hadn't, because the two Courts rarely mixed with one another, and non-Gatekeepers had never possessed any real means of defending themselves against Faerie's hazards. Ilsa's talisman, powerful though it might be, wouldn't be a guarantee of protection.

"That one," said the Unseelie Queen. "You will bring her to me immediately."

"You can't—" I broke off. Who was I kidding? She absolutely *could* order me to bring Ilsa here against her will. "Ilsa lives in the mortal realm, and she has little experience with Faerie. Besides, her talisman can only banish human ghosts, not faerie ones."

"I told you not to lie to me," she said. "I know for a fact that she banished your mother."

My blood iced over. "My mother was human."

"Not in the end." She rose to her feet, the folds of her dress pooling around her feet, while I found myself having to crane my neck to look up at her. I wasn't used to that, when most Sidhe were only slightly taller than I was, but with her magic at full power, she appeared as towering as a skyscraper.

"My apologies," I said, my throat dry. "It's my understanding that Ilsa did banish my mother's wraith, when she was human, but when she became immortal, it was iron that killed her."

I was pretty sure her talisman *had* played a part in my mother's second banishment, but I'd never seen her banish the conscious ghost of a Sidhe. Wraiths weren't the same. Or so I thought.

"Bring her to me." Her hand shot out, her fingers digging into the side of my face. "Or I will ensure you pay the price for your mother's transgressions as well as for your lies."

Bile burned the back of my throat. My heartbeat raced wildly, and for a horrible moment, shadows stirred beneath my fingertips while I fought to keep them in check. If the Morrigan's magic leapt at her, then my doom would be sealed.

Before it did, however, she let go. I touched a trembling hand to my cheek, expecting it to come away bloody, but she hadn't broken the skin.

"If Ilsa dies," I began, my voice a faltering whisper. "If she dies here, then the Ancient that dwells in her talisman will enact revenge on the entire Court. I have no control over what it might do."

"I will not harm your cousin," she said, her tone almost pitying. "She has not done me any wrong, unlike yourself and your family, and I am sure she will have more sense than you do. I will give you until the day after you return to the mortal realm to bring her to me. Do not delay."

Her words rang out with finality, and her eyes

brimmed with power which could do much worse than turn me into an ice statue. Even the Morrigan had been unable to fight back after she'd been encased in chains for her actions during the Huntsman's attack on the mortal realm.

Movement stirred behind me, jerking my attention away from how dangerously close I was to looking her in the eyes. Several ogres and redcaps had crept into view, watching our standoff, while I spotted the pale form of the banshee she'd adopted lurking in a corner. My throat tightened, and I managed a couple of steps backwards before I regained full control over my limbs.

"I will endeavour to fulfil your request," I choked out, before turning away and leaving the cave as fast as my human legs would carry me.

The cold breeze outside brought a swirl of snowflakes which stung my cheeks, but hot anger burned away the chill. *She has to be joking.* How the hell was I supposed to tell Ilsa's boss why I was taking away one of the necromancer guild's most crucial members when the city was in dire need of her help? If I didn't know Lady Montgomery for the no-nonsense sort, I'd expect her to laugh in my face at the mere question. Ilsa, of course, would know of the potential backlash to refusing the Unseelie Queen's invitation, but for most humans, the Sidhe were nothing more than a hypothetical force of terror, not an enemy they expected to see in the flesh. Like a meteor strike or a rare plague. The fact that they *had* brought calamity on Earth twenty-something years prior made them a cut above a myth or superstition, but not typically someone you ran into in your everyday life unless you willingly walked into their domain.

Never mind that most humans who entered Faerie were *un*willing. Even the Gatekeepers. Cursing Thomas Lynn under my breath, I crunched down the snowy path until the snow became slush and then leaves. A black crow flew in front of me and then shifted into Puck, causing me to stop mid-step with my hand on my weapon.

"It's me," said Puck. "Lord Lyle is waiting back there."

"Excellent." My hands fisted. "I need a punching bag."

"Why?"

"She wants Ilsa. To banish a ghost. Yes, a human who's never set foot in the Unseelie Court."

Puck blinked. "She asked you to bring your cousin here?"

I swung my glare on the approaching figure of Lord Lyle. "I can see why you didn't want to tell me yourself that she's asking me to bring my cousin here. As if I don't know exactly what she does to most humans she invites into her domain."

"I did not know the nature of her request, only that there's a specific ghost she wishes for you to help her with," said Lord Lyle. "No Sidhe has been able to rid the Court of the spirit, but your cousin is experienced in the area, is she not?"

"No, she bloody well isn't," I said. "I told your queen that she's never used the book on a Sidhe ghost before, certainly not here in Faerie. I might as well try teaching algebra to an ogre."

"Does her talisman not contain the power of an Ancient?" Lord Lyle dropped his voice, as though concerned the trees were listening in on our conversation. Which, given that we were in Faerie, was a fair possibility. "Our predecessors' magic should suffice to banish a simple spirit."

"Her talisman is designed to be used in the mortal realm." The guy was as stubborn as his Queen. "Not here. I didn't think Faerie *had* its own Gates of Death."

The Death Kingdom was more of a crossover area, through which the Wild Hunt had been responsible for escorting the dead to be reborn. If any kind of necromancer-style system had existed in Faerie before immortality, I didn't know of it.

"I am not an expert," said Lord Lyle. "I have never died."

"There's a first time for everything." The words slipped out before I thought better of them, but he was the one who'd landed me in this mess to begin with. "Would you be so keen to drag a defenceless human into your realm if you didn't know your capricious Queen would as easily turn *you* into a statue as she would the rest of us if she didn't get her way?"

His moment's hesitation made me roll my eyes. *Thought not.* He might be loyal to his Queen to the detriment of his own comfort, but that didn't mean he wasn't scared witless at the notion of experiencing one of her brutal punishments first-hand. She'd gained her position by murdering the competition and claiming the talisman nobody else in the Court was strong enough to master. That made her the most magically accomplished person in Winter by default. Her only potential challenger had been the Morrigan, who was no longer a threat to her, which left the rest of the Sidhe with the choice between unquestionably doing her bidding or being exiled.

"I will convince your cousin she will not come to harm," Lord Lyle said.

This just got better and better. If an Unseelie knight wandered into the middle of the necromancer guild, then it was safe to say my uninvited visits would be at an end. "I don't think that's a good idea. The guild is warded with iron against trespassers. If you march in there waving your sword around, they'd be within their rights to declare war on you for threatening their place of safety."

The necromancers likely wouldn't start an outright conflict when they were already fighting one impossible battle, but sometimes the best way to get through to the Sidhe was to talk in terms they'd understand. A similar transgression in their own realm was likely to result in war, after all.

"That won't be necessary," said Lord Lyle. "I will meet your cousin elsewhere, not within the guild."

"Our realm has its own ghost-related problems, you know, and she's one of the few people who can handle them. Death is screwed up. The guild needs her."

I couldn't picture Lady Montgomery handing her over to Faerie without a fight, but now I thought about it, River himself was half Summer fae. That meant his mother, Lady Montgomery, must have been intimately acquainted with a Sidhe at one point, which meant she must have some understanding of the tricky nature of faeries' requests. That might be our saving grace... but that didn't mean Ilsa had the time or ability to banish the Unseelie Queen's unwanted spirit.

"She speaks the truth," added Puck. "I imagine the guild will look poorly on you if their Gatekeeper goes missing in Faerie."

"My Queen has no desire to harm the Gatekeeper," insisted Lord Lyle.

"What if she fails, then?" I asked. "If Ilsa can't banish the ghost, will the Queen throw one of her infamous temper tantrums and take out her anger on everyone in her path? Because her promise not to harm either of us seems to be contingent on Ilsa doing something which has never been achieved in Faerie before."

Or as far as I was aware, anyway.

Lord Lyle's mouth thinned. "Why would she fail? Is it not the same as banishing a ghost in your own realm?"

"No, it isn't," I said. "Also, you know the Morrigan is missing, don't you? Isn't she usually in charge of Death-related matters?"

It was probably my fault the Unseelie Queen was being haunted in the first place, but over my literal dead body would I admit it to his face.

"The Morrigan keeps to herself," said Lord Lyle stiffly. "None of us is aware of how her abilities work, except perhaps my Queen, but she does not speak on the subject."

"I bet she doesn't," I muttered. "Isn't she actually looking for the Morrigan at all? I know they weren't exactly friendly with one another, but if her absence is causing ghosts to appear where they aren't supposed to be…"

I dangled the possibility, heart in my throat, hoping he wouldn't make the connection with my own last visit here.

Lord Lyle stared at me for a moment. "This has been going on for much longer than the Morrigan's disappearance, mortal. Since the source of immortality was broken, there have been many more ghosts appearing in Faerie.

This is the first to enter the Court, but it will not be the last."

Did that mean it *wasn't* my fault? I'd bet the reason the ghosts had started wandering into the Courts was due to the Morrigan no longer being able to keep them in check, at the very least, but it wasn't like I could rip away the Morrigan's magic from my veins and give it back.

On the other hand, the Morrigan's power had enabled me to do some serious damage to a ghost in the mortal realm. Might *I* be able to get rid of the spirit? I'd need to be careful if I did, but it would at least help get Ilsa off the hook if her own talisman was unable to carry out the banishment. Regardless, the only way I'd be able to try was if I kept my word to the Unseelie Queen and brought Ilsa with me. However little she deserved to be made into a pawn.

Puck cleared his throat. "So, are you going to speak to Ilsa once we're back?"

"The Queen gave me until tomorrow to convince her," I said. "At least we have that."

"Then I will take you home." Lord Lyle beckoned us after him. "I will return within a day for your answer from her."

"I don't suppose there's a slight chance you can talk some sense into Her Majesty?"

"No," said Lord Lyle. "She has exhausted all other options. Think what it means for her to ask a mortal for help."

Yeah. She was desperate, all right, but that didn't make her any less likely to lash out if Ilsa wasn't able to solve her ghostly problem. Which meant putting the burden on *me,* and on the magic which I wasn't supposed to have in the first place.

In a flash of light, Lord Lyle dropped us off on the other side of the Ley Line. The sky in Edinburgh was dark, signalling more than a day had passed since we'd left.

"I will come back in a day's time," said Lord Lyle and vanished before I could answer.

"That was generous of him," said Puck. "I reckon we missed a few days again, though."

"Figures." Damn, I was tired. "So… want to come with me to tell Ilsa the bad news?"

8

"You're joking," said Ilsa.

"I'm really not."

I'd had to wait until the following morning to meet with Ilsa as she was on an all-night mission at the guild, and while Cassandra's Cafe wasn't exactly a private place to talk, the small supernatural-run cafe was crowded enough that nobody paid any attention to our table in the corner.

Ilsa, who'd been imbibing coffee at a slightly alarming rate, rested her head in her steepled hands. "A day? That's all they've given me?"

"I was lucky to get that much." I absent-mindedly touched my hand to my cheek, where the Unseelie Queen had dug her nails into my skin. "Saying no wasn't an option."

"I can't go to Faerie," she said. "I'm needed here."

"I know." Roseanne had said as much when I'd told her the bad news last night, while my plan to employ the Morrigan's powers on the ghost had been shot down as far too risky. I'd hoped Ilsa and I might come up with a viable alternative, but first I needed to convince her to come with me in the first place.

It didn't help that Jas and her vampire boyfriend, Keir, were at the next table, with Pepper the faerie puppy running around and drawing rather a lot of attention from the other patrons. The vampire kept glancing in our direction, for some reason, but I didn't think he'd have any reason to eavesdrop.

"I wish I could help," Ilsa said, "but there's no way I'll be able to convince the guild to let me disappear at a time like this. Lady Montgomery might understand why, but what would happen if I ended up vanishing for days? Or worse?"

"The Unseelie Queen told me she'd see to it that you didn't come to any harm," I said. "For what it's worth, I wouldn't ask you to do this if there was another way, but I'm pretty sure refusal will mean Lord Lyle will be vow-bound to march directly into the guild in person and haul you straight into Faerie."

Ilsa rubbed her eyes. "I realise that telling the Sidhe the universe doesn't revolve around them is like trying to negotiate with a toddler, but who *is* this ghost who's bothering the Unseelie Queen so much?"

"Haven't a clue, but it sounds like it got into the Winter Court and won't leave," I said. "If you could use your book to get rid of it, then it'd be a quick job, but if not…"

"If not, then we'll both end up skewered to the walls."

"Not necessarily." I dropped my voice. "There's a chance I *might* be able to remove it myself, but I'd rather Her Majesty didn't bear witness to that."

Ilsa's eyes bulged. "Lying to the Sidhe? Seriously?"

"Can you think of a better option?" I sure as hell couldn't, and unlike her, I hadn't spent the last few days running around the city trapping ghosts in candle circles on no sleep. "If we get her out of our hair, then it'll be one fewer thing to worry about."

"I was blissfully unaware that I *needed* to worry about her until you told me." Ilsa drained the dregs of her mug of coffee. "Besides, you don't work for her anymore. Why's she still giving you orders?"

"Because she thinks I owe her," I muttered, not wanting to get into a discussion on that. Ilsa knew perfectly well why the Unseelie Queen would see me as in her debt—and that wasn't even getting into my possible link to the Morrigan's disappearance. "Lord Lyle dragged me before her. Almost in a literal sense."

"Damn." Ilsa drummed her fingers on the table. "I really thought the curse being broken would get them out of our lives, you know?"

"You and me both." Never mind that we wouldn't have had to deal with the Wild Hunt at all if the Sidhe had arrested the lot of them after Fionn's death. "In fairness, I haven't quite abandoned the theory that whatever's going on in Death has its roots in Faerie."

"If the ghosts are acting anything like the ones in this realm, the banishment won't be permanent, then," Ilsa said. "Not that I think the two are connected, but that's another issue to consider."

No kidding. "What's the guild doing to contain them? I notice the city looks pretty normal, all things considered."

Her eye twitched. "It's a facade. What we ended up doing was setting up circles in the guild's spare rooms and summoning the strongest ghosts into them so they wouldn't wreak havoc in the rest of the city. Unfortunately, there are only so many candles to go around, and we weren't able to spare any to give to the half-faeries."

"I hope they managed to get through to the mages, then." I cast a glance around the cafe and locked eyes with the vampire at the neighbouring table again. This time, the stark hostility in his stare caught me off guard. Granted, I wasn't exactly *friendly* with the guild members, but I'd got on okay with Jas, his girlfriend. What was that dude's problem? Had he overheard our conversation and figured out I was about to send the guild's best necromancer to Faerie?

I returned my attention to Ilsa, who wore a thoughtful expression. "I have a suggestion, but it's... well, it's possibly a worse idea than going to Faerie, to tell you the truth."

"Come on, now you'll have to tell me what it is."

"Summon the Morrigan," she said.

"You're right... that *is* a terrible idea." I shook my head. "Is that even possible? She's not a ghost."

"I bet she can be summoned," said Ilsa. "If you can summon Ancients and related creatures from hellish dimensions, then surely we can summon her from wherever she ended up after she disappeared."

"Not sold on the 'hellish dimensions' part." If anyone with connections among the mages or the upper ranks of the necromancers found out, we were liable to end up being arrested for so much as contemplating the possibility of summoning a death goddess into the mortal realm. "How many laws would that break?"

She winced. "A lot."

"Thought so." Blood magic was barely legal, but summonings were dodgy territory, and summoning death faeries landed firmly in the "nope" category. Add in the fact that the Morrigan was supposed to be under house arrest by the Unseelie Court for the havoc she'd wreaked during her last trip to the mortal realm, and we'd be lucky not to be sentenced to death. And honestly, I wouldn't blame the mages a bit. "Ilsa, summoning *her* makes taking on a faerie vow seem like a relaxing beach holiday."

"Is that really any more dangerous than the pair of us going to the Unseelie Court?" she asked.

Fair point. "I'm pretty sure you couldn't put the Unseelie Queen in iron chains without leaving a mark on her. And she at least didn't fight on the side of the invaders."

"Yeah… true." She rubbed her tired eyes. "I wouldn't forgive myself if we ended up with a situation like the last time she got loose in the mortal realm, under Fionn's orders. A lot of people died. Ivy told me."

"Exactly." I heaved a sigh. "Besides, summonings are risky territory. Didn't you say the reason you ended up with a faerie puppy is because Morgan tried summoning something else and Pepper showed up instead? I realise a cute puppy isn't the worst thing to accidentally summon, but still."

Ilsa snorted. "Everyone thought he was a hellhound at first. Anyway, forget I suggested it. I just think it's more doable than banishing a ghost in Faerie without making things worse than they already are."

"*Have* you banished any ghosts from Faerie?"

"I banished some wraiths." Her mouth twisted. "The backlash knocked me out cold. I was lucky to survive."

My heart lurched. "Fuck. I didn't know."

"Not like I wanted to repeat it." She checked her phone, scrolling down the screen with her fingertip. "I thought the Morrigan might be able to solve the problem…"

"The Unseelie Queen would know if she can," I said. "Lord Lyle said it's not a subject she's discussed with the other Sidhe, but there's a chance Her Majesty might know where she typically vanishes to before she's reborn into a new body. Pity she's unlikely to share that information with us mere mortals."

"If she *did* tell you, then we might be able to get her back," Ilsa said. "In the meantime, I can't exactly carry a bunch of candles into the Court. They don't work that way over there."

"I figured." Even the mages lost most of their magical prowess when they set foot in Faerie, which was partly why they liked to pretend it didn't exist. The mortal realm might have comparatively less magic, but it at least obeyed clear rules. Faerie operated on its own bizarre type of logic, a lot of which even the Sidhe didn't seem to fully understand.

Take the Morrigan, for example. If only there was someone other than the Unseelie Queen who might have the knowledge as to whereabouts she might be hiding, but in Faerie, you never got anything for free.

Ilsa pushed back her chair. "River is on his way. If you don't want to be here when I tell him, I'd suggest you get out."

Great. "I need to go back to half-blood territory anyway, to see how they're dealing with the ghosts."

I hadn't asked what'd happened to the one who'd been

lurking in Leyton's house yet, so I had to check with Roseanne. Or Hawk. My phone buzzed as I rose to my feet, and I glimpsed a new message from Puck saying he was heading over to half-blood territory as well.

Jas and Keir got up from their table, and the latter reached the door before I did. Coldness shot through me when we locked eyes. That was the vampire effect, I supposed, though I wasn't totally clear on how Keir's abilities differed from a regular necromancer's.

Other than that, the vampire's sculptured features and tangled shoulder-length dark hair might have put me in mind of a fae if not for the fact that I stood a head taller than him and could probably have taken him in a fight. Besides, I refused to be intimidated by a human, given that I'd faced the Unseelie Queen less than a day ago. "Is there a problem?"

His gaze raked over me. "What are you?"

"What?" I said blankly.

"Keir!" Jas grabbed his arm. "What are you doing?"

"Asking me bizarre and personal questions," I said. "If you mean what species, I'm human. If you mean what kind of supernatural, ask the faeries if there's a word for a human with the Sight."

"Your soul doesn't look like a human's."

"I'm sorry, what?"

"What he means to say," Jas said, "is that we're all stressed out and it's been a long week. Sorry he ambushed you. Your soul looks perfectly human to me."

"But—" Keir cut off as the faerie puppy barrelled into his legs and began chasing his tail around in circles.

"Thanks," I said to Jas. "See you later."

I walked away before the vampire waylaid me again,

though for all I knew, he was right. Had the Morrigan's magic had some permanent effect on my *soul?* That was all I needed. For all I knew, next I'd be shifting into a giant crow every time I lost my temper. I'd come dangerously close back there when the Unseelie Queen had threatened me, and I didn't like to think how badly that might have turned out.

Suppressing a shudder, I headed back to half-blood territory as fast as I could walk. I'd forgotten to reply to Puck's message, but I almost walked straight past him near the front gate to half-blood territory.

"What's going on with you?" he asked. "Did you get my message?"

"Yes, but a vampire just told me my soul doesn't look like a human's, so I was a little distracted." I checked my phone and reread his message, which said he and Hawk were on their way to check out the ghost situation.

"That's pleasant," said Puck. "I can't say I've ever met a vampire. They're not fae?"

"I had the same question when I first came to Edinburgh," I said. "They're necromancers, and they get their name from the way they drain people. Except they don't drink blood. They... wait, they feed on spirit energy. Maybe he *would* know if my soul isn't fully human."

Puck stared at me. "The Morrigan...?"

"I don't have time to think about the state of my soul when the world is in chaos," I said, wishing I'd never brought up the subject. "Ilsa suggested summoning the Morrigan ourselves, but we threw that idea out pretty quickly."

"Summoning her?" he said. "You mean with a ritual like the Wild Hunt's?"

"She freely admitted it was a bad idea," I said. "Especially as we'd probably need a blood sacrifice to do the summoning. Granted, if anyone can summon her, it's Ilsa, but she's run off her feet and I don't think I helped when I dropped the Unseelie Queen's request on her head."

"She said no?"

"She said she'd think about it, but we both know that you don't just refuse a request from Faerie."

His expression darkened. "The Unseelie Queen might have agreed not to harm your cousin, but I understand why she wouldn't want to take the risk."

"I wouldn't either," I said. "Not that summoning the Morrigan isn't risky, too, but she'd certainly be able to take care of the ghost. She might even be able to explain what's going on with Death."

"I'm not convinced she would know," he said. "Faerie would be better off if she were back where she belongs, of course, but that doesn't mean… ah, there's Hawk."

Puck's friend waved at me from behind the gate. "Thought I heard your voice out here. Congratulations on surviving another trip to Faerie."

"Thanks, I think," I said. "Did Puck tell you why I went there?"

"Your cousin must be thrilled," he said. "Almost as thrilled as I am that the mages sent us a grand total of *one* set of candles to protect half-blood territory from the ghosts."

"Of course they did." I gave an eye roll. "Otherwise, how's the situation?"

"Not great," he said. "If we want to get the most out of the candles, we'll have to set them up around the whole of half-blood territory, which means driving out *every* ghost in here. Including the one we trapped in Leyton's house."

"You mean the one *we* trapped," said Roseanne, bounding over to us. "While you watched."

"Everything okay?" I asked her.

"Sure," she said. "Need me to scare off some ghosts?"

"Brook is coordinating everything," Hawk added. "We need to get every single ghost outside the boundaries of the territory before lighting the candles, which means a coordinated effort. Last I checked, there were at least thirty spirits drifting around."

"Wonderful." At least it'd take my mind off my looming trip to the Unseelie Queen's home. "How are you going to go about driving all the ghosts outside the territory without the help of a necromancer?"

"Salt, candles, and yelling, mostly," said Hawk. "We'll need a necromancer for the last step, but I'm sure your cousin will volunteer."

"If her boyfriend doesn't show up with his talisman and murder me in my sleep."

"You mean River?" Puck said. "He's that pissed off with you?"

"It's not like he can take it out on the Sidhe, can he?" I pointed out. "Look, I backed her into a corner, and she *told* me that last time she banished ghosts in Faerie nearly got her killed. River is pretty mild-mannered for a fae, but who wouldn't be angry with me after bringing an ultimatum from the Unseelie Queen?"

"Me," said Roseanne. "And I haven't even met her."

"Better hope you never do," I said, suppressing a shudder at the reminder of the close call she'd had. "Right, let's get rid of some ghosts."

Brook had already assembled a team of half-faeries, both Seelie and Unseelie, to help scare off the ghosts while others set up the circle of candles around their territory. I was pretty impressed with how quickly he'd put together a game plan, handing out canisters of salt to everyone who volunteered and organising them into groups. I stepped in to help, glad of the chance to temporarily push the impossible situation the Unseelie Queen had put me into to the back of my mind.

Roseanne, Puck, and I teamed up, while Hawk said vaguely that he was going to help Leyton "prepare to move the ghost" and then disappeared for an hour. While I'd mentally prepared to have to defend Roseanne from more derisive comments, the others were more occupied with the ghosts than with my harbinger companion. While the other groups scattered throughout half-blood territory, we went to divest Leyton of his unwanted guest.

Puck knocked on the door to Leyton's house, while Roseanne and I prepared what was left of our salt. After days of being trapped in the cloakroom, I suspected the ghost would be keen to escape, but that didn't mean it wouldn't do some damage on the way out.

Roseanne knocked on the door when he didn't answer. "Hey, open up!"

"What have they been doing in there?" I checked on my salt supplies. Not much left. I might have to resort to using the Morrigan's powers again. "Not banishing the ghost, evidently."

Roseanne shot me a sideways grin. "Unless the ghost was helping them take one another's clothes off."

"Huh?" I'd known he and Hawk had got over their

initial coolness towards one another, but I'd clearly missed something while Puck and I had been in Faerie.

Puck laughed, but luckily, Leyton opened the door before he could make a comment. He looked a little flushed but thankfully had all his clothes on. "Oh, you're back."

"We've come to evict your ghost," I said. "But if you're busy…"

"I'm not," he said. "Hawk has been helping me out."

"Bet he has," said Roseanne.

I shot her a warning look. We were supposed to be professionals, after all, though when two of our four-person team were a teenage death faerie and a trickster fae, the word 'professional' might be a questionable choice. "Has the ghost stopped raising a fuss? Or didn't you get the chance to do anything yet?"

The flush on his neck deepened. "I did get a silencing charm to put on the cloakroom door to keep it quiet."

"I didn't know you had any witch charms." I spotted Hawk behind him, hovering near the cloakroom door. "Anyway, ready to get rid of that ghost?"

"One second." Hawk darted past me, out of range of the ghost's route out of the house. Roseanne rolled her eyes after him, while the rest of us entered the living room.

A flash came from the cloakroom door as the spell deactivated, and then the ghost's voice rang out. "How dare you keep me imprisoned in here? This is a violation of my human rights."

"You're a ghost." Roseanne yanked on the door handle. "And you've outstayed your welcome."

A bolt of bright blue energy blasted through the open

door, while the rest of us ducked behind the furniture to avoid being struck. Roseanne, who'd thrown herself flat to the carpet, lunged into the cupboard and grabbed one of the candles, yanking it out of line.

At once, the ghost shot out of the cupboard with the force of a bullet, straight out of the house through the front wall.

"That was easier than I expected," said Hawk. "We've washed our hands of that guy."

"Don't forget we have to drive him off half-blood territory." I followed Puck out of the house via the front door, one-handedly texting Ilsa to tell her that we'd soon need a necromancer to help light the candles.

As I'd predicted, the ghost hadn't gone far from the house, and he turned on us with a shriek when we emerged. "You'll pay for that!"

"Catch me if you can." Roseanne darted past, sticking her tongue out at him and waving her salt canister in the air.

Leyton wasted no time in upending his own salt canister in front of the house, while Hawk remained at a sensible distance from the ghost. Puck, meanwhile, shifted into a bird and flew at the spirit, and Roseanne shifted and joined him. The pair of them made a good team, flying close enough to goad the spirit into trying to grab them before flitting out of range. What the ghost didn't notice was that each movement brought him closer to the fence dividing this side of half-blood territory from the rest of the city.

Elsewhere, the other groups of half-faeries drove out the other lingering spirits, while I spotted a dark-cloaked figure approaching our territory from the outside. Not

Ilsa. She was too short to be my cousin, but I recognised her.

Jas flipped down her hood when she saw me near the gate. "Hey, Holly."

"You volunteered to help us?" I was kind of surprised, given how her vampire boyfriend had thought I was some kind of evil spirit earlier, but I'd bet Ilsa was tied up elsewhere.

"Yeah, Ilsa really needs a nap," she said. "I just have to light the candles, right?"

"They're self-lighting ones, so work your necromancer magic the instant we get that dude out of here."

I indicated the ghost, who was attempting to blast Puck's bird form out of the air. Bright blue magic shone in his palms, but when he spotted Jas, he turned his attention on her instead. "I will not be banished, necromancer."

"Oh yeah?" Roseanne popped up in front of him in human form and threw an entire canister of salt straight through him.

The spirit recoiled, while Brook signalled at me from the other end of the road. The other ghosts were gone. One left.

"Hey, dickhead!" I shouted at the ghost, giving him the finger. When he flew at me, I stepped swiftly backwards, grimacing when the chilling touch of the grave washed over me at his touch, but he'd failed to notice the invisible barrier between the candles on either side of him.

At a faint nod from me, Jas snapped her fingers, and white-blue lights ignited around the territory as all twelve candles turned on at once. The ghost spun on his heel and grabbed for me, but the invisible barrier kept him from entering half-blood territory again. He shrieked, howling at the top of his lungs, and the echo of a dozen other ghosts drifted from outside.

"We'll need to invest in earplugs for tonight." I gave Roseanne an approving nod, and she grinned in return. "Nice job."

"You bet," said Jas. "Uh, sorry about what Keir said to you earlier, Holly. I think he's seeing hostile vampires everywhere."

"He doesn't think *I'm* a vampire, does he?" I lowered my voice so nobody else could hear us except for Roseanne. Jas didn't know I'd kept the Morrigan's power, but did it really matter if I told her? It wasn't like she was familiar with Faerie, after all.

"No," she said. "I was telling the truth when I said *I* didn't see anything weird about you."

"I think I might know what the issue is," I said. "Remember the magic I borrowed for the fight with the Wild Hunt?"

Her brow furrowed. "The Morrigan gave you a loan, right? Ilsa said."

"Some of that magic lingered behind," I said. "Maybe it made my ghost look weird, I don't know. Not like I can see it."

"Ah, that makes sense," she said. "Should I mention that to Keir?"

"Best keep it quiet, but you can tell him I'm not a vampire if he asks," I said. "Thanks for the help."

After all the effort we'd gone to, we'd better hope nobody found any surprise ghosts hiding in their cupboards when they went back home.

9

Instead of Lord Lyle, the following morning brought another surprise visitor altogether. Shortly after I'd got back from checking on the circle around half-blood territory to make sure nobody had knocked over any of the candles overnight, someone knocked on my front door. Bracing myself to face the grumpy Sidhe, I opened the door to find none other than Hazel Lynn standing on the other side.

"What are you doing here?" I was not mentally prepared for the former Summer Gatekeeper to appear on my doorstep wearing a glaringly bright-orange T-shirt which said, "I met the dragons of London and all I got was this crappy T-shirt."

"Ilsa called me," said Hazel. "She said it was urgent."

Instead of asking how she'd got here so fast when I'd thought she was way down in Cornwall, I found myself asking, "What's with the shirt?"

"I bought it from some dragon shifters in London," she said. "Can I come in?"

"Go ahead." What the hell. She'd already come all this way, after all. "Did you come here directly from London?"

"Yeah, I came via the spirit line, which is a bloody nuisance, I might add." She sauntered past me into the living room. "Anyway, what's this I hear about the Unseelie demanding that you bring Ilsa to the Court to solve their problems?"

"They have a ghost wandering around the Court," I explained. "Ilsa's the Gatekeeper of Death, and the Unseelie Queen won't accept any alternative. Not that there is one, since the Morrigan is missing."

"She's *what?*"

I pinched the bridge of my nose. "You've been out of touch with Faerie, haven't you? Hang on, I'll get my housemate. She'll want to hear this."

"You have a *housemate?*"

I ignored her incredulous tone and ran upstairs to Roseanne's room, knocking on the door. "Hey, Roseanne. We have a visitor."

No reply came. I tried to open the door but found she'd wedged something under it which meant I could only get it open a crack. In the gap, I glimpsed her sitting on the bed, reading a book.

"I don't want to meet any visitors," Roseanne grumbled.

"Are you reading one of Ilsa's books, by any chance?"

"Yes, it's a really weird fantasy series set on an alternate earth in which all the magic users live in an apocalyptic wasteland ruled by a zombie king."

"Sounds fascinating, but my cousin Hazel wants to meet you," I said. "You know, the former Summer Gatekeeper and the person who broke the curse on our family. Ilsa's twin sister. Interested now?"

"Oh." She let the book fall from her hands onto the bed. "Does she know...?"

"Nope, because she just showed up."

Roseanne darted across the room and removed whatever was blocking the door. "All right."

On the way downstairs, I messaged Ilsa and Morgan saying their sister was in town, doubting she'd opted to warn them she was on the way up north either. In the living room, Hazel had made herself comfortable, sprawling on the sofa to display the ghastly orange T-shirt she'd procured. Despite her casual jeans and Converse, I spotted a couple of iron knives poking out of her pockets. Some habits were hard to shake.

Her attention flickered over to Roseanne. "Nice place you've got here. That your housemate? Wait, she's a minor?"

"Long story," I said. "This is Roseanne. Roseanne, this is Hazel, the former Summer Gatekeeper."

And the reason we're in this mess, I refrained from adding. Roseanne nodded shyly, evidently trying to gauge Hazel's likely attitude towards her. Which would take about four seconds, but Hazel was anything but subtle. Sure enough, she gave a wide grin. "Wow, who'd have thought it? Holly Lynn taking care of a teenage faerie. I knew you had a heart buried somewhere under all that ice."

"Hazel." Annoyance flickered through me. "If you came all the way up north to help Ilsa, why did you come to visit *me* first? Wait, who gave you my address?"

"Ilsa did," she said. "She told me to wait for her and Morgan here."

"Who designated my house as a meeting room?" I folded my arms across my chest. "I swear, if you make this one disappear—"

Hazel rolled her eyes. "You're still pissed off at me about that?"

"She made your *house* disappear?" Roseanne wanted to know. "How'd she do that?"

"It was a side effect of the Gatekeeper's curse breaking," Hazel explained. "The original Lynn house had split into two copies so each of the Gatekeepers would get their own separate base, and when the curse broke, they merged into one house again. My house vanished as well as yours did, remember? Don't go getting your facts mixed up."

"And your mother moved into the one house which was left behind."

She sniffed. "Did you expect me to let my poor old mother live on the streets?"

"She's hardly ancient or frail." Also, I was the one who'd ended up on the streets in lieu of taking charity from my estranged relatives. Including Hazel herself. Not that she had any idea, because she'd immediately taken off with her boyfriend for a long holiday to celebrate her newfound freedom.

Hazel snorted. "You're lucky I didn't invite my mum to this family reunion as well. Anyway, tell me everything."

Where to start? "Did you bring Darrow with you?"

"Yes, but he's staying in a hotel," she said. "We both are. Unless you'd like to let us camp out in your house for a couple of nights?"

"Not a chance, because I won't be here," I said. "I have until tomorrow to convince the Sidhe to leave Ilsa the hell alone, and I stand more of a chance of learning to ride a unicycle."

I gave her a quick rundown of the last few weeks, starting with the murders and our discovery that the Wild Hunt was responsible. When I told her the Morrigan had loaned me her magic, she whistled. "That's impressive. You must have been really convincing."

"I have regrets now." I pushed ahead, telling her about the issues which had emerged in the aftermath, including our current ghostly problem. "So the Morrigan is gone, leaving the Unseelie Court without anyone who might be able to get rid of their unwanted spirit except your sister."

"You killed the Morrigan?" Hazel asked.

"She vanished," I corrected her. "Left her chains behind and everything. I *think* she went to wherever she goes when she's reborn…"

"Which means she *is* dead, technically."

"It's not a permanent state with her, is it?" I pointed out. "Never mind the semantics. Do *you* have any idea how long it'll take her to come back?"

"No, of course not," she said. "I thought *you* were the expert on the Winter Court."

"The Death Kingdom has its own rules." To say the least. "The Unseelie Queen might know, but she's pissed off with me at the moment."

Hazel shook her head at me. "You've really got yourself in a bind, haven't you? And poor Ilsa has to be the one to get rid of the Unseelie Queen's ghost. I wonder if it's the spirit of someone the Queen killed?"

"I honestly couldn't give a crap," I said. "Without the

Morrigan… I don't know what role she actually has in handling the dead, but her absence is a glaring imbalance if I ever saw one."

"Do you think the Unseelie Queen might soften up and tell you where she's hiding out if you and Ilsa get rid of her unwanted spirit?"

How had she figured that one out? I'd always thought of Ilsa as the more intelligent sibling of the two of them, and honestly, Hazel would agree, though admittedly, she was the one who'd grown up wise to Faerie's tricks and learned to think like one of them. That didn't change the fact that we were seriously short on any other available options. "If you have a better plan, I'm all ears."

"Ask the Seelie Court."

"Your solution is to ask the Unseelie Court's enemies?"

"The new Summer King is fair," said Hazel. "He'll hear us out."

"Absolutely not happening," I said. "Do I need to describe what the Unseelie Queen will do to us if she finds out we've told Summer she's being haunted by a ghost and asked a human for help?"

"Okay, you've got me there."

My phone buzzed with a message from Ilsa, who was on her way to my house, probably with Morgan in tow. "Your sister and brother are on their way here. I can't believe she decided to designate my home as your meeting room."

"*I* can't believe you took the Morrigan's magic," she said. "Can you show me?"

"No."

"Spoilsport."

Figuring it'd at least distract her attention for a few

seconds, I held up my palms. Shadows swept my hands, and Hazel's eyes sparkled with awe. "Nice."

"During the battle, she full-on shifted," said Roseanne. "Into a giant bird. Do you think that's what pushed the Morrigan over the edge?"

Hazel swung to face me again. "You think you overused her powers?"

"I know she didn't intend me to keep them," I said. "I can't exactly ask her now, though, can I?"

A loud hammering came from the front door. I went to answer and got out of the way swiftly as Hazel's siblings swamped her in an awkward group hug. I shuffled around them and back to Roseanne, who raised a brow at me. I gave a shrug in return. I didn't have siblings either, and frankly I was better off that way, given what kind of parent my mother had been.

When the others piled into the living room and took the remaining seats, I perched on the arm of Roseanne's chair. She hadn't actually met Morgan yet, but he seemed more fixated on his sister's sudden appearance than on my housemate.

"I can't believe you came back without telling us," he said to Hazel. Then to me, he said, "I can't believe *you* want to drag Ilsa to Faerie."

"Hazel came here to help us out," I said. "Ilsa, you directed her to my house… why?"

"Because I'm not doing this at the guild," she said.

"I take it River isn't waiting with his talisman ready to ambush me when I walk outside?"

"He's just worried about me," she said. "He said *he'd* come to Faerie if that's what it took."

"Why do *any* of you want to go to Faerie?" Morgan

asked. "Didn't you break the curse so this crap would stop happening?"

"*I* didn't break the curse," I reminded him. "Besides, it's not us the Unseelie Queen wants. It's a necromancer. *Any* necromancer. Theoretically, River would fit the bill, if he wants to take Ilsa's place, but I doubt the Unseelie Queen would go for that."

"Only you would get an invitation from the most inhospitable part of Faerie," said Hazel. "Hell, even the Grey Vale is more of a known entity."

"Not to me, it isn't," I said. "Besides, Lord Lyle has agreed to escort both of us directly to the Unseelie Queen and then lead us home afterwards. He's honourable enough, for an Unseelie knight, and he claims he'll see to it that we won't come to harm."

"See?" Ilsa said to Morgan and Hazel. "I've got this covered."

"The hell you have," said Morgan. "Tell the Sidhe to get stuffed."

"Like *that'll* end well," said Hazel. "Ilsa, are you positive you'll be able to use your talisman to banish a Sidhe ghost the same way you would a wraith? I remember what happened the last time…"

"If she can't, then I'll do it myself," I said. "We just need to get the ghost out of the Unseelie Queen's Court, right? Banishment doesn't necessarily have to be involved."

"*You'll* banish her?" Hazel's brow crinkled. "Wait, do you have the Morrigan's ability to rip out souls?"

"Not that I'm aware of, but transforming into her scares the shit out of ghosts," I said. "Ilsa, did you ask your boss for permission?"

"I told River, and he said there was no chance she'd

want to risk my death," said Ilsa. "Yes, I know the Unseelie Queen told you she wouldn't harm me, but the guild's in a bad way."

Hazel's teeth worried her lower lip. "If you're sure you want to go, then I can always help the guild in your place."

Ilsa shook her head. "You're not a necromancer."

Right. I hadn't thought much about it, but like me, Hazel hadn't walked away from her Gatekeeper's vow with any other magic except for the Sight. She, at least, didn't seem unhappy to lose her powers, but she was the one who'd broken the curse and willingly given up her magic, whereas I'd had it ripped away from me without any warning. It was her the Unseelie Queen ought to be ticked off at, considering she was the reason I'd abruptly resigned from my position as Gatekeeper without handing in my notice.

Hazel grinned. "Just an idea. Honestly, the guild will be fine without you for a couple of days. Might teach them not to rely on the Gatekeeper."

"They aren't relying on me," Ilsa said. "Not on purpose, anyway. I'm the only person who can banish any ghosts in the city, even temporarily, and they'll be in a bad way if I disappear."

"You're supposed to be talking her out of this ridiculous plan," Morgan said accusingly to Hazel. "Traitor."

Hazel stuck her tongue out at him. "In all seriousness, do *you* want to end up on the Unseelie Queen's bad side? Because I never got the impression that's a nice place to be."

"Can confirm." My gaze flickered over their group. "Ilsa, my offer stands. I'll come with you as backup and help get that ghost out of the Court by any means necessary."

"Have *you* tested your powers on a ghost in Faerie?"

"No…" Good point. It wasn't like I'd had an abundance of opportunities, but for all I knew, the magic of the Morrigan wouldn't work the same for me on the other side of the Ley Line. "We can do a test run. Lord Lyle won't mind."

If he did, then it wasn't my problem. I'd rather know in advance if there were likely to be any issues with our approach *before* we got within sight of the murderous faerie Queen.

10

Lord Lyle showed up late that afternoon. We'd all expected him to be early, so Ilsa had gone to ask the necromancer guild for permission to disappear for a couple of days while I'd bought Roseanne enough snacks to last for the duration of my trip and texted Puck asking him and Hawk to keep an eye on her.

I'd barely had time to hit send on the message when Lord Lyle appeared outside the house in a flash of light bright enough to see even with the curtains drawn. Roseanne darted upstairs at once, while I waited for the sound of her door closing behind her before I went to greet our visitor. "You're early."

His gaze went straight to Hazel, who'd appeared beside me. "You have the Summer Gatekeeper with you?"

"She came to help her sister," I said. "You didn't knock over any candles on your way in, did you?"

"Candles?"

"We had to put them around the entirety of half-blood territory to keep the ghosts out," I said. "I was telling the truth when I said things were just as bad in this realm as they are in Faerie, if not worse. Luckily for you, Ilsa is willing to humour Her Majesty's whims, on a couple of conditions."

"What conditions would they be, then?"

"We'd like a test run," I said. "To see if Ilsa's talisman can actually be used to banish a ghost. That way, she wouldn't have to make her first attempt in front of the Unseelie Queen."

"Very well," he said. "Where is the Gatekeeper?"

"On her way." I checked my phone, but Puck hadn't replied yet. "We'll meet her at the Ley Line."

"Cool." Hazel hopped off the doorstep to join Lord Lyle, while I climbed the stairs to say goodbye to Roseanne through the closed door of her room.

"I'll be back soon," I called to her but received no response. There was no way for Lord Lyle to know who I was talking to, but I didn't blame her for being wary of showing her face.

I retreated downstairs and locked the door behind me, while Lord Lyle eyed Hazel, who'd thankfully changed out of her bright-orange T-shirt and now wore dark clothes and a jacket which covered the knives at her waist. "You're coming too?"

"Only as far as the borderlands," Hazel said. "If you want to hire one Lynn, you'll get all of us."

"This wasn't the plan," I muttered to her out of the corner of my mouth.

"No plan survives contact with Faerie." Hazel strode into the lead and opened the gate out of half-blood territory, while Lord Lyle easily overtook her and turned the corner. Ilsa and River waited on the

Ley Line, along with Morgan and Pepper the faerie puppy.

Hazel came to a halt. "Morgan, you're seriously bringing the puppy with you?"

"He's trained to attack ghosts," Morgan said. "Just in case Ilsa's plan doesn't work."

"Nice to know someone has faith in me," said Ilsa. "I think I'm on the boss's shit list forever. This better be worth it, Holly."

"I'd opt for pissing off the necromancers over being eviscerated by the Unseelie Queen." I glanced over at our Sidhe companion, who was studiously ignoring the newcomers. "Assuming you aren't set upon by an army of redcaps the instant we set foot into Faerie. This was supposed to be a low-key mission, not a family reunion."

"Tough," said Hazel. "Okay, where's our first stop going to be? The Summer Court?"

"Excuse me?" Lord Lyle was the only person who looked even more disgruntled than I did at the new arrivals, but his glare was entirely fixated on me. "You have been asked to come to the Winter Court."

"We're doing a trial run first, right?" Hazel asked. "You don't want us wandering all over Winter looking for ghosts, but I know Summer inside out. If our banishment works out, we'll come and get rid of your spirit."

I was starting to wonder how she'd made it through her training as Summer Gatekeeper without one of the Sidhe turning her into a human-sized pincushion. Lord Lyle's jaw tensed. "One ghost, but I never said I'd protect any of you from Summer's wrath if you choose to trespass on their territory without an invitation."

"Do we really want to draw the Seelie King's attention?" River asked. "Aren't the borderlands a safer bet? We have allies there too."

"We do," Hazel agreed. "That'll do, then. Let's move."

"Agreed," said Puck from by my shoulder.

I damn near jumped out of my skin. "What the hell are you doing here?"

"Hey, we have company." Hazel eyed Puck with curiosity. "Who're you?"

"You know this guy?" asked Morgan.

Annoyed at the fright he'd given me, I swivelled on my heel, noting that Puck had changed from his work clothes into a dark outfit not unlike Hazel's. Unless it was all a glamour, of course.

"This is Puck," I told the others. "He's a detective who's helping the half-faeries here in Edinburgh deal with their ghostly infestation, and he's going to keep an eye on the situation while I'm gone."

Amusement flickered in his eyes. "Did you read my message?"

"Didn't know you sent one." Conscious of the others' curious stares, I pulled out my phone without reading the message on the screen. "Puck, you and Hawk are in charge of making sure nobody accidentally knocks over the candles around half-blood territory until we can permanently shut those ghosts out."

"I beg to differ," he said. "Hawk can handle half-blood territory. I, however, would like to ensure that you don't run into any difficulties in Faerie."

I slid my phone back into my pocket and tugged the zip closed. "I don't think so."

Tagging along to ensure Lord Lyle didn't leave me to

rot had been an understandable choice on his part, but I already had more than enough companions, all of whom were currently staring at me as if the Morrigan herself had volunteered to bodyguard me.

"Enough delays." Lord Lyle had run out of patience, it seemed. "I will not take responsibility for making sure any of your friends get out of Faerie in one piece, Holly Lynn. You have wasted enough of my time."

"You're the one who showed up half a day early." I cast a glance around at the others. "He's not kidding. If you land yourselves in a trap—"

Lord Lyle interrupted by taking a decisive step forwards. The entire street warped around our group, and a leaf-strewn path replaced the tarmac, the street lamps and houses vanishing beneath densely packed trees. At once, Pepper started chasing the leaves around, while Hazel shielded her eyes against the sunlight streaming through the trees. "I forgot how *bright* it is in here."

Lord Lyle's flinty gaze landed on me. "Don't take too long with your trial run, mortal. I will be waiting here."

"Sure, because finding and banishing ghosts is easy business in *Faerie*," said Morgan. "Honestly. This is the place where nobody wants to acknowledge death is even a thing. Where do we find a ghost?"

"I suggested the borderlands," River said, "but given how many of us there are…"

"I thought you had allies there." I'd have preferred for Ilsa and me to hunt down a ghost on our own, but it looked as though we wouldn't be able to ditch our entourage until we went into Winter itself. The borderlands lay somewhere off the path amid the dishevelled tangle of trees which filled the gap between the Courts, but considering how much everything moved around in Faerie, it was anyone's guess as to how long it'd take to track down these allies of theirs. Besides, we hadn't the time to pay social calls.

Ilsa rested a hand on her pocket, where I glimpsed the square shape of her talisman. "I can draw the attention of any nearby ghosts. We just need to pick the right spot."

"If you're sure," said River. "Better not do it here, though."

"All right." Since nobody else seemed obliged, I walked off the path and into the tangle of trees at the side, seeking a deserted clearing where we could safely set up a trap for our unlucky ghost. Or lucky, depending on whether or not Ilsa could send them to a peaceful afterlife.

As I walked, Puck fell into step with me. "I didn't know you had this much of an extended family."

"It's only one extra person," I said. "I know Hazel is loud enough for three people, but still."

Puck's mouth tilted in a grin. "You don't get along?"

"No more than the Summer and Winter Sidhe do," I said, not particularly caring if Hazel overheard us. "Luckily, I only had to see her and the others a couple of times a year when I was Gatekeeper."

Namely, at the solstice balls, held at either my house or Hazel's, and one of the few times the Winter Lynn house wasn't an empty house of deserted corridors and draughty rooms. Too bad the last one had been overshadowed by my mother's vengeful wraith being imprisoned inside the house.

Puck watched the back of Hazel's head. "The ex-Summer Gatekeeper."

"That's her," I said. "I'm surprised you never ran into one another while she was making a mess out of your Queen's territory."

His expression flattened at my words, even though I hadn't mentioned the Aes Sidhe by name. "I wasn't there at the time."

Hazel hadn't recognised him as Aes Sidhe yet, but she'd figure out the connection sooner or later, given that she had more experience with them than most.

Our group reached a clearing, where Ilsa wasted no time in pulling out her talisman. "Don't stand so close, River. This won't take long."

A blue glow spread around the book, and brightness pinged on my vision from the tangle of trees surrounding us. A shadowy form wreathed in bright magic.

Hazel's attention veered in that direction. "There's your ghost."

"That," said Ilsa, "is not a ghost. Not the type I was looking for, anyway. Everyone stand back."

A shiver of unease raced down my spine. Sidhe who died in a place they couldn't move on from turned into wraiths when their magic turned inward and devoured their essence from the inside out, turning them into husks which had no will of their own except for the tenuous need to continue existing. Could they be banished? That was up to Ilsa to determine, not me, but the Morrigan's magic reacted at once, flooding my palms with shadows. I clenched my fists to dispel it, standing back to let Ilsa do her job.

The wraith swooped upon the clearing, shimmering with bright green light which indicated it'd once been a Summer Sidhe. Otherwise unrecognisable, it resembled a cloud of malevolent energy, and when its tendrils swept across our group, a sudden rush of weakness washed over me. The others staggered in unison, hit by the same sensation.

Ah, shit. The wraith was draining our life force, collectively. Ilsa better handle this one fast.

She raised the talisman and shot a jet of blue-white light at the wraith. River, meanwhile, drew his blade, which shimmered with bright-green Summer magic. While the wraith was immune to physical damage, River's talisman stored enough magical energy to block its attacks and drive it backwards.

"I banish you." Ilsa advanced on the wraith. "I banish you… wherever you're supposed to go."

"Yeah, fuck off," said Morgan, his hands aglow with necromantic energy. "Or I'll make you."

"Morgan, stand back." Ilsa swayed on the spot as another wave of draining energy washed over all of us, but she held her ground and raised the talisman again.

The wraith reeled back from her strike, but a second shadow swept in from outside the clearing. River noticed first, spinning on his heel and slashing with his talisman. The blade stabbed through the creature's transparent form without leaving a mark, but the magic within the sword did seem to have an effect on the ghostly being. The wraith recoiled away from him and flew at me instead.

The Morrigan's magic was more than happy to sink its claws into a new victim. Shadowy magic pulsed from my hands and through the wraith's transparent form, causing it to shudder and fade around the edges. Shadows crept higher and higher up my arms, revelling in the chance to freely unleash their wrath upon an obvious target.

The wraith hit out at me. My back hit the ground, feathered wings breaking my fall, and I lifted my head in time to see Ilsa raising her talisman, taking aim at both wraiths at once.

A blast of necromantic power struck the wraiths head-on, and they exploded into nothingness as if they'd never existed. I sprang to my feet and saw Hazel goggling at me. "Whoa. I see what you meant about having a *bit* of the Morrigan's power left."

How far had I shifted? From Puck's raised eyebrows, a lot. With difficulty, I pulled the shadows back underneath my skin until the claws became hands again. "Okay, so banishing wraiths doesn't work. Where do we find an actual ghost?"

"Stab someone?" Morgan suggested.

Ilsa tutted. "*Morgan.*"

That was when several Sidhe stepped out from the bushes, wielding crossbows and longbows, swords and daggers—all of which were pointed at our group.

"I thought," I whispered, "you had allies out here."

The newcomers sure as hell didn't look friendly, but I was at a loss to figure out which Court they'd come from. Their attire was understated, greens and browns blending into the surrounding forest. Some had Summer-green eyes, others hazel or brown, but from the notable absence of any sparkling jewels or gleaming talismans, they didn't appear to be Summer Court members.

"Who are you?" A tall female Sidhe with vibrant

orange-red hair which contrasted with her dark clothing stepped to the front of their group, a crossbow in her hands. "Who let humans into the borderlands?"

I knew bringing all these people was a mistake. If Ilsa and I had come alone, we'd have avoided drawing attention, but together with Morgan, Puck, Hazel, and River—not to mention the puppy—anyone within a mile's radius would have heard the ruckus from our fight with the wraith. I just hoped none of them had seen me shape-shift into a likeness of the Morrigan.

Hazel put on a wide smile. "I don't suppose you've seen a ghost we can borrow?"

I groaned inwardly. Ilsa looked as though she wanted to do the same, but she cleared her throat and addressed the Sidhe with careful politeness. "I wasn't aware we were trespassing on anyone's territory."

"Last I heard, the only territory in the borderlands belonged to the half-faeries," added River. "Who are you?"

Were they half-blood? It was hard to tell, since River himself would have been indistinguishable from a Sidhe if I didn't know him to be half-necromancer.

"My name is Adria," said the female Sidhe. "You came from the mortal realm, did you not?"

"Yeah, we did," said Morgan. "You're welcome for destroying those wraiths."

I really should have left them at home. I scanned the other newcomers, fighting the urge to just use the Morrigan's magic to scare them off so we could get the hell out of this forest and find an actual ghost. I counted at least a half dozen more hidden in the bushes, watching us. How long had they been there? Had they glamoured themselves to spy on our movements from the moment we'd stepped off the path?

Glamour...

"Human." The female Sidhe's disdainful gaze travelled among our group. "Three humans… no, four, a cu sidhe… and two half-bloods."

"Trickster!" The voice came from a blond male Sidhe standing among the bushes, who pointed straight at Puck.

Puck, who seemed to have been expecting an attack, shifted into a bird in time to avoid a dozen arrows loosed from their bows. My whole body tensed as the arrows struck the ground where he'd been standing, forming a quivering line.

"Shit, they're *hers*," muttered Hazel.

She didn't need to say the word for the truth to hit me, entirely too late. *Aes Sidhe. They're Aes Sidhe.*

"What are you doing?" I demanded. "What gives you the right to shoot at us?"

A strangled gasp escaped one of the soldiers as Puck descended on him in a swoop of wings, shifting into his monstrous bearlike form. My shout of warning went unheard as more soldiers moved in on my allies. While the archers remained among the trees, the soldiers seized each of us by the arm and pressed knives against our throats. The Morrigan's magic itched to escape, but the cold bite of the blade on my neck was proof enough that running would risk any of the others' deaths—and worse, I'd lost sight of Puck at some point when he'd shifted.

I should have known the Aes Sidhe wouldn't have quietly integrated into the Summer Court after Hazel had turfed them out of their home. This was more her fault than mine, but the glare she levelled on me above the blade pressed to her neck suggested she blamed *me* for our predicament.

"This is a mistake," River warned them. "You can see I'm carrying a talisman from the Summer Court. I am the son of Lord Torin."

"Did *he* give you permission to be here?" asked one of the soldiers.

"I thought this territory belonged to the half-faeries." Hazel grimaced when a stream of blood trickled down her neck from the knife's touch. "Ouch! Dammit, I know the new Seelie King. He won't let you hurt us."

"That remains to be seen."

Silently hoping that she wouldn't give away my former Gatekeeper's status, I had little choice but to let my captor steer me out of the clearing and among the trees. While we could hardly be in a worse position, learning I was currently working for Winter would not endear me to them. I'd bet there *were* Unseelie spies in the borderlands —the Unseelie Queen was not known for leaving any corner of Faerie unwatched—but it wouldn't help us get out of here alive if the Aes Sidhe thought we'd come to spy on them for the Winter Court.

The Aes Sidhe marched us up to a tunnel entrance which plunged below the leafy ground. Apparently unconcerned by our predicament, Hazel twisted to face her captor. "Wow, you kept up the 'dark tunnel' aesthetic even after you were finally allowed to see daylight again?"

"Quiet," snapped the Sidhe holding her arm, giving her a shove into the tunnel.

The rest of us followed into a warren of tunnels, lit by what looked like glowing white fungi which sprouted from the walls and floor. If this was a mirror of the Aes

Sidhe's old home, I'd have to take Hazel's word for it, but Puck's absence gnawed at me as they marched our group through a wooden door built into the tunnel.

All of us except for River, who stood in the doorway before they could shut us in. "If I may, I would like to speak to your leader. I'm sure we can sort out this misunderstanding."

"Fine," one of them said. "The rest of you are to stay here."

The door slammed, leaving our group trapped in a cave around the size of my living room, minus any furniture. Ilsa shot her sister an exasperated look. "Could you not keep your mouth shut for five seconds?"

"Nope," said Hazel and Morgan simultaneously.

"If I were you," I said through gritted teeth, "I'd let the grown-ups do the talking next time."

"Stop bitching," said Morgan, attempting to calm a trembling Pepper. "It's your bullshit that brought us to Faerie to begin with."

"He has a point," said Hazel.

"Guys." Ilsa sat cross-legged with the Gatekeeper's book open on her lap. "Quiet. I'm trying to concentrate."

"On what?" Hazel scooted over to her, and Ilsa swatted her away with a hand. "Ah, yeah, your book won't let anyone read it except you. Can it tell us how to get out of here?"

"No," Ilsa said. "Please keep the noise down. You know they're looking for an excuse to stick their knives in us."

And they have Puck. Unless he escaped. If he had, he'd better come back for the rest of us. I shifted my hands to claws and dug them into the earthen wall, but the soil was packed tight and breaking through would likely bring the ceiling down on all our heads.

While Morgan sat against the wall with the faerie dog curled up on his legs, Hazel paced in circles around the room. "I can't believe they copy-pasted the lifeless underground design their tyrannical queen imposed on them. That's just *sad*."

My claws flickered in and out of view as I examined the door, wondering if I could yank it out of its frame. "Clearly, they're the sensitive sort. Which is why pissing them off was a mistake."

"Hey, I didn't start it," said Hazel. "'Trickster,' they called that Puck guy. Does he know them?"

Was that an attempt at a truce? I wasn't particularly keen to spread Puck's secrets around, but if we were stuck here for the duration, the truth would come out sooner or later. "I'd guess yes, but it's not like I had time to ask before they chased him off."

"He's Aes Sidhe." Hazel halted mid-pace. "Trickster... not *that* trickster?"

"Robin Goodfellow?" Ilsa's head lifted from her book. "You didn't mention your detective friend was related to him."

"I didn't see the need," I said, "considering he's a distant descendant and half-human besides."

"I didn't see him in the Aes Sidhe's Court," said Hazel. "Though I was kinda busy when I went there."

Yeah. You just flew through the place and left a trail of chaos behind you. "I'm guessing you didn't see any signs of the Wild Hunt, either."

"Should I have?"

Had she not listened to a word of my explanation

earlier? "The Wild Hunt taught the Queen of the Aes Sidhe how to use blood magic. They might even have put her in touch with the death god too."

Hazel's jaw went slack. "Ah, yeah… the one our ancestor was nearly sacrificed to."

Morgan jolted to his feet. "You mean the people who just kidnapped us were once part of the Court who tried to sacrifice our ancestor?"

"Did both of you miss that part?" I glared at him and Hazel, who opened her mouth to respond.

Ilsa cut in. "Stop arguing. Holly's right… we need to figure out what we're up against here."

"You're taking *her* side?" Morgan asked.

It surprised me, too, though I knew from what I'd witnessed as a kid that the Lynn siblings were constantly arguing with one another. I at least knew that nobody got under your skin like family did.

I did my best to keep my tone calm when I went on. "What we're up against is a bunch of people who belonged to the Court we now know to have worked with the Wild Hunt—who are extremely pissed off that Queen Etaina is dead. Hence their attempt to summon the god of death by murdering half-faeries in Edinburgh."

Hazel's forehead scrunched up. "The Wild Hunt wanted to summon him… why? For revenge?"

"That, and the fact that their immortality source is gone," I said. "They figured they'd kill two birds with one stone: avenge their Queen and obtain a new source of lifeblood to rebuild the cauldron of resurrection. Given the timing, we can't afford not to assume these rogues aren't their allies too."

"The Wild Hunt's soldiers are in jail in Winter,

though," said Ilsa. "Besides, most of the Aes Sidhe didn't know Etaina captured our ancestor, did they? They didn't know about the Gatekeeper's curse."

"No," I acknowledged. "According to Puck, anyway."

"You told *him* that?" asked Hazel.

"It's not like we're sworn to secrecy." I wished I hadn't mentioned his name, given the thoughtful expression which appeared on her face. "I wanted to know if he was involved in any of their schemes, but he said he wasn't in the Court when it all went down... and neither were the Wild Hunt. They didn't see the battle. Unlike us."

"Yeah, we had a front-row seat," said Hazel. "The Wild Hunt must have given Etaina the tools she used to mark her soldiers with blood magic symbols. I did wonder where she got them, considering she never left her Court."

Blood magic symbols. If Hazel had been around a few weeks ago when the Wild Hunt had been on a killing spree among the half-faeries, we'd have figured out their plan a lot sooner. "If these guys came here direct from the Aes Sidhe's Court after the battle, we can't rule out the possibility that they brought some of their Queen's strategies here. Besides, you said the borderlands are supposed to belong to the half-faeries. Does that mean they moved in here by force?"

"I don't know." Hazel's teeth worried her lower lip. "Makes more sense that they negotiated for a piece of their territory. Not all of them would have wanted to rejoin the Summer Court after centuries of exile."

"None of that explains why they locked us up." Morgan gave the puppy a stroke. "They didn't even ask our names."

"They must know who the Gatekeepers are," said Hazel.

"Not necessarily." Puck hadn't until I'd told him myself. "Besides, the curse broke, didn't it? If they've never met us before, then as far as they're concerned, a bunch of humans just randomly showed up on their territory without an explanation. We'd better hope River is better at negotiating than you are."

"There's nothing in here on the history of the Aes Sidhe and the Wild Hunt, anyway." Ilsa turned the page of the Gatekeeper's book. "It also doesn't know where Sidhe go after death, only that it's to another realm."

"Wait, *that's* what you asked?" I strode over to her, stopping short of trying to read over her shoulder. "Does the book know the Morrigan is missing?"

"It doesn't know the details of where the Morrigan goes before rebirth," said Ilsa. "Only that I shouldn't try summoning her back."

"Told you so," said Morgan.

"And the Wild Hunt?" I asked. "Where do they fit into this?"

"The book has little to say on the Wild Hunt," said Ilsa. "Except what we already know—they were entrusted with escorting departed souls to be reborn, which might also account for the ghosts ending up stuck in Faerie now the Wild Hunt are no longer doing their jobs and the Sidhe are dying for real."

"They stopped doing their jobs a long while ago." Hazel spun to the door when footsteps sounded in the tunnel outside.

The door opened, and River appeared in the entryway,

flanked by two Aes Sidhe. "We can leave, but please be quick about it."

"Seriously?" said Hazel. "What did you do, threaten them with your father's wrath?"

"No," said River. "They're not interested in capturing humans, and they figured we're more trouble than we're worth."

"That's nice," said Morgan.

I shot him a warning look which I then directed at Hazel, crossing my fingers behind my back that she didn't open her mouth and get us locked up again. Ilsa, having already put away her Gatekeeper's book, rose to her feet to follow me out of the cave. Pepper didn't need any encouragement to hurry after us. That just left—

"Where's Puck?" I asked. "Is he in here?"

One of the soldiers shot me a cold look. "The trickster is ours, mortal."

My heart leapt into my throat. "No way. He's not—"

Hazel gave me a prod in the spine as she walked past, joining the others in heading out of the tunnel. Meanwhile, I dropped back to River's side and whispered, "Did you see where they took him?"

River shook his head. "I've no idea, sorry. They wouldn't say."

I ground my teeth. "I *knew* he should have stayed behind."

Our escorts herded us towards the tunnel opening and into the forest again, while the others gladly walked out into daylight. I walked alongside them despite the sharp tug in my chest urging me to turn around and head back into the darkness to find what they'd done with Puck. Did they believe him to have betrayed their Queen? Was that why they'd taken him?

"See to it that you do not trespass again," said one of the Aes Sidhe.

The soldiers retreated back into their base, leaving us alone in the forest clearing. Hazel and the others headed back towards the path at once, but I followed at a slower pace, my thoughts with the mound of earth behind us. I'd need to go back inside to figure out where they'd taken Puck, but without getting myself caught again. Easier said than done.

Ilsa slowed her pace, glancing over at me. "You want to get Puck out of there?"

I began to walk faster in case any Aes Sidhe were hiding in the bushes and listening in. "They were prepared to shoot him full of arrows, remember?"

"I knew it." Hazel swung around, a grin on her face. "I knew there was something between you two. He wouldn't have followed you all the way here if there wasn't."

Anger spread through me like a wave of icy water, and I clenched my hands to keep them from shifting into claws. "I don't give a crap why he came with us, but those Aes Sidhe bastards wouldn't have been as keen to let us go if they knew who *you* were."

Without her circlet or green eyes, she resembled an ordinary human, blending in among her siblings. I had little doubt that the Aes Sidhe would have locked her up along with Puck if they knew she'd personally brought about the death of their Queen.

The amusement vanished from her expression, to be replaced by the hint of a challenge. "What?"

"You know what?" Shadows swept up my arms. "I'm done letting you steamroller through everything in your path without caring how much of a mess you leave behind."

"Whoa," said Morgan. "Simmer down."

"You're almost as bad." I shot him a glare. "You both got us all captured. If Puck dies, it's on the pair of you."

"This isn't just about him," said Hazel. "You've had it in for me since I broke the curse."

The rivalry between our sides of the family had persisted for far longer than that, but she was right. Breaking the curse had upended both our lives, and every round of shitty luck I'd landed in since then could be traced back to her.

"That," I said, "is because you never take any goddamn responsibility."

"Holly." Ilsa shot me a pleading look. "Now isn't the time."

I forced down my temper, knowing exactly where it came from—or rather, who. "Ilsa, I'd be more than happy to help you get rid of Her Majesty's ghost, but I have to do this first. Hazel, Morgan, do whatever you like, and I'll conveniently forget you got my friend captured. Deal?"

Hazel had the decency to look abashed, while Morgan busied himself watching Pepper chase leaves around the forest path.

"I really wouldn't turn against the Aes Sidhe," warned River. "It was hard enough to convince them to set you free the first time around."

"And you missed Puck off the list?" Ilsa reprimanded him.

River flushed slightly. "I don't know him. Do any of

us? He *lived* with the Aes Sidhe, and I've only heard Holly vouch for him."

The truth in his words bit into me like the point of a sword.

"Go on." I waved an impatient hand at all of them. "You don't have to stick around, but I owe him my life, and besides, the Aes Sidhe's former Queen tried to kill us all. That's reason enough for me to have a snoop around inside their base."

"You're right there," said Ilsa. "All right. I reckon we can manufacture a distraction."

11

I frowned at Ilsa. "What did you just say?"

"You heard me," she said. "You guys are all free to leave, but I'm going to help Holly find Puck and get him away from the Aes Sidhe. They only have one entrance to their base, so it shouldn't take more than one diversion to lure their security elsewhere."

Damn. I'd expected it to come to a fight between Hazel and me—and she still didn't look like she'd object to trading a few blows—but instead Ilsa had decided to help me out. I didn't need to ask why. She and her siblings shared the same trait: they unthinkingly rushed into danger to save one another's necks when any sensible person would cut and run. After all, they'd been brought up by someone who would have laid down her life for her children, not someone who'd tried to sacrifice her child to prolong her own existence.

Yet the instinct to go back for Puck reared up like a tidal wave, and it was all I could do to keep the shadows under my skin in check as I gave Ilsa a relieved nod. "All right, but make sure you stay out of range when they come out and start shooting arrows again."

I left her to argue it out with her siblings and retraced my steps towards the tunnel leading to the Aes Sidhe's base. While part of me remained on the lookout for more hidden archers in the woods, I'd seen most of them go back into the base, so I concealed myself in the undergrowth and waited until a loud crash echoed through the forest which sounded like several trees falling over.

Figuring that was Ilsa's distraction, I crept closer to the base, taking care to keep to the undergrowth when several Aes Sidhe emerged from the tunnel and scattered amid the surrounding forest. Once they'd vanished from sight, I hurried towards the vacated tunnel entrance, one hand on my iron knife. I'd had zero expectations that my cousin's diversion would have drawn every single one of the bastards outside, so I was ready when two male Aes Sidhe barred my way into the tunnel.

I brought the hilt of the iron knife down on the first guy's head and stuck out a foot to trip the second before hammering my fist into his forehead. When he went down, I ran through the tunnel and around a corner. A female Aes Sidhe with dark-brown hair and a pair of sharp knives in her hands blocked my path, but she came to a halt when the iron of my blade met the skin of her neck.

"Step aside," I said. "I'm here to get my friend out, not kill anyone, but I'll gladly cut you down if you get in my way."

Her eyes narrowed, but the merest touch of the iron to her bare skin left an ugly grey mark on her neck. "The trickster is no friend of yours, mortal. You're a fool."

"Forgive me if I don't take your word for it." I gripped the knife hard, the greyness spreading around its edge. "Tell me where he is and I'll let you walk away alive."

She jabbed a finger over her shoulder in the direction of a door. "Take him if you must, but you'll come to regret spurning our goodwill."

"Kidnapping people doesn't count as goodwill." I kept my knife pressed against her throat as I stepped around her, and when I removed the blade, I waited to be sure she wouldn't lunge at me from behind before I ran towards the door she'd indicated.

A sharp kick sent it flying inward, revealing another cave. Puck sat on the earthy floor in his human form, his hands bound together with thick ropes. His face was bleeding from a long cut, but he could have been a lot worse off, considering how close those arrows had come to skewering him earlier.

Surprise flickered in his eyes. "Holly?"

"You're welcome." I strode to his side and severed the ropes with my iron blade, careful not to make contact with his skin. "What did you do to them to make them want to kill you on sight?"

He grinned sardonically. "Oh, nothing much."

My questions would have to wait until later. I held my knife at the ready as I returned to the door. "Ready to run?"

"Ready." His breath was hot on my neck, closer than I expected, and tension zipped up my spine in response.

I ran out of the room and sprinted through the tunnel towards the exit, skidding to a halt to avoid colliding with Adria coming the other way. The fury in her eyes was palpable. "How dare you set the traitor free after we so generously let you walk away?"

"Don't pin the blame on me." I raised my knife. "Want to step aside like your friends did? Trust me, it's better this way."

"Trust you." Her gaze lingered not on my mark, but on my face. No, on my forehead, as though scrutinising me for something. "You are no ordinary human, are you, mortal?"

My throat went dry at the sudden suspicion that she'd expected to see the Gatekeeper's mark which had once stood out in the centre of my forehead, but I took my chance and kicked at her kneecaps.

She moved smoothly aside, but before she could strike me in return, Puck shifted into a bird and flew into her eyes, his beak jabbing at any skin he could reach. As she moved her arms to shield her face, I swept her legs out from underneath her and hammered a strike into her solar plexus, driving her breath from her lungs.

Hoping Puck stayed close behind me, I ran the rest of the way out of the tunnel and sprinted through the clearing into the forest. Puck flew ahead, dive-bombing anyone he unearthed in the bushes and shifting forms dizzyingly fast to drive them out of our path. I kept sprinting until the trees thinned out and I spotted the others waiting ahead of us on the path leading back to the Courts.

Only Ilsa looked visibly relieved to see me halt, breathless, beside them. "Good, you made it out."

No thanks to your siblings. I bit back the comment and gasped out, "Where's Lord Lyle?"

"Back in Winter, I assume," Ilsa said. "Waiting for us. Where's your friend?"

Puck swooped down as a bird and shifted to human form again, his face covered in more blood than before—though most of it didn't appear to be his. "I wouldn't advise any of you to travel back into the borderlands."

"We need to find a ghost, though," Ilsa said. "Going to Summer would take us back in range of the Aes Sidhe… though I have to wonder if they got permission from the half-faeries to build a new base in the borderlands instead of rejoining the Court."

"From what I heard, they didn't want to move back to Summer after losing their own Court," said River.

"You talked to them," said Morgan. "Did they mention whether they let the half-faeries know before they invaded their territory?"

"Supposedly, they have an agreement," said River. "I doubt the half-bloods would have felt they had much of a choice, though, given the power discrepancies between full Sidhe and half-fae."

"They're not that tough," Hazel said. "Not great strategists, either."

"I wouldn't underestimate them," said Puck. "They only agreed to let you go because they believed you had allies in the Summer Court, and they will not take kindly to you venturing near their territory again."

"We do have allies in the Court," said Hazel. "I'm pretty tight with the new Seelie King."

"Good for you," I said. "Ilsa, we need to find another ghost, and I reckon the only place we might avoid another ambush from the Sidhe is the Death Kingdom."

"Not ideal, but you're right," said Ilsa. "Hazel, Morgan… you should head home while you can."

"No," said Hazel. "If we leave you here, then you'll have no way out if the Winter Sidhe decide to keep you."

"Lord Lyle gave his word that he wouldn't allow her to come to harm." We'd wasted enough time already, but if they didn't shut up when we entered the Death Kingdom, we'd have a contingent of banshees on our backs. "You can come, but if you do anything to draw unnecessary attention, I'll throw you into the Morrigan's moat."

"Ooh." Hazel grinned but wisely shut up when I flashed my claws at her. "Fine, fine. Let's go nab us a ghost."

It didn't take long before we ran into our first ghost on the path into the Death Kingdom, without Ilsa even needing to use her talisman as a beacon. A sad-looking transparent male Sidhe drifted into view, his long hair fluttering in the breeze. Unlike the wraiths, he resembled his living self, somewhat, and hope flickered through his expression when he saw us. "Is this the way out?"

"Depends." Ilsa raised her talisman. "You want to move on, right?"

"Who are you?" the ghost asked.

"She's the Gatekeeper of Death," Hazel interjected. "We're here to send you to the afterlife."

Ilsa shot her sister an annoyed look. "It won't hurt, I promise."

Brightness spread outward from the pages of the Gatekeeper's book, bathing the ghost in white light. He flinched. "What are you doing?"

"Banishing you," Morgan said. "Go on, hop to it."

"I banish you," Ilsa said. The light continued to burn from the book's pages, but the ghost simply shuddered on the spot and didn't budge. "I banish you… dammit. I can't…"

"Can't what?" I took a step towards her, but River reached her first. He took hold of Ilsa's shoulders and let go a second later as the brightness intensified, forcing us all to cover our eyes.

Squinting against the glare, I fixed my gaze on Ilsa. "Ilsa, hang on. Don't force it if it's hurting you…"

I should have known this was a mistake.

Ilsa swayed on the spot, the talisman resembling a glowing blur in her hands, radiating light which covered the ghost from head to toe.

The light faded, and then a yawning blackness appeared behind the ghost. He fell back with a cry, the darkness swallowing him into its depths.

Ilsa sagged against River, her eyes closing, yet the patch of darkness remained intact despite the ghost's absence. *Is that the Sidhe's afterlife?* It looked more like a black hole hovering above the forest path, a chill breeze whipping from its depths. Cold fear clenched within me. It looked all too similar to the hole in reality the Wild Hunt's ritual had ripped open, and which only the Sidhe had managed to close.

"Ilsa!" Morgan yelped. "Close that thing before we fall into it."

"She's passed out." Holding her shoulders, River looked at the rest of us in alarm. "Shit."

Hazel gasped, shocked into silence for once, while Pepper the dog howled in terror, straining against the lead in Morgan's hands. The black hole didn't budge, but neither did it disappear.

I strode towards Ilsa with no clue what I could possibly do, short of shaking her until she woke up. The talisman in her hands continued to glow despite its owner's state of unconsciousness, while River gripped her shoulders hard, peering into her eyes. "Ilsa. *Ilsa.*"

That was when the first wraith appeared, sweeping downhill as though drawn to the darkness. Unfortunately, Ilsa and River stood directly in its path.

"No you fucking don't." I ran at the wraith, but Puck shifted before I could get there, transforming into a flame which struck the ghostly figure. The wraith veered towards him instead of the others, while I shifted my hands to claws and positioned myself between the wraith and its target. "Want to fight?"

The wraith couldn't speak, of course, but I could have sworn a cry of rage or excitement escaped when it flew at me in a haze of white light. My claw raked across its front, leaving a trail of shadows. An odd sensation rose from where I'd touched the beast, and to my own shock, when I reared back for another strike, the wraith came with me. Its shadowy form had snagged on my claw, resembling a fluttering piece of fabric caught on a hook. *Holy shit.*

"Get off me!" I gave another wild swing of my claw, then common sense caught up to me. Catching my balance, I took aim at the gaping hole of darkness Ilsa had opened and flung the wraith with everything I had.

The wraith came free of my grip and flew into the darkness without so much as a single cry. Before the others could do any more than stare in shock, River let out a choked exclamation. My gaze snapped to him as Ilsa stirred, her eyes flickering open. "Go beyond… I banish you."

Light speared the void from Ilsa's talisman, and the patch of darkness vanished from sight. I lowered my clawed hands, relief sweeping over me.

Until I spotted Lord Lyle standing nearby. His jaw hung slack, his gaze fixated not on Ilsa, but on me—or to be more precise, at the Morrigan's claws.

"It worked," said Hazel. "See?"

"Your sister nearly *died*," I snapped at her, willing my claws to disappear. The shadows folded away and left my human hands behind, but Lord Lyle had already seen them. My heart hammered wildly against my ribs. Never mind the hole into the afterlife Ilsa had almost opened on top of us—I was the one who'd done something unforgivable.

"That was *way* too risky." Ilsa swayed on the spot, grabbing River's arm for balance.

"I told you this was a bad idea," said River. "It nearly killed you last time."

"Why did everyone ignore me when I said so, then?" Morgan said.

Puck landed in human form at my side. "I think it's settled, then. None of us can help the Unseelie Queen."

"I beg to differ." Lord Lyle's icy glare landed on me. "Come with me, Holly Lynn."

"Oh, shit," Hazel muttered.

I didn't budge. "As you can see, our trial run was unsuccessful, exactly like I told you it would be. Are you sure you want Ilsa to do the same in the Unseelie Queen's territory?"

"You saw for yourself that she speaks the truth," said Puck.

"Quiet, trickster," Lord Lyle said. "Come with me, mortal."

I raised a hand to silence the others before anyone could speak. "Wait here. *Don't* follow me, any of you. That clear?"

Ilsa hardly looked capable of walking on her own two feet, but it was Puck who I levelled a glare on as he made to walk after me. He'd come close to death once today already, and it seemed I'd never find out why the Aes Sidhe had been so angry with him that they'd tried to shoot him with a dozen arrows.

The instant Lord Lyle and I were alone together, his sword came unsheathed in a vibrant blue glow. Taking a step back, I let the shadows wash over my hands, and Lord Lyle's eyes bulged at the sight of the Morrigan's claws. "You thieving human."

"I didn't steal this magic." I ducked when he swung his blade at me, raising my claw to deflect the end of his sword before it took my head off. "The Morrigan loaned me her magic for the duration of the fight with the Wild Hunt."

Lord Lyle's weapon snagged my clawed hand. "That is… forbidden."

"It was her choice." I released his blade, which he lowered, his gaze still distrustful. "I won't apologise for wanting to do everything I could to stop the Wild Hunt from summoning the god of death and declaring war on the mortal realm. The Courts ought to be glad of it too."

"The last person who used the Morrigan's magic stole

it from her against her wishes," he said. "I cannot help but believe the same of you."

"Who stole her magic?" This was news to me, though perhaps it shouldn't surprise me, given that she'd been chained up in a vulnerable position, unable to free herself or otherwise use her magic to fight. Not without loaning it to another person, which had brought about its own set of consequences.

"That is none of your business, mortal," he said. "I cannot return to my Queen without informing her of what you have done. My vows to protect the Court would not allow it."

As I'd thought. "Even if it means my death? What would happen to the Morrigan's powers if I'm killed before she returns?"

His expression shadowed. "That, I cannot say."

"Then I can't let you tell her." My hopes of asking the Unseelie Queen if she knew whereabouts the Morrigan had vanished to had thoroughly evaporated by now, but I didn't need to see her in person to know she would never forgive me for this. "I won't walk with you to my execution."

"And I will not betray my Queen."

"Then I'll go alone." Ilsa strode up to us, her face pale but her expression resolute. "If I must, I'll banish the ghost in the Winter Court by myself. You can go and report to your Queen after you've seen us safely back home."

"You are still asking me to lie by omission," he said. "I cannot do that."

"Ilsa." Banishing a single ghost had almost killed her. Doing the same in the Unseelie Court was out of the question, but I was at a loss as to think of another way out of this situation which didn't end with me dead. "You know that's not a possibility. Lord Lyle, I'm pretty sure your Queen wouldn't want a repeat of… whatever happened back there."

His expression shadowed at her words. The Morrigan's magic lurked beneath my skin, preparing to leap at him, as though it knew that I was about to face my doom and refused to accept it. She hadn't given me her magic to beat the Wild Hunt only for me to get killed by one of the Unseelie Sidhe instead.

"Nevertheless," he said, "given your family history, I cannot let your theft go unreported."

Of course he couldn't. My mother's actions had followed me long after her wraith had departed… and it made a depressing kind of sense that they might be the end of me after all. "You once served my family and trained me as Gatekeeper. I thought you were honourable."

For a moment, a flicker of genuine regret simmered in his gaze. Then it was gone. "My honour is reserved for my Queen."

12

Lord Lyle grabbed at my wrist, but before I could block his strike, Puck descended in a shower of feathers and transformed into his giant bear form mid-movement. Sidhe might have impeccable balance most of the time, but a bear falling out of the sky was enough to make Lord Lyle hit the path with a thud which knocked the blade from his hands.

"Puck," I warned, as his claws found the Sidhe's throat. "Don't kill him. Trust me, it'll be worse for us all if you do."

Lord Lyle jerked to the side, his fingers closing around the hilt of his blade, and he swung the sword at Puck. The bear became a bird, flying high enough to avoid being struck, while my hands shifted to claws. "Don't do this, Lord Lyle. You don't have to betray your Queen in order to spare my life."

"I beg to differ."

His sword flashed out. The thick layers of feathers on my clawed hand caught most of the blow, but the momentum sent me flying backwards into a tree. My back hit the trunk, the breath flew from my lungs, and I lifted my head to see Puck slam into Lord Lyle in his bear form, shifting to a bird too fast for the blade to make contact. When Lord Lyle turned on me again, Pepper the faerie dog leapt out of the bushes and sank his teeth into the Sidhe's leg.

"Get him, Pepper!" Morgan yelled.

"What are you doing?" I staggered towards the enraged Winter Sidhe, but Hazel ran into view and River followed, his own talisman gleaming in his hands.

"It is not my desire to make an enemy of the Winter Court," he said to Lord Lyle. "But I will do what is necessary to protect the Gatekeepers."

"You have given me no choice." Lord Lyle faced our group, white-faced and bleeding from a cut on his face which had come from either me or Puck. "*Stop.*"

The invocation rippled through the air, freezing every single one of us to the spot. I'd never heard Lord Lyle speak the gods' language before, but the ringing echo of the Ancient's command locked my feet together and rendered me helpless to move. Even as he advanced on me, his blade pointing at my neck…

Shadows burst from under my skin of their own accord, claws sinking into his chest. Blood sprayed out, while the spell released me as he dropped to his knees, his talisman clattering onto the path. My vision wavered. If he died, we'd all be sentenced to death.

"Stop," I said hoarsely, as the others moved in on him. "We can't let him die. We have to help him."

"Uh, no." Hazel shook off the effects of the paralysing spell. "The other Sidhe will kill us."

River took a faltering step forwards. "We've already committed treason."

"Exactly," said Morgan. "If he dies, they'll assume he got clawed to death by a wild beast."

Bile coated the back of my throat, and I swallowed it down. "I can guarantee he'll have told at least one person he was coming to meet Ilsa and me. They'll know we did this."

"Then what do you suggest?" Hazel said. "I'm guessing he doesn't have healing magic."

"No… but if we take him to the boundary with Lady Rive's territory, she'll help him." It was still one hell of a risk to take, but I knew better than to think leaving him to die would do anything other than seal our own doom.

"Why are we saving him when he tried to kill us?" asked Morgan.

"Because the Unseelie Queen is a terrifying tyrant," I said. "You know how impossible it is to disobey a vow, don't you? She ordered him to bring me to her. If he'd defied her, he'd have been obligated to tell her I have the Morrigan's magic anyway. Then I doubt being in the mortal realm would have spared any of us from the backlash."

"Why not hide the body, then?" Morgan asked.

"Have you forgotten the Court is haunted?" Ilsa said. "If he dies and his ghost stays in Faerie, then he'll go straight to her side. If he lives, on the other hand, he might take pity on us and find a way to defy her."

"That's putting a huge stress on *might,* but you're right." River strode over to his limp body and lifted the prone Sidhe into the air, while Ilsa grimly picked up his sword.

"Hey, can we steal that?" Morgan said.

"No," said Ilsa. "You can't even use a throwing-knife correctly. I'd rather you didn't get your hands on a Sidhe's talisman."

Hazel snickered, and I glared at her. Since I was the one who'd struck him down, I could theoretically try to claim Lord Lyle's talisman as my own, but the last thing I needed was yet more volatile magic in my possession which wasn't supposed to belong to me in the first place.

Puck said nothing at all. He'd barely spoken since his intervention in the battle, nor did he meet my eyes as River followed my instructions and carried Lord Lyle to the boundary between Lord Lyle's territory and the sprawling estate where Lady Rive lived. I'd better hope she came looking for him soon, because we had to make a swift retreat in case the Sidhe caught us next to his bleeding body.

What a fucking mess. Leaping to the Sidhe's defence wasn't in my nature, but the Unseelie Queen was likely the most powerful person in the entirety of Faerie at this point in time. Even the Morrigan's magic wouldn't put a dent in her, and to top it all off, whatever dimension Ilsa had accessed when she'd tried to banish the ghost didn't seem to contain the Morrigan at all. Which meant I was out of ideas as to how to bring her back in time to stop the Unseelie Queen's wrath from crashing on all our heads if she found out I'd dealt a mortal wound to one of her favoured advisors.

Snow crunched beneath my feet as I strode through Winter's forests and in the vague direction of the path between the Courts. As we walked, a loud rustling came from behind us, like a hundred trees shedding their snowy coatings. I turned around, my heart sinking as the trees *moved,* icy branches rising to point in our direction.

"Run!" Hazel's unnecessary shout rang through the trees as a dozen sharp icicles slammed into the ground on either side of us. One skimmed my cheek, drawing blood. Puck shifted into his bird form, while the others ran, faster and faster. At a guess, Lady Rive had found the body, and the Unseelie Court itself had weaponised against us. That meant its master, or someone linked to her, knew we'd betrayed its Queen.

When we neared the path to the Courts, a final wave of icy spears slammed into the ground, melting into the leaves. Breathless, we skidded to a halt, while Puck shifted into his human form, dishevelled and covered in dirt and blood. He favoured one leg over the other, suggesting he was injured.

"Good job we brought Pepper," said Morgan. "C'mon, take us home."

The puppy gave such a violent tug on the lead I half thought he'd run off and leave the rest of us behind, but the path shifted below our group, becoming cold tarmac. We emerged into the mortal realm to the sound of sirens blaring from somewhere nearby.

"Crap." Ilsa bent double to catch her breath. "What did we miss?"

"A lot, I'm guessing." The sun shone overhead from a cold blue sky, its dazzling brightness suggesting it was morning. Given the time we'd spent on the other side, I guessed that we'd skipped two or three days again.

On the plus side, we'd left the Courts in one piece. On the minus side, I had a price on my head in Faerie, and so did everyone else. For a moment, silence spread among our group as everyone took stock of their injuries. I'd got away with a few scrapes, luckily, but Puck looked a little battered as he began to limp away from the Ley Line.

I stepped in behind him. "Where are you going?"

"To look for Hawk," he said. "He needs to know the Aes Sidhe are hiding in the borderlands."

Hazel straightened upright. "I'm gonna find Darrow and tell him about those Aes Sidhe too. I'm sure he'll be interested to learn they stuck around."

Does that mean you'll mention how you got us all captured? I held my tongue, aware that my fuckups infinitely outweighed hers. Even Ilsa was avoiding my gaze.

"So… what do we tell the boss?" she asked River. "That we never banished the Unseelie Queen's ghost after all?"

"Tell her whatever you like." The words tasted sour in my mouth. "Hell, you can place the blame on me. It's not like I'm joining the guild anytime soon."

If the guild elected to lock me in jail, at least I'd be relatively safe if the Unseelie Sidhe came back for me. I'd heard the necromancer guild's jail was built of solid iron, after all. Not that anyone responded to my offer. Instead, the others departed, even Puck, who walked ahead towards half-blood territory.

I caught him up, which wasn't hard when he was limping. "You should fix those wounds."

"Hawk will heal me." He didn't slow, and his face looked pale underneath all the blood. "He'll also give me a lecture and a half about leaving him alone to handle the ghosts."

The ghosts. I didn't see any glowing candle lights among the trees near half-blood territory. Oh boy. "You said he'd easily be able to deal with them while you were in Faerie."

"I may have exaggerated a little." He limped on towards the gate to half-blood territory, leaving a trail of blood behind him. When he came to a sudden halt, I almost walked into him. "Looks like someone broke the candle circle."

I swore under my breath. "Wonder how long it lasted?"

"A day." Brook opened the gate to beckon us into half-blood territory. He looked like he hadn't slept since we'd left. "You're late."

"There are ghosts on the loose in there?" Puck asked.

"Yes, but the rest of the city is worse."

Guilt struck me like a blow. I'd dragged Ilsa and River away from dealing with the ghosts for no good reason. When Puck walked ahead of me down the path, I veered towards my own home. "I need to check on Roseanne."

"Go ahead," Puck said. "Is Hawk around?"

"Yes, he is." Brook beckoned to him. "Need a healer, do you?"

"Not as much as you need someone to reset those candles." Puck limped on without so much as glancing back at me. The tight sensation in my chest intensified. Biting my lower lip, I headed back home and unlocked the door.

Roseanne wasn't in. She'd left a note saying she'd gone to help Hawk drive off some ghosts. I was not in the mood to face Hawk and his relentless questioning and cheeriness after the day I'd had, so I went upstairs to change out of my muddy clothes and wash every trace of Faerie from my skin.

The sound of the door opening downstairs got me out

of the shower pretty quickly. I tugged on a fresh outfit and hurried downstairs to find Roseanne in the kitchen, rifling through the cupboards. "Hey, Holly. You look like shit."

I grunted and went to the cupboard, figuring I should probably eat something as well. "How many days did I miss?"

"Two, but things started to go to shit almost as soon as you left." Roseanne emerged from the cupboard with a box of cereal in her hand. "Some clumsy troll knocked one of the candles over."

"So you've been banishing ghosts ever since." I reached out a hand for the cereal box, past experience having told me she'd eat the whole thing with her bare hands if I left her to it. "Didn't anyone ask the guild to redo the circle?"

"Dunno." She hovered by the counter as I tipped cereal into two bowls. "I think they're rushed off their feet."

I closed the cupboard door. "Guess it didn't help that two of their best members were in Faerie on a pointless quest."

"Pointless?" She grabbed her cereal bowl and sat down at the table. "Did it go that badly?"

I let out a humourless laugh. "You might say that. I'm barred from the Unseelie Court for life, and there's a price on my head if I ever set foot in Faerie again."

Her eyes widened. "Didn't Ilsa banish the ghost?"

"She never got that far." I sat down opposite her and dug my spoon into my cereal bowl, though I'd already lost my appetite.

She began shovelling cereal into her mouth. "Why'd they banish you, then?"

"Three guesses." I shifted my hands to claws in answer.

"Fuck."

"Yeah." I let my hands turn human, leaned my head against the back of the chair, and closed my eyes. "Lord Lyle said he was obliged to kill me on behalf of his queen. I fought him off, and we barely escaped in one piece."

"That's unfair," she said. "You didn't steal her powers on purpose."

"Tell that to him, not me." I rubbed my temples with my thumbs. "To top it off, we got locked up by a bunch of vigilante Aes Sidhe in the borderlands, and when we broke Puck out of their prison, we landed on their shit list too."

She rocked back in her seat. "Didn't he used to be one of them?"

"Yes." I pushed my cereal bowl towards her. "Go ahead. I'm not hungry."

"Bollocks." She sprang to her feet. "You know this isn't your fault, right? Blame that gormless troll for kicking the candles over."

"You wouldn't have needed candles if I hadn't taken away the one necromancer who might have been able to help." To placate her, I started eating. "The others *did* make it clear I'm at fault for dragging them to Faerie at the worst possible time, so there's a fair chance the guild will be the next to come after me."

"Then they're blaming the wrong person." She sat back down. "I remember you told *me* to ignore the people who blame me for shit that's not my fault."

My mouth parted. "I think getting my family exiled by the Unseelie Court is a little different than a bunch of superstitious half-bloods spreading gossip. Not that they aren't wankers anyway. They didn't give you too much trouble while I was gone?"

"Nah, Hawk drove them off," she said.

"*Hawk did?*"

Roseanne filled me in on everything I'd missed, which mostly consisted of anecdotes about chasing ghosts around. Hearing she hadn't been holed up in her room the whole time did improve my mood a little, though the topic soon returned to unwelcome territory.

"So Puck just took off as soon as you got back?" she asked. "I saw him on my way here. He was covered in blood."

"He claimed Hawk would patch him up," I said. "Probably wants to see if he can do anything to help drive out the ghosts."

"There's no point," she said. "They always come back. The guild never sent another necromancer."

Great. There was zero chance of them letting Ilsa out of their sight now she'd returned to their ranks, so we'd need to find an alternative solution. "And the Mage Lords?"

"They dumped a pile of salt on our doorstep this morning and then buggered off again."

"Figures." That, at least, I'd be able to help with, though I didn't know what to make of Puck's odd silence since I'd stabbed Lord Lyle. Did *he* blame me for the way our trip to Faerie had spun out of control? Whatever the case, I still needed to find out why the Aes Sidhe had greeted him with a storm of arrows. "All right, let's see how much of a mess the ghosts have made."

13

A lot, as it turned out. Signs of spiritual destruction lined the path as Roseanne and I walked through half-blood territory. Bushes and plants had been pulled up by the roots, roof tiles and broken glass littered the ground, and I spotted Hawk and Puck carrying hefty sacks of salt over their shoulders. That must be the Mage Lords' generous delivery. I assumed Hawk had healed Puck's injuries, because he'd stopped limping despite the blood staining his face and clothes.

"Hey, Holly," said Hawk. "Come to help us out?"

"That's what the Mage Lords gave you?" I indicated the sacks piled near the gate. "A shit-ton of salt? They do realise you're dealing with ghosts and not zombies, don't they?"

Not all ghosts would be deterred by salt. Reapplying the candle barrier seemed the only solution, assuming we could get a necromancer to re-light the candles. Which depended on whether or not Ilsa told her boss just how badly our mission had gone.

"Yes, but Brook told us we have to apply a salt barrier around every home on the territory," said Hawk. "Too late for some, of course, but I reckon the guild will be quick to send a necromancer to check up on us now they've got two of their best members back."

"I wouldn't be so sure." I risked a glance at Puck, but he'd walked past us towards the nearest house with his giant sack of salt. "Anyway, what are we supposed to be doing? Putting salt around all the houses?"

"Brook told us to start here." Hawk gave a sweeping gesture to the street we stood on. "Put salt in a line in front of each house, leaving no gaps. Pretty straight-forward."

"Unless there's already a ghost in there." I walked towards the pile of sacks near the gate. "Shit—Leyton's ghost is back, isn't it?"

"He's back to his old tricks, yes."

"Bloody perfect." Before picking up a sack, I checked my phone, then berated myself for thinking Ilsa would message me right away. She was probably enduring a grilling from her boss as we spoke. Guilt clenched inside my chest, and I put my phone away and seized a bag of salt from the pile at the side of the road. Roseanne wandered over, and I beckoned to her. "Come and help me with this."

"I can manage." Roseanne tried to drag one of the giant sacks single-handedly but almost fell flat on her back under its weight. Hawk moved in to help her, while I found myself fighting a smile at the sight of the two of them getting along so well. He'd won her trust when he'd defended her from those judgemental half-fae, and I was glad of it. I couldn't be her sole ally, especially when I hadn't exactly set a great example lately.

I hauled the bag of salt to the nearest house and began scattering handfuls in a straight line. This would take all day, but at least it kept my hands busy if not my thoughts. When I finished the line, I picked up the giant sack to carry it to the next street and found myself working near Puck. He gave me a nod of acknowledgement and nothing more, prompting another guilty twinge.

Dammit, just tell me you're mad at me and we can move on. Why stabbing Lord Lyle would be where he'd draw the line, I hadn't a clue. Silence surrounded us, thick as smog and yet as fragile as glass, while the urge to shatter it became stronger by the second. Not just because I wanted to know if he blamed me for getting us banned from the Courts, but due to the equally strong urge to ask why the Aes Sidhe had captured him.

They called him a traitor. Had they been mad at him for leaving them behind while they'd been sent to fight for their Queen, or were they in league with the Wild Hunt after all? I hadn't seen any clues that they might be, but it wasn't like I'd had the chance to explore the warren of tunnels in which they'd made their new home. Besides, Hazel was the only one of us who'd actually *been* to the Aes Sidhe's old Court.

I continued to scatter salt, and the next time I glanced in his direction, I found him watching me. "What is it? Need more salt?"

"No, we need a necromancer."

Yes, I'm aware of that. "Don't get your hopes up. You saw the others after we came back."

"They don't blame you for how our trip to Faerie turned out, Holly," he said.

I gave a humourless snort. "I know half-fae can lie, but that's obviously bullshit. Ilsa might be too nice to apportion blame, but River, Morgan, and Hazel made their thoughts on our excursion clear from the start."

"Yet they chose to come with you."

"So did you, so you're one to talk."

A smile flickered across his features. "Yes, I did, and I still think they're fools."

"'Lord, what fools these mortals be.'" The quote escaped before I'd quite considered how it might sound to someone who'd grown up in the realm which Shakespeare had been referencing.

He grinned. "So you're familiar with a certain play concerning lovestruck humans being bewitched by faeries."

"I assume the real story involved a lot more bloodshed," I said. "Ever given anyone a donkey's head as a prank?"

"No, I can't say I have," he said. "Need help with that?"

I glanced down at the salt spilling from the bag in my hands while I hadn't been paying attention. "No, I've got it."

He wasn't mad at me. Instead, we were talking *Shakespeare*. How did I even get myself into these situations? I returned my attention to applying salt to the road instead. "This is going to deter any wildlife from coming near the place for months. Not to mention melting the Winter Sidhe's snow."

"Small price to pay for being ghost-free."

I made a sceptical noise. "I suppose at least the spirit of

the Winter Court is going to haunt the Unseelie Queen for the rest of her immortal life."

"Serve her right," he said. "I've been shunned by Winter for years. They aren't worth bothering with."

My hands clenched. "Maybe not, but if this Death-related crap originated over there, these ghosts are here for the long haul."

"I don't think it did," said Puck. "I saw that black hole Ilsa banished the ghost into. That wasn't the afterlife, was it? Not the same one we see here."

"No." I moved the bag of salt along. "Unfortunately, the part that *did* originate in the Courts is the disappearance of a certain feathered death goddess. Which is no doubt why that ghost got the impetus to go and haunt Her Majesty."

Puck was silent for a moment. "The Morrigan knowingly loaned you her powers with full awareness of the potential consequences."

Not all of them. I'd brought him back to life, and I'd *felt* the Morrigan's magic react to the violation. But admitting that would result in needing to explain why I'd done it, and I simply didn't have the words. "This realm *is* linked to Faerie, through the Vale if nothing else. Sidhe have been visiting since the time of the Ancients."

My known family history only went back a few hundred years to Thomas Lynn's big mistake—which I gathered was shortly before the Aes Sidhe had left Summer and set up their own territory—but I knew the Sidhe had been tormenting mortals long before then.

Speaking of which… "Puck, why were the Aes Sidhe so pissed off at you? Were they mad at you for ditching your

Queen and running off to the mortal realm instead of fighting for them?"

"In a way," he said. "I was on a mission at the time, and I came back to the Court to find chaos had broken out and that Queen Etaina had ordered her entire army to travel to the Summer Court immediately."

"How'd you get out of that one?"

"We weren't bound to be part of her army," he said. "Hawk was a healer, not a fighter, and I was…"

"A trickster," I said. "What exactly did that entail?"

He tilted his head to one side. "Does that mean you're going to answer some questions from me too?"

"Depends what they are." If he ventured too far into my family history, he'd hit a door marked Do Not Disturb. "Besides, you know what my job as Gatekeeper involved. I have no idea what a trickster does aside from play pranks on people."

"Traditionally, a Court's trickster is either a spy or a saboteur depending on who gives the orders," he said. "I was sent to hinder the various potential enemies of the Aes Sidhe and to ensure nobody came close to stumbling across our hiding place."

Made sense. The Aes Sidhe had been believed extinct even by the Court they'd originally belonged to, although Hazel had implied the former King of Summer had been aware of their survival, as the person who'd kicked them out to begin with. Until, that is, they'd had him murdered. "So the others think you should have stuck with them?"

My thoughts drifted back to the group of outcasts who'd made their home in the forest, creating an exact imitation of their old Court. What would have happened if they *did* guess that Hazel and I had once been the Gate-keepers whose actions had destroyed their Queen?

"No, there's likely nothing I might have done to satisfy them," he said. "I was a Court trickster. They believed my loyalty to the Queen ought to outlast her death."

"You don't think they're scheming like the Wild Hunt were?" I suggested. "Because if they were, it's a good job they didn't realise they captured the Gatekeepers."

"No." He stared at me for a moment. "How did they not recognise you if they were present during the battle?"

"No Gatekeeper's mark." I jabbed my forehead. "No circlet, no glamour, no fancy clothes. We registered as ordinary humans to them, nothing more. I guess they assumed the Gatekeepers ran as far away as possible once they were free of the curse."

Which, in fairness, was exactly what Hazel had done, until this recent screw-up had forced her to come straight back to Faerie.

"I suppose," said Puck. "Looks like my assessment that Queen Etaina's entire army shared three brain cells between them wasn't far off the mark after all."

I fought a smile. "Try two brain cells. Hazel wasn't wrong when she said they had zero imagination, consid-ering they built a carbon copy of their old Court in the borderlands."

"Speaking of Hazel."

I spun around, suppressing a groan. Hazel walked down the pavement towards us, eyeing the lines of salt on either side of the road. "You seriously think that'll keep out the ghosts?"

"I didn't sign up for the opposite of a pep talk." I made

a shooing motion at her. "Thought you were with Darrow."

I'd also thought she was mad at me after our return from Faerie, come to that. Hazel, however, pursed her lips. "Ilsa is with the Council of Twelve."

"Am I supposed to know who they are?"

She blinked. "You don't know the Council?"

Puck stepped in. "Neither do I. I take it they're important?"

"You might say that," said Hazel. "They're a cross-supernatural group with ties to the regional mage councils, put into place to help defend humanity from the backlash of the faerie invasion. Ilsa is one of their consultants because of that talisman of hers, and they're demanding answers about where she disappeared to."

"Shit." If Ilsa got into trouble with this Council, then they'd come for me next. "Did she tell them she was in Faerie?"

"Haven't a clue, because she's been in questioning for the last hour," she said. "Her boss at the guild is in there, too, along with the highest members of Edinburgh's mage guild. It's not like *they* have a representative in Faerie, but I don't know what they'll do when they find out we burned so many bridges with the Court."

My throat went dry. I wouldn't blame Ilsa if she told the Council the truth about her reasons for being in Faerie, but if they were anything as stringent as the Mage Lords, a jail sentence might be in the near future for me after all. Making enemies of the Courts did not strike me as being in line with the goal of defending humanity from the fae.

I drew in a breath. "On a scale from 'mildly screwed' to 'locked up for all eternity,' what's the likely consequence?"

"Huh?" Hazel said. "They know how volatile the Sidhe are. I got banned from Summer not that long ago, before they had a new ruler."

So she had. I'd forgotten entirely, given that her exile had immediately been followed by the breaking of the curse. "How'd you make it up to them?"

"I helped them crown a new ruler and averted a war."

"Great." So much for there being an easy solution. "Yeah, that's not gonna work for us this time. Winter doesn't want a new ruler, and as for averting a war, we're more likely to *start* one if we go back to Faerie at all before the Morrigan comes back."

"I know," said Hazel. "Just thought you should know the Council's here. I'm sure Ilsa will text you when they let her go."

If she isn't in jail. How many more pieces of unwelcome news could fall on us in the course of a single week? "That should be 'if they let her go.' If not, I guess I have to go and turn myself in."

"What?" Puck said. "No. Absolutely not. You aren't taking the heat for what the Sidhe did."

"Then tell me what you would do in my situation." I looked between him and Hazel. "Ilsa doesn't deserve to take the blame for a mission I got her ensnared in. The Mage Council might be less likely to turn us into ice statues than the Unseelie Queen, but they're no less hard-core when it comes to punishing lawbreakers. Without the knowledge of who started this crap, they're looking for someone to blame."

"Nah, they want rid of the ghosts more than anything."

Hazel backed down the path, waving at Roseanne. "Just thought I'd give you an update."

"Thanks." I watched her leave. "Great. I assumed it'd be the necromancers who stuck me in a cell, not this Council. Might be the coward's way out, but being imprisoned is better than being executed by the Sidhe."

"The last thing I'd call you is a coward, given what you did in the borderlands." Puck spoke in a low voice, and warmth travelled up my neck. "You got me out of the Aes Sidhe's hands when you'd already walked free."

I addressed the bag of salt instead of him. "Maybe I wanted your death off my conscience."

He smoothly stepped in behind me, almost close enough to touch, but not quite. "Bullshit."

"Holly." Roseanne's voice came from nearby, causing me to startle. "What did Hazel want?"

"To warn me Ilsa's being interrogated by this Council of Twelve, whoever they are."

"Incoming!" Hawk yelled.

I spun on my heel as Leyton's ghost appeared hovering above our heads. "I've been waiting for you to come back. You'll pay for locking me out of my house."

His hands lit up with Winter magic, which he blasted at me. I ducked and rolled, the Morrigan's magic reacting without conscious thought and shifting my hands to claws. My already fraying temper snapped. "Oh, fuck off."

Aes Sidhe rogues, wraiths, Lord Lyle, even my own allies—I'd seen enough conflict today that the sight of the annoying ghost was enough to push me over the edge. He wheeled above our heads, firing off blasts of magic which sent the others scattering throughout the street.

Shadowy wings folded outward from my back and

carried me forwards, and I slammed down in front of him and thrust my claws through his transparent form. My grip snagged on something almost solid, or fluid, and the ghost screamed. "Let me go!"

I hadn't imagined grabbing that wraith earlier. The Morrigan *could* interact with spirits.

"I won't," I said. "I banish you."

Not that there was a hole into the afterlife for me to throw him into this time around. My claws remained lodged in the ghost's squirming form as I struggled to shake him loose, imagining a pair of gates appearing at his back. Without the spirit sight, though, banishment remained beyond reach.

I did the next best thing instead—I threw him like a javelin. The ghost screamed, high and loud, as I pitched him headfirst across the rooftops and out of sight.

"Holy shit," breathed Roseanne. "Ah—Holly, we have company."

My claws vanished, and not a moment too soon. A woman strode up the path, carrying a sword which glowed in a manner which resembled a faerie talisman. Yet she was human, dressed in a leather jacket and jeans, with her long brown hair tied in a ponytail. Had she seen what I'd done? I *hoped* not, but the look on her face was assessing as she took in the chaos around us.

"Looks like I got here just in time," she said. "I'm Ivy Lane. Which of you killed the Morrigan?"

14

I stared at her for a good five seconds. How did this Ivy Lane know the Morrigan was missing, let alone dead? My mind ran through the possibilities, but I drew a blank.

She addressed me. "I'm guessing nobody told you I was coming? You're one of the Lynns, right?"

I found my voice. "Yes. I'm Holly, the former Winter Gatekeeper. This is Roseanne."

"We've met," Ivy said, startling me. *Does that mean she knows Roseanne's parentage?*

"Uh, yeah." Roseanne looked distinctly uncomfortable. "A while ago."

"Three years or so, right?" Ivy said. "Didn't expect to find you all the way up in Scotland. What is it about Edinburgh always being the centre for this kind of madness?"

I glimpsed Puck and Hawk watching from the end of the road, but I gave a faint shake of my head to tell them not to intervene. "You mean, this isn't happening anywhere else in the country? The problems with Death, I mean?"

"No, except the disappearance of a few of the necromancer guardians," Ivy said. "They were last seen in this city, which is why the council and I came here."

She's with the Council of Twelve. I'd thought her name sounded familiar, but she appeared to be a regular human to me, despite the glowing sword in her hand.

Wait a moment. Hadn't Ilsa said Ivy Lane was the person who'd killed Fionn, the former leader of the Wild Hunt?

A brief thread of hope rose inside me despite my lingering wariness. If Ivy was in the know about the Wild Hunt, she might be able to help us find a solution after all.

"If it's centred on this city, then why did you mention the Morrigan?" Bringing up the subject again might not be a wise idea, but she was the one who'd levelled the accusation at me to begin with. "Is her disappearance linked to what's happening here?"

"So you're admitting that you killed her, then?"

"No, I didn't kill her." I looked between her and Roseanne. "How do you even know about any of this? You're human."

"Really? I had no idea." Ivy rolled her eyes. "I know because I've worked with the faeries for years, and because I was in the middle of touring England with the Council of Twelve when we were interrupted by a flood of calls from the mages here in Edinburgh begging us to help figure out what was wrong with Death. On top of that, I went to pay the Morrigan a visit and found a hysterical ogre in her cave wailing that she'd vanished."

So she'd been to Faerie herself? At least it meant

nobody in my own contacts had blabbed to her. "Did he say *I* was the one responsible?"

"He said a human caused her disappearance," she said. "He said she loaned her magic to someone and disappeared shortly afterwards. Given what I just saw you do to that ghost, I'm taking a wild guess it's you."

Oh boy. The ogre had guessed more than I'd expected, but despite the accusatory note in Ivy's tone, she hadn't used her sword on me yet. Maybe she wanted to hear my side of the story first, which was an improvement on the Unseelie, if nothing else.

"That's not precisely true," I said. "I don't know how much you know about the Wild Hunt's recent attack on the city, but when I asked for the Morrigan to help me stop them, she loaned me some of her magic as part of a vow."

"She made a deal with you?" Her brows rose. "How'd you convince her?"

If Ivy was in the habit of paying social calls to the queen of the death fae, she presumably knew the entirety of her unpleasant history with the Wild Hunt. "She's scared of the Wild Hunt."

Her mouth formed an *O* of understanding. "She was willing to do anything to ensure they didn't get their claws in her again."

"I hardly expected her to vanish immediately afterwards," I added. "Nobody has seen her body, so I assume she's going to be reborn at some point, but there's a lag."

"I believe you," she said. "Mostly because I'm pretty sure nobody *can* kill the Morrigan, including the Unseelie Queen, for that matter. She's designed to be indestructible."

"She's taking her sweet time reviving herself from the dead, though," I said. "You really don't think there's a connection with how Death is screwed up here?"

"I can't see how she would be," said Ivy. "I wouldn't claim to know everything about Faerie, but she doesn't escort *our* dead to the afterlife. Neither did the Wild Hunt."

Which meant it wasn't my fault after all. Not all of it, anyway. Didn't change the mess I'd made of things in Faerie, but if the Morrigan's disappearance hadn't caused Death to lose control of its gates, then what had? "Why's the Council of Twelve interrogating Ilsa, then?"

"Who told you that, Hazel?" Ivy asked. "I reckon they're probably finished with her by now."

That sounded ominous. "Are they going to punish her for getting kicked out of Faerie?"

"No. Wait, you got kicked out?"

She didn't know about our mission. No surprise, if she'd arrived in the city while we were already in Faerie. "The Unseelie Queen had a ghost she wanted Ilsa to get rid of, but I guess it's not linked to the issues in this realm."

"Tell me on the way to the guild." Ivy began to walk back towards the gate out of half-blood territory.

I didn't move. "The guild's management is ticked off with me for taking her and River into Faerie at a critical time."

"Pity for them." She kept walking.

I gave Roseanne a bewildered look. "Is she normally like this?"

"Yes," said Roseanne. "She won't let you get arrested, though. I'll tell the others…"

"They know." I cast my gaze around and saw Puck and Hawk picking up the bags of salt the ghost had knocked over. "I'd better see what this Council has to say."

I didn't *want* to step within ten feet of the guild, but Ivy was not to be deterred. She got the entire story out of me on the walk to Edinburgh's Old Town—both the conflict with the Wild Hunt and our recent disastrous trip to Faerie.

"Damn," said Ivy when I'd finished. "That's one wicked streak of bad luck. I had no idea the Wild Hunt were even still around."

"Yeah, that's why I needed to borrow the Morrigan's magic," I said. "I hadn't a hope of beating them on my own, and neither did anyone else. They captured Ilsa and Roseanne and came within seconds of summoning a god of death. If one of the victims hadn't faked his death to put them off their guards, they'd have succeeded."

"They're imprisoned in Winter, then," she said.

"Yes, so I don't see how they can possibly have any connection to what's going on at the moment."

"They might," she said. "They got pretty far with that ritual."

So they had. "Yeah, but Etaina actually *did* summon the god, and it never screwed up Death."

"True, but the Ancients are unpredictable," said Ivy. "This wouldn't be the first time one of them caused an adverse effect on the spirit realm. They can travel between realms, after all."

From the way she talked, she sounded like she ran into Ancients every day of the week. Before I could probe her further, we reached the oak doors of the necromancer guild. Ivy didn't hesitate for a second before pushing open the door and crossing the lobby in a confident stride. Everyone in the vicinity stared at her, but the sword at her waist kept them from challenging her.

I swiftly followed before they looked away, and we headed upstairs to the archive. Inside the small room, Ilsa sat at the desk, while Morgan, Lloyd, and Jas crowded behind her. None of them looked surprised to see Ivy walk in.

"Thought I'd find one of you in here," said Ivy. "The council finally finished with you?"

"Just about." Ilsa rested her head on her steepled hands, her face drooping with tiredness. No surprise, given that she'd been dragged here straight after returning from Faerie. "I figured you were checking in with whoever could get you up to speed on the latest catastrophe."

"Meaning me," I said. "Ilsa... what *did* you tell the council?"

All eyes turned towards me, and it took every ounce of self-control I possessed not to lower my gaze.

"She told them you all got kicked out of Faerie," Jas said.

Great. Everyone knew, and no doubt River and Morgan had made it quite clear where the blame lay.

"That wasn't their concern," Ilsa said. "They wanted to know about the problems in Death."

"They weren't interested in Faerie?" I guessed the rampant ghost issue in Edinburgh was a more pressing concern, but still. "Ivy said it might be linked to the god of death."

"I said 'might.'" Ivy didn't blink when everyone turned their attention to her instead. "Without seeing the spirit realm for myself, I don't have much more than guesswork to go on. Whatever the case, banishing individual ghosts is a waste of time until we fix it."

"You do think it's fixable?" I asked.

Ilsa lifted her head. "We've checked Death countless times. It doesn't look any different until you try to push a ghost through the gates."

"You haven't walked between realms to check?" asked Ivy. "I can have a look, but I assume you're more of an expert on this city."

Walked between realms? She couldn't be talking about simply using the spirit sight. "I didn't know you were a necromancer."

"I'm not." Ivy hefted her blade. "This allows me to travel between realms… to some degree. I still can't get into Faerie without an invitation, though."

"That's a talisman." A genuine Sidhe talisman. "How'd you get it?"

"Stole it from a Sidhe," she said. "Or won it, technically, in a way which is actually pretty similar to how *you* ended up with magic which shouldn't have been yours."

Meaning with a vow. No wonder she'd easily accepted the idea of me taking the Morrigan's powers. Then again, she wasn't part of the Courts, and she knew I hadn't *killed* the Morrigan.

Unable to hold back the questions rising within me, I said, "You killed Fionn of the Wild Hunt. Is that where you got it?"

"No, but I used this weapon to kill him," she said. "The magic inside it originally came from an Ancient, which gives me the ability to travel on the spirit lines, necromancer-style. Ilsa can do the same, so we'll head straight over until we find the source of the trouble."

"That sounds… risky." I glanced over at the others, who were all staring at Ivy, too, even though I'd assumed they already knew about her talisman. "Especially if you think the death god was partly responsible. Or the Wild Hunt."

"The Wild Hunt never summoned the god of death," Jas said. "The ritual failed."

"Holly said the same," Ivy said. "They can certainly cross realms themselves if the desire takes them, but I don't see one of *them* making trouble in Death. They'd have nothing to gain from it."

"You didn't know the Wild Hunt worked with the Aes Sidhe, then?" I asked Ivy.

"No, I didn't," Ivy said. "Are the Aes Sidhe the ones Hazel found hiding underground?"

"Yep," said Ilsa. "Queen Etaina put the Gatekeeper's curse on our family, but we didn't find out until recently that the Wild Hunt was giving her lessons in blood magic. They never showed up to defend their Queen during the battle, so they missed how her reunion with the god of death backfired on her."

"How loyal of them," Ivy said. "I figured some of the Hunt must have survived after I killed their leader, but it's not like I've had the time to hunt them all down. That's supposed to be the Sidhe's job."

"No shit," said Morgan. "You want to drag Ilsa into Death when she just blew out her magic banishing ghosts in Faerie, then?"

"I'm fine," Ilsa insisted. "Ivy, if you think this is the only way to find the source of the trouble, I'll come and take a look."

"You want to do this now?" Jas asked. "I realise we

need to alleviate the pressure on the guild, but I don't know that walking into Death without a plan is a good move."

"We have a plan." Ilsa pushed to her feet. "Look out for trouble. Ivy has more experience walking between realms than I do."

I didn't think it was the best idea, but I had no alternatives to suggest, and at least I wouldn't take the blame if this plan went tits-up. While Ivy left the room, I went to speak to Jas. "If you have time, the half-faeries might need the help of a necromancer again when they've finished evicting their unwanted guests."

Her forehead scrunched up. "What happened to the candles?"

"A troll knocked them over," I said. "They're salt-proofing their houses at the moment, but we'd appreciate it if you could help."

"Sure, no worries," she said. "You should keep an eye on Ilsa and make sure she doesn't tire herself out."

I was fairly sure she wouldn't be asking me to do that if she knew I'd been responsible for her current state in the first place, but it seemed the others hadn't opted to share all the details of our trip to Faerie with the others at the guild.

Meanwhile, I headed downstairs behind Ivy and Ilsa and through the front doors out of the guild.

"Are you sure you want to do this alone?" I asked Ivy. "I mean, I can't travel into Death like the two of you, so I wouldn't be able to see if you ended up in trouble on the other side."

"Two of us should be fine," Ivy said. "We can watch

each other's backs. Better pick a spot farther from the guild…"

They walked down the cobbled street and turned a corner.

"Ilsa," I said. "Aren't you going to tell River?"

"No," she said. "He's stuck in a meeting with the boss, and this will only take a few seconds."

Unless you get stuck in Death. They took one hell of a risk when they left their bodies behind and fully crossed over to the other side, and most necromancers couldn't pull it off without being unable to return to their bodies at all.

Ivy rounded another corner, leaving the two of us hurrying to keep up.

"Did you say your talisman enables you to use necromancy?" I asked her.

"No," she said. "I mean, I can see ghosts, but I'm not guild-trained and it's more of a side effect of my talisman. I can walk between this realm and Death for the same reason. I think it used to be common for the Ancients."

The talisman had been an Ancient's. Like Ilsa's. That explained the commonalities between their talents, despite Ilsa being a necromancer and Gatekeeper and Ivy being… well, I wasn't exactly sure *what* Ivy was, except someone I'd prefer not to end up facing on a battlefield.

Regardless, I felt a little better now we had a purpose. Ivy and Ilsa picked out a bench to sit down on and cross into Death, while I scanned the near-empty street. "You're doing this in broad daylight?"

"Nobody can see us except senior necromancers, and they're all in a meeting with the boss at the moment," Ilsa said. "Let's go into Death."

15

Ivy and Ilsa both went completely still, their expressions blanking out as they tapped into the spirit realm. As I waited in front of them, Morgan strode over with Pepper in tow.

"I thought you were staying at the guild." Maybe he didn't trust me to keep an eye on Ilsa when she was in a vulnerable position. Pepper climbed protectively onto Ilsa's lap as though to back up my suspicion, while Jas and Lloyd strode over to join him.

"Who wants to draw on their faces?" Morgan asked. "Anyone got a pen?"

"No, and I don't have a death wish, either," said Jas. "I'm not drawing anything on Ivy."

"I wouldn't screw with the person who killed the Huntsman," I added. "Even if she did just entrust us with her personal safety."

"Pretty sure that sword's enough to deter anyone from attacking her," Lloyd said. "What're they looking for in Death, anyway?"

"I have no idea," I said. "Not like I can see what's going on."

Ilsa and Ivy remained in their zoned-out state until, in a sudden movement which startled the puppy into falling off Ilsa's lap, they both blinked back to alertness. Ivy leapt to her feet and drew her sword. "Crap."

Without so much as another word, she broke into a sprint down the street, while Ilsa fumbled in her pocket for her own talisman. "We got ambushed on the spirit line."

"By what?" I hurried after her with the others on my heels, while Ivy had already rounded a corner ahead of us.

When we caught up to her, we found Ivy battling two shadowy forms in a narrow alleyway. *Wraiths.* From the way the temperature had plummeted, they were from Winter. Ivy fought both at once, her talisman a blur of bright blue magic. One wraith slid out of her reach and targeted the rest of us instead.

Ilsa barred the wraith's path. Bright whiteness spun from her hands and knocked it backwards, but an exclamation from Morgan drew our attention to a third wraith approaching from behind, followed by a fourth. They had us surrounded.

Morgan, Lloyd, and Jas all conjured necromantic magic to their hands, while Pepper leapt at one of the wraiths, barking at the top of his lungs. Necromancy did have an effect on wraiths, if not as strong as Ilsa's power— or Ivy's, which shattered the first wraith into nothingness. Unfortunately, we still had three of the bastards to deal with.

When one of the wraiths pushed Lloyd and Jas into retreat, I ran into the fray, revelling in the shadowy magic which shielded me against the coldness of its touch. My claws slid through the wraith, and I gripped onto the near-solid part as I'd done with the wraith I'd fought in Faerie. *Gotcha.*

"Whoa." Jas goggled at me. "How'd you do that?"

"I need a hand over here, Ilsa." The wraith wriggled like a fish on a hook, unable to free itself from the Morrigan's claws. "I banish you, wraith."

"Go beyond the Gates of Death." Ilsa's shout came from behind me, and the shadow of the Gates of Death appeared behind the wraith amid the fog of Death.

A wild impulse seized me. Instead of pushing the wraith through the gates, I flew forwards, my claws still hooked into its cloak-like form as I squinted, trying to see what lurked in the gap between the towering gates.

The wraith broke from my grip, propelled beyond the gates—which abruptly vanished as I hit the alley wall. Hard. Pain spiked from my nose to my cheekbones.

"Holly, what are you doing?" Ilsa asked.

I reeled back, one hand clutching my face. *Ouch. That failed, then.* Blood dripped from my nose, but I didn't think I'd broken anything. "Did you manage to banish it?"

"What do you think?" Morgan said. "Why'd you fly headfirst into a wall?"

Heat crept up my neck. "I was trying to see through the gates."

"You *threw* the wraith," Jas said. "Is that one of the Morrigan's tricks?"

"A new one." I wiped my bleeding nose on my sleeve. "I can't banish anything without the spirit sight, though."

"There's something off with the gates, all right." Ivy strode down the alleyway, having presumably dealt with the remaining wraiths. "Have you managed to get through to any of the necromancer guardians?"

"No." Ilsa pocketed her book. "Actually… the guild says they haven't been able to contact any of them since before all this started. Summoning them results in a dead end."

"Does that mean they're dead?" Lloyd asked. "Deader than dead, I mean?"

"I don't know, but Lady Montgomery told me in confidence that they haven't been seen since all this started," Ilsa said. "I'm not supposed to tell everyone, but I don't see how we're supposed to handle this if we hide vital information."

"The Council knows, I assume," said Ivy. "Damn, maybe I shouldn't have skipped that meeting."

"Where'd the wraiths come from, then?" asked Jas. "You were attacked in Death, right?"

"On the spirit line," Ilsa said. "When we tried to check out the gates. I'm wondering if there's something similar on the other side of the gates, screwing around somehow there so the ghosts can't stick. It's as good a guess as any."

"What?" Lloyd stared at her. "That's not possible, is it? If you go to the other side of the gates, you disappear."

"Even wraiths do, right?" added Jas.

"Usually." Ilsa didn't elaborate, but unease trailed long fingers up my spine. After all, we'd both encountered a wraith who'd lingered behind the gates even after being banished from the mortal realm. She'd lurked there for weeks, in fact, until she'd seized the chance to return to life again.

"How…" I swallowed. "I mean, how can we check the other side of the gates? Without dying ourselves, I mean?"

"Yeah, I'm not volunteering," said Morgan.

"I *might* be able to," Ilsa said. "I did it once before, but I was close to death myself and my talisman kept me grounded. I wish I knew what happened to the guardians. I wouldn't have thought it'd be possible to *kill* one of them."

"Considering being dead is in the job description," said Jas. "Ah… I saw part of the other side of the gates myself once, in similar circumstances, but Ilsa stopped me from drifting away."

"What the hell is wrong with you people?" Ivy said. "Do you waltz over to the other side of the Gates of Death for fun?"

"Speak for yourself," said Ilsa. "Anyway, the gates aren't designed to let anyone escape. Once you're on the other side, you're more or less cut off from your body. Even in the first layer of the veil, it's hard to keep a grip on your conscious self."

Does the same apply to the Morrigan? When I'd seen the gate up close, I hadn't felt myself being tugged through, but my collision with the wall hadn't exactly been the desired outcome either. Maybe one of the other necromancers would be able to volunteer, but they'd be running one hell of a risk.

Then the obvious hit me. "Wraiths can't think for themselves. Who put them up to this?"

"That's the question, isn't it?" Ivy strode out of the alleyway. "I'm going to tell the Council. Ilsa, I'll mention you were with me when we found the wraiths, but they shouldn't drag you in for questioning again."

"Good, because I have to explain myself to River, too," she said, as Ivy strode away down the street.

"Rather you than me," said Morgan. "Nah, he won't

stay mad at you. He knows this is your thing. Getting stuck in Death, I mean."

"C'mon." Lloyd let the faerie puppy walk into the lead. "Let's get back to the guild before Ilsa gets any more of her risky ideas."

While the others headed in the direction of the guild, Ilsa lingered for a moment to speak to me. "Why *did* you fly into the wall? Could you actually see through the gates?"

"I came close," I said. "Do *you* really think there's a wraith or two hanging out on the other side, clinging onto existence?"

"I have no idea." She looked down. "I know there were special circumstances involved with—you know."

With my mother. "The Winter Gatekeeper's magic was powerful. That's why she hung on. These wraiths... they were just regular Sidhe, right?"

"The ones we fought were," she said. "You—grabbed one of them. How long have you been able to do that?"

"Since we were in Faerie," I said. "It makes sense that the Morrigan can grab hold of the dead. She wouldn't be able to capture souls to devour otherwise."

"Please don't start devouring souls, Holly." Despite her light tone, a worried undercurrent in her voice drew my eyes to her face, which was pinched with tiredness.

"I won't if you go and take a nap without any more sojourns into Death."

She smiled. "Consider it done."

While she went to rejoin her friends, I turned towards home. Roseanne would be waiting for an update, and I couldn't begin to figure out what our next move should be. Wraiths had no real independent thoughts, nor any will of their own except pure destructive instinct. My mother had been a glaring exception, but otherwise, wraiths were incapable of speech, let alone hiding themselves in Death until someone came looking. Whether they could take orders or not, I didn't know.

The sky had begun to darken by the time I reached half-blood territory again, and I found Roseanne waiting for me outside in the form of a crow, perched on a low wall.

"Are you okay?" I asked, surprised she was out in public alone, even in her shifted form.

Roseanne shifted into a human again. "I should be asking you the same question. Were you interrogated by the Council of Twelve?"

"No," I said. "Ivy and Ilsa went looking for the cause of the trouble in Death and drew some wraiths on our tail, but we dealt with them. On that note, do you know if wraiths can take orders from living people?"

"Wraiths?" Her nose wrinkled. "No clue. Why?"

"Just a thought I had," I said. "The wraiths ambushed the others in Death, but I thought they had no will of their own."

"So did I," she said. "Puck's still here, by the way."

"Wait, he is?" I followed her through the gates. "Is he still putting salt around the territory?"

"Yeah, very slowly." A smirk appeared on her mouth. "Or waiting for someone."

"The necromancers." I rubbed my sore nose. "I told Jas we needed her help to get the candles lit again, but we need to get rid of the ghosts first."

"Not the necromancers." She gave me a gentle but surprising shove. "He's waiting for you, dimwit."

Sure enough, I found Puck waiting around the corner from my house beside an empty sack of salt, while Hawk was nowhere to be seen. "There you are, Holly. What happened to your face?"

"Wraiths." I'd rather not mention the specifics of my collision with the wall. "Ilsa and Ivy decided to check Death to see what was going on behind the gates, and someone didn't want them to look."

"Wraiths?" Puck blinked. "They're not autonomous. What were they doing hiding deep in Death?"

"I think someone sent them there."

"You do?" Roseanne looked at me in surprise.

"Yes." I drew in a breath. "The Aes Sidhe."

Puck's mouth parted. "You think the Sidhe in the borderlands sent them? Holly, I'm fairly sure they've never set foot in the mortal realm since the battle."

"They don't need to if they send wraiths in their place," I pointed out. "I'm not an expert on wraiths, but they absolutely *can* lurk behind the gates after death. If someone else gave them orders to attack anyone who tries to get through, I think it's safe to say that's where the trouble lies."

"What motive would the Aes Sidhe have for meddling with Death?" Puck asked. "I never saw a wraith near their territory in my life."

"They worked with the Wild Hunt," I said, undeterred. "Maybe *they* did it. And yes, I know they're locked up now, but they might have given the orders beforehand."

"When would they have had time?" he asked. "During the siege on the city? Besides, I wouldn't risk going back into Faerie again on a hunch."

"Right." Of course not. My hunch was just that, and yet

I was sure the Aes Sidhe weren't lingering in the border-lands with no purpose. They might have let us go, but they'd come close to skewering Puck with a dozen arrows over a perceived slight.

Puck himself looked doubtful. "I'll ask Hawk, but I don't think…"

"You think I'm wrong." It wasn't like I had any desire whatsoever to set foot near Faerie again after our last disastrous visit, but I'd hoped he at least would believe me. "You know what, never mind. I'm tired. I'll see you tomorrow."

"Holly—" He broke off as I made for the door, the exhaustion of the past day and who-knew-how-long in Faerie catching up with me. "Okay, but I'll tell Hawk your theory and see what he thinks. It's possible the Aes Sidhe in this realm might know more about the outcasts' reasons for settling in the borderlands."

"Except for hating the Courts." That much, at least, we had in common. And while Puck didn't try to change my mind, the obvious disappointment in his eyes as I left him on the doorstep was difficult to shake off.

16

The following morning, I took my theory to Ilsa at the guild, to be met with incredulity from her and downright scepticism from Morgan.

"You think the *Aes Sidhe* sent the wraiths?" Ilsa perched on the table in the archive, looking considerably more alert than she had the previous day after a decent night's sleep.

"They have a motive, considering they worked with the Wild Hunt before," I pointed out. "We ran into wraiths in the borderlands too."

"Not the first one we've found in the borderlands," said Ilsa. "It's close to the Vale. Besides, the Aes Sidhe and the Wild Hunt can't have been in communication for a while, otherwise the Hunt would have come to lend a hand in the battle."

"Exactly," said Morgan, who sat behind the desk on archive duty again. "Those wraiths didn't need a reason to attack you yesterday."

"They were blocking the gates." I fixed my attention on Ilsa. "You and Ivy saw them, right?"

"Ivy," she said, "is with the Council of Twelve, who are attempting to figure out a way to contact the necromancer guardians. I think it's safe to say that until we speak directly to them, we can only guess at what's happening on the other side of that gate."

"But you *saw* them." I had the distinct sense I was hammering at an invisible wall, but Ilsa at least must know I had some first-hand experience of what happened when a wraith with a purpose clung to life on the other side of the gates until the time came to strike.

My mother hadn't needed anyone to give her orders. The wraiths yesterday, though? If they really had gained enough awareness to trap the necromancer guardians on the other side of the gates, they couldn't have done it alone. While the Wild Hunt members were in jail, the Aes Sidhe were a different story.

Ilsa shifted position on the desk. "Why not ask your friend Puck? He's at least had experience with the Aes Sidhe."

That was a dismissal if I ever heard one. "He doesn't believe me either. Where's Hazel, anyway?"

"No idea. She and Darrow are staying in the same hotel as the rest of the Council of Twelve," she said. "She doesn't care much for the necromancer guild. Most likely she's with Ivy, making herself useful."

"Or making trouble." Hazel and I had been at odds for long enough that there was no way I'd be able to convince her to believe my theory if neither of her siblings did, especially after our major disagreement the day before.

"If she and Ivy are in the same room, probably," Ilsa

remarked. "Holly, I'm not trying to dismiss your idea, but you know the Sidhe won't exactly welcome us back with open arms if you want to go back to Faerie to check."

"You couldn't pay me to go back there," Morgan said. "Also, don't you even think about dragging Ilsa with you again."

"I'm not." Even if my theory proved to be true, how was I supposed to get into Faerie to confront the Aes Sidhe with the Winter Court out for my blood? The whole venture seemed a lost cause. "See you around, then."

"Sure." Ilsa's tone carried an apologetic hint, but she didn't call me back when I walked out of the archive and headed downstairs. While I was on my way out through the guild doors, I narrowly avoided colliding with River walking the other way.

"Holly." His voice was tight with disapproval. "What are you doing here?"

"Not recruiting your girlfriend to come to Faerie," I said. "Keep your hair on."

He backed out of the door to join me outside. "I would appreciate it if you didn't ask her to travel into Death, either."

"That was Ivy's idea, not mine," I told him. "I can't even *see* the afterlife unless one of you wants me to."

An image entered my mind's eye, unbidden, of the first time I'd set eyes on the grey emptiness of Death. River had used his own magic against me, back when he and the others had believed me to be their enemy, and while I didn't like to remember that incident, I found myself wondering if he'd regretted not shoving me into Death permanently instead.

River's eyes narrowed, as if he too was remembering the day in which he'd shown me the world on the other side of the veil. "Ivy isn't here at the moment, so I assume you had a theory of your own."

"I did." Yet it was another idea which struck me at the memory of that day, more than a year ago. "Did Ilsa tell you the gates were blocked by wraiths?"

"No," he said. "She said wraiths attacked her and Ivy when they attempted to see the other side. I advised her not to try again."

"What if *I* were to try?"

"You're not a necromancer."

"You wound me." My heartbeat quickened at the reminder of the close call I'd had when he'd used his magic on me. I'd been helpless to resist even with my Gatekeeper's magic intact at the time. Yet this time, I had another type of magic entirely.

River reached for the doors to the guild again. "I don't have time to play games with you, Holly."

"It's not a game, River," I said. "Show me the afterlife, and I'll take it from there."

"Show you—what?" From the blank shock on his face, he *had* forgotten that incident. Small wonder, considering he'd been the perpetrator and not the victim. "You want me to show you the veil?"

"Yes," I said. "I can *almost* see the gates when Ilsa uses her magic, but not enough to confirm what I think I saw behind there. When I tried to take a closer look, I hit a wall."

Literally.

River frowned. "What's in this for you?"

"Answers." Did he still think me the villain? Maybe he

did. Most of Ilsa's family did, after all. "It won't take more than a few seconds, right?"

"No." He stepped away from the necromancer guild. "We'd better hope none of the other necromancers asks what I'm doing."

"Tell them I was hassling your girlfriend, then." I walked a short distance behind him and stopped when he did.

He rotated on the spot, looking into my eyes. "Ready?"

"Sure." Blue light filtered around the edges of the bright green of Summer magic gleaming in the depths of his eyes, and then fog rolled in all around me, masking the world on the other side. River disappeared, while the afterlife remained, an endless field of grey punctuated with the bright shapes of ghosts. I lifted my head, seeing the shadow of a large, endless pair of gates stretching across the horizon. Focusing my attention on the gates, I watched the cloud of bright ghosts flocking towards the gap to the other side. The gates became more distinct even as the world on the other side blurred, flickering around the edges. A dark flickering. Kind of like—

Glamour.

The greyness disappeared in a flash as the real world snapped back into place. I swayed on the spot, while River studied me. "Did you get what you wanted?"

"Glamour," I muttered. "Thanks, River. I think I know what's going on there."

Before he could ask what on earth I meant, I took off at a fast stride, barely paying any attention to where I was walking. I kept on at a punishing pace until I reached Puck and Hawk's office and pushed open the door without knocking.

Both of them looked at me with startled expressions. Puck spoke first. "Holly, what—?"

"The wraiths behind the gates are using glamour to hide themselves," I said. "What're the odds of them being Aes Sidhe?"

Puck's mouth parted. "Holly... wait, how did you see behind the gates?"

"I asked River for a favour," I said. "The others at the guild don't believe me, but I know what I saw."

"Hang on, what?" Hawk looked between us. "Puck said you thought the Aes Sidhe might be ordering wraiths around, but not that they *were* the wraiths."

"Not all of them are, but it makes sense," I said. "There was a glamour over the gates. I have no idea what's really going on over there, but nobody who dies can stay put for long. The gates force them out again."

"The gates?" Hawk said. "As in the gates from which nobody can return?"

"Except necromancer guardians," I said. "They've all vanished, though, and I think they're stuck behind the Gates of Death, while ghosts are being forced to return to the land of the living."

"Does the council know?" Puck asked.

"No, because I only just figured it out," I said. "At least some of the wraiths are Aes Sidhe, I'm sure of it. I'll tell the council myself, but I have a feeling they'll need proof. And that's assuming they don't get suspicious of how and why I asked a necromancer to show me the afterlife in order to have a look through the gates."

Hawk blinked. "I didn't know it was possible for a necromancer to give someone the ability to see into the afterlife."

"Only for a powerful necromancer," I said. "And it's generally used as a punishment or intimidation tactic against someone who really ticked them off."

"They can't check *behind* the gates, though," Puck said. "Can they?"

"No." Which left one way to get proof… find the people who'd given them orders. "Not without dying first."

Hawk whistled. "That almost makes Faerie seem reasonable."

"Precisely my thinking." Not that I'd expected anyone to agree. Including Puck. "When the top-ranked necromancers in the entire country can't figure this one out, it's got to be caused by the group of Sidhe everyone thought was extinct for centuries."

"Or the Wild Hunt," said Hawk. "Sure there weren't more of them?"

"Would they have the patience to hang out behind the Gates of Death?" I glanced at Puck, who still wore a doubtful expression. "The council needs to know, anyway. Maybe one of them will be nice enough to volunteer to go to Faerie and see what the Aes Sidhe are up to, assuming they don't laugh in my face."

I pushed open the door, ignoring the sting of Puck's disbelief, only for him to appear directly behind me in a movement which made me jump. His hand brushed my shoulder, but he released me just as quickly. "Holly, wait. I'm not saying I don't believe you, but…"

"But going back to check on the Aes Sidhe is a death wish, I know."

"Not necessarily," he said. "Provided your entire family doesn't come with us this time around."

"What?" Hawk said. "You're not going back *again*, are you? You've lost your minds."

"It's only a matter of time before the ghosts get into our office too," Puck said. "It's a miracle they haven't already."

"Well, *that* changes everything." Hawk folded his arms across his chest. "No, seriously. How do you even plan to get there now the Sidhe want you dead?"

"We can borrow your friend's puppy," Puck said. "The Aes Sidhe failed to get the better of us last time, and it's not like they have as many resources as the Courts do."

Relief swept over me. "I don't see the other Sidhe keeping a close watch on the borderlands either. We probably only have to worry about the Aes Sidhe... and their wraiths."

And we'd better hope they don't realise I'm Gatekeeper. They'd been close to guessing the last time around, which made this doubly risky for me, but compared to the Winter Court, it was no contest.

"I can shift and avoid attention," Puck said. "You're more at risk than I am."

"Maybe, but it's my risk to take." He didn't have to come with me. No more than he had last time... or the time before. He might believe my theory, but it made no sense for him to stand beside me after the myriad times I'd pushed him away—partly out of guilt which had turned out to be misplaced, since I hadn't broken Death after all.

Now? If I caught the Aes Sidhe in the act, I might just be able to fix the damage. As for Puck? Once again, dealing with my confused feelings about the trickster fae would have to wait.

Puck nodded. "Right. Can you get the faerie puppy? I'll check in with Roseanne, if you like."

"Sure, but she's not going to be happy with me."

I left the office, launching into another speed-walk back towards the necromancers' headquarters. A potent cocktail of emotions ranging from gratitude to disbelief and nervousness whirled within me, and it wasn't until I reached the guild that I realised Puck had followed me in crow form. I gave him an awkward wave as I ducked into the lobby, once again heading for the stairs to the archives.

Inside the small room, I found Morgan sitting alone at the desk, doodling in the margins of a book which I sincerely hoped was his and not the archive's, mostly because I knew how Ilsa felt about defacing old books. He looked up when he heard me come in. "Back already?"

"Yeah," I said. "Can I ask a favour?"

He rolled his eyes. "Let me guess, you want to borrow my puppy to get you into Faerie."

"How'd you guess?" Maybe my refusal hadn't entirely fooled him, or Ilsa either. "Never mind. Is he around?"

"Keir took him out for a walk," he said. "Also, the answer is no. I'm not letting you run off into Faerie with Pepper."

"I won't be alone," I said. "Puck is coming with me. If we get into trouble, I'll tell him to order Pepper to run. I'm pretty sure the puppy understands every word he says."

"Yeah, I saw." He scowled. "You're not going near the Courts, are you?"

"Not at all," I said. "Only the borderlands. We'll ask the

puppy to wait outside of the Aes Sidhe's lair while we do some snooping."

"Fine." He shook his head. "Keir ought to be back soon, so you can try to convince *him* instead."

I had zero desire to speak to the vampire either, but if it got us into Faerie, I'd deal with it. "Thanks."

After heading downstairs and across the lobby, I left the guild. Upon seeing me, Puck transformed back into a human. "He said no?"

"Nah, the puppy's out at the moment. With Keir."

"Who's that?"

"The vampire. He was at the fight with the Wild Hunt."

He'd also thought I was some kind of soulless monster because of the Morrigan's magic, but that seemed a minor consideration at the moment.

I didn't have to wait long before I heard a familiar excited bark. Pepper ran into the street, followed by Keir, who raised a brow at the sight of me. "You again. Still hanging out at the guild?"

"Actually, I need to borrow the puppy." My gaze went to Pepper, who attempted to hide from sight behind the vampire's legs. "Morgan gave us permission to take him to Faerie."

"You think I'd take your word for it on that?" Keir eyed Puck, who beckoned to the puppy. "Who's he?"

"Call me Puck." The puppy happily bounded over to him and rolled over at his feet. "Holly and I have reason to believe the Aes Sidhe hiding in the borderlands of Faerie are behind the current issues you're experiencing in Death."

"Have *you* seen behind the gates?" I asked him, curious as to whether vampires had other special privileges aside from the unpleasant ability to drain someone's life force at a touch.

"Have I what?" His blank expression said no. Then again, he didn't have the Sight. Few at the guild did, aside from River and Ilsa, after all. "You think the Sidhe are responsible for this, do you? I thought you already looked in Faerie and failed to find anything."

"We looked in the wrong place," I said. "Check with Morgan or Ilsa if you want to know more, but we can't delay any longer if we want to stop this."

Keir's gaze landed on Puck, who'd started a game of fetch with the puppy using a screwed-up piece of newspaper. "He likes your friend, at least. You can take him, as long as you bring him straight back."

"Thanks." I took the puppy's lead from Keir, while Puck rose to his feet and watched the vampire walk back to the guild.

"He doesn't seem to care about our mission," Puck said.

"From what Jas said, the vampires are kind of an independent entity." I handed him Pepper's lead. "They're not on the council and most of them don't want to be part of the guild, either. Not sure how he ended up joining. Anyway, we should leave."

"C'mon, Pepper." He coaxed the puppy into the lead, and I walked alongside him to half-blood territory.

As we neared the Ley Line, Roseanne stepped out of the shadows to bar our way down the road. "Going somewhere?" She folded her arms. "Going to *Faerie,* specifically?"

"Roseanne, you can't come with us." I'd guessed Hawk wouldn't be able to convince her to stay put, but there was zero chance I'd let her set foot near Faerie even *before* the Winter Court had put me on a hit list.

"Why are you going back?" she said. "They want you dead."

"We're not going to the Court," I said. "The Aes Sidhe are meddling with Death. We need proof if we're to stop them."

Her mouth pressed together. "I can help you. I'm sick of hiding."

"You've been helping Hawk and the others handle the ghosts, right?" I pointed out. "Look, if we get into trouble, we can send Pepper to warn you and you can pass on word to the council."

"Really?" Roseanne frowned. "The council won't listen to me."

"Ilsa will," I said. "And Ivy. You know how to find her, right?"

Her expression brightened. "Yeah, I do."

And just like that, the argument was won. Roseanne departed without any fuss, while Puck and I made our way around half-blood territory to the place where the Ley Line crossed through the nearby streets.

"You never asked *me* if I could use Pepper to pass on a warning to her," he remarked.

"I figured you could, given that you're the puppy whisperer."

A grin tugged at his mouth. "Animals are easy. People… they're trickier. Some more than others."

Meaning me? I'd have asked, but Pepper was already straining to get away from me. Not the first time I'd had that issue. At one time, I'd assumed the lingering essence of my Winter Gatekeeper's magic had been the culprit, but maybe it was just me. In any case, I stepped over to Puck's side as the faerie puppy led the way through the Ley Line and onto the path stretching between the two Courts.

Here we are, in Faerie again. Tension gripped me, part of me expecting to see Lord Lyle lurking in the bushes ready to strike. Nobody confronted us, though. I breathed out. "Right. Did you see any other secret entrances into the Aes Sidhe's home while you were in there?"

"No," said Puck. "I can shift into a bird and fly in, but you…"

"I can shift into a bird, too, just a human-sized one." Which wasn't exactly inconspicuous. "I won't ask you to go in alone."

"I can use my ability on others too," he said. "If you don't mind, that is."

"Turn me into a woodland creature, Sidhe-style?" One of the Summer Court's favoured tricks was to turn any stray humans who stumbled into Faerie into deer, which was barely better than Winter's propensity for turning them into ice statues instead. Didn't mean I was any keener to be trapped in an animal form where I wouldn't be able to access my magic. "It wouldn't be permanent?"

"Of course not." He hesitated for an instant, then reached out a hand. "I'd need to touch you first."

I took a wild guess that he'd seen my tensed reaction whenever he got too close: an instinct leftover from a life-time of watching my back. "Turn me into a crow."

It'd be appropriate, and besides, having wings would give me the ability to escape if we got caught. He reached out a hand, which brushed my wrist. "This okay?"

My pulse fluttered, my heartbeat kicking up. "Yeah."

Magic zinged up my arm, startling me into pulling away from him, and the world shrank and spun around me in a blur of colour. I tried to stagger back but instead found myself off the ground, wings beating behind my shoulders.

If I hadn't had practise flying as the Morrigan, I might have panicked even more. Even so, I flew in dizzying circles until I managed to halt by grabbing a low-hanging branch with a pair of claws which seemed unnaturally short compared to the ones I'd grown used to.

"Holly?" Puck called to me. "Caw twice if you want me to turn you back."

I forced my trembling wings to fold against my back and perched on the branch, shaking my head. The sight of a yellow beak in front of me almost made me lose my balance again. This couldn't be over fast enough.

Puck crouched beside Pepper to whisper some instructions to him before shifting into a bird himself and flying up to land next to me. He made it look so easy. I drew in a breath, then took flight, circling the trees until I'd adjusted to the motion. Being small enough not to be noticed by anyone below went some way towards dispelling my nerves about potentially running into Lord Lyle, though I was no keener to go into the borderlands than I had been previously.

At least from this view the paths weren't as much of a tangled maze. Puck took the lead, swooping ahead of me until we came to the mound of earth which comprised the Aes Sidhe's base.

Puck descended in a sweep of wings before I could caw a warning at him, and there came several alarmed noises from the entrance. The Aes Sidhe around the entrance scattered, while Puck himself took flight as a crow and flew up to me again. Perching on a branch, he turned human for a few seconds in order to whisper, "Better get in there fast. Pepper will warn us if they're likely to catch us."

I flew down from the branch, Puck shifting into a crow once again behind me, and soared through the entrance into the tunnel. At once, I wished I was out in the forest again. My wings could only carry me so far with an earthen ceiling blocking any chance of escape, while the tunnels contained no hiding places to speak of. The Aes Sidhe didn't seriously *like* living this deeply underground, did they? Maybe it was just what they were used to, but we had to figure out if their attachment to their old Court applied to their deceased Queen too.

When we heard voices up ahead, our wingbeats slowed, and Puck perched above a doorframe. I did likewise, glimpsing several Aes Sidhe standing inside the cave-like room on the other side of the door.

"Give me that." The impatient voice came from the female Aes Sidhe who'd led the group who'd captured us last time. Adria. "It's no wonder we're at a standstill."

"Nobody has ever done this before," protested an Aes Sidhe with a deeper voice. "The Queen never told me—" He cut off in a hiss of pain.

Unable to restrain my curiosity, I ducked my head under the doorframe and saw one of the Aes Sidhe holding out a forearm while another scrawled swirling symbols on his bare skin with a pen.

Blood magic.

They were using blood magic. If I needed any proof that they were in league with the Wild Hunt, this was it.

"Command." The Sidhe shook out his arm with a wince. "Command the dead. You said yourself this has never been used before. It might not work."

"It did work," said Adria. "For me, at least. I successfully convinced the half-bloods to give us this part of their territory with the aid of a wraith, and I also sent a spirit to Winter Court."

"Then why have we not made any progress?" asked the Sidhe with the gleaming marks inked on his arm.

My blood chilled. *Command the dead.* They *were* using blood magic to command spirits… not just wraiths, but the ghost who'd taken up residence in the Unseelie Queen's home.

"Be patient," said Adria. "The Wild Hunt's warriors are waiting for an opening, nothing more. If all else fails, we can send assistance to them. And then?"

"And then our Queen will be avenged," said another Sidhe, with barely contained excitement. "And the Gatekeepers will die."

17

My heart lurched as if trying to escape my chest. Not at the news that they wanted the Gatekeepers dead—that part didn't surprise me—but the rest. *They're going to break the Wild Hunt out of jail.*

The ghost in the Unseelie Queen's home wasn't a random haunting… it was a trap. Not a very good one, given their lack of success in freeing the Wild Hunt thus far, but that didn't mean their use of blood magic to control the dead hadn't succeeded in other ways. Like, for instance, on Earth.

I remained perched on the doorframe as the Aes Sidhe moved around inside the room, unaware that one of the Gatekeepers they detested so deeply was close enough to hear their every word. If nothing else, we knew for certain that they hadn't known who'd walked into their trap when they'd freed us at River's request. After all, if there was one constant with the Sidhe, it was how very little they considered humans to be worthy of notice. The sheer obviousness was almost laugh-worthy, but when Puck's eyes met mine, my brief spark of amusement fled. He'd realised the danger, too… and that their next target would be the Winter Court. Someone had to warn them.

The sound of loud barking drifted down the tunnel. *Pepper.* Had they caught him? Or was he warning us? Puck immediately launched into flight, and so did I. We flew down the tunnel, wings beating fast, but the tunnel's low ceiling gave us nowhere to hide when two Aes Sidhe barrelled into our path.

Puck transformed into a leaping flame, and both Aes Sidhe recoiled with sharp noises of surprise. I took the opportunity to fly past them, and Puck shifted into a bird to join me a moment later. We flew out of the tunnel opening and into the sky, while the Aes Sidhe outside exclaimed in fury.

"Get them!" An Aes Sidhe fired an arrow in our direction, which clipped my wing but didn't penetrate deeper.

Several other arrows hit the canopy, bringing a shower of leaves on our heads. Panicking, I pumped my wings faster and faster until I soared high above the trees. The arrows were no longer able to reach me, but I no longer had the faintest idea how to get back to the path from here.

Puck's crow form surfaced from the canopy, and relief flooded me when he indicated a clear route to the path below. As I ducked below the trees, Pepper leapt in and out of the bushes until he reached the path between the Courts. Puck shifted back into his human form and gave him a stroke. "Good job."

I landed beside them, alarmed at how even the puppy dwarfed me while I was in this form. Upon spotting me, Pepper started to bark, only for Puck to shush him. "C'mon, Holly, I'll change you back."

I cawed at him in response, while he held out a hand. I took flight, warily perching on his hand, and magic zipped up my spine again. He let go, but not fast enough. As I abruptly shifted to human size, I fell forwards and caused us both to tumble backwards into a pile of leaves. For an instant, I lay there, breathless and reeling from my abrupt shift to human size again.

Puck's gold-flecked green eyes looked up into mine, startled, and while I knew I should get up, part of me remained too stunned to move. At least part of that was because the sensation of my body pressing against his wasn't objectionable. The corner of his mouth tilted up. "You know, I'd be happy to lie here all day, but we're still in Faerie. Also, I can't feel my legs."

"Sorry." Wondering what in hell had got into me, I pushed off him and clambered shakily to my feet. "That was a close one."

"I know." Puck sprang upright. "Holly, you were right. The Aes Sidhe are using blood magic…"

"To control the wraiths," I finished. "They sent a ghost to Winter. Someone needs to warn the Queen they're planning to set the Wild Hunt free."

"I'd rather get captured by the Aes Sidhe again, to be honest."

I know. But if the Aes Sidhe's plan to free the Wild Hunt from jail succeeded, then it was only a matter of time before they came back to the mortal realm to finish the job they'd already started—and kill the Gatekeepers.

"You're not seriously thinking of warning Winter, are you?" Puck asked, when I didn't reply. "Lord Lyle will have you skewered, assuming he survived."

"The Wild Hunt want revenge on all of us and so do the Aes Sidhe," I reminded him. "What do you think will happen if their plan succeeds? They won't stop with the Courts, though a potential war in Faerie is bad enough on its own."

His mouth pressed together. "The Winter Sidhe will never listen to either of us, Holly. You know they won't."

There must be a way to warn them. Short of sending a messenger… "Hang on."

As Puck watched, baffled, I surveyed the nearest tree, then dug my claw in to scrape off a large piece of bark. Then I applied my claw to the surface, scratching a few words in the faeries' language.

"Are you… writing a letter?" Puck looked at me as if he thought I'd cracked. "To the Unseelie Queen?"

"I figured you'd object to me flying into the Court as a crow and pretending to be the Morrigan's messenger." I delicately clawed out a few more symbols. "I can at least send them a warning, not signed."

My memory of the fae's language was rusty, but I knew enough to scratch out a basic message: *The Aes Sidhe in the borderlands sent that ghost. They're planning to break the Wild Hunt out of jail.*

"I can't believe you're writing the Unseelie Queen a *letter.*"

"Technically, it's not me. It's the Morrigan." I held up my claw in demonstration. "I delivered hundreds of letters between the pair of them. I know her handwriting."

"She's dead, though."

"Missing," I corrected him, finishing the letter. "Where's she most likely to find this? I guess it depends if Lord Lyle survived."

Puck exhaled. "I'll drop it off."

"You don't know the Court."

"I saw some of it," he said. "When I followed you."

"When you..." Right. Of course he'd shifted and flown behind me when I'd explicitly told him not to risk his neck by coming to Winter. "Fine, but for god's sake, don't get caught."

He shifted into a bird and took the letter in his beak before flying above the trees. I, meanwhile, sat down on the leafy path next to Pepper, who pointedly turned his head away from me.

"Don't you start," I said to the puppy. "This is the only way to warn the Court without risking certain death. It doesn't matter if they don't believe the Morrigan wrote the note. We'll be long gone by the time it matters."

Pepper lifted his head, his gaze roving around the nearby bushes, and then he barked out a warning. I was on my feet an instant later. A chill breeze washed over me, and a cloud of dark energy swept out of the trees, coalescing on the path in front of us.

I was willing to bet the Aes Sidhe had sent that wraith after the intruders. Meaning, us. The cold breeze which drifted in its wake told me it'd once been a Winter Sidhe. I shifted my hands into claws, the Morrigan's magic more than ready to strike it down. Shadows flowed beneath my skin, and when the wraith struck, I snagged it on my claw. "Go to hell."

The wraith flew back when I released it, crashing

through the trees in a wave of icy energy and knocking a shower of leaves onto the path. The sound of a muffled exclamation was my only warning before an arrow pierced the ground next to me.

Fuck.

Several Aes Sidhe warriors appeared amid the bushes, and Pepper barked at the top of his lungs as a stream of arrows flew in my direction. I flung myself into the undergrowth to dodge them, and alarm flickered through me when Puck's crow form flew into view.

No. Get out of here.

Adria stepped to the forefront of the group, her red hair streaming around her face and her crossbow levelled on Puck.

I didn't stop to think. As the crossbow fired, I summoned my wings and leapt into flight, tackling Puck in mid-air. The momentum sent both of us crashing into the bushes, and when I lifted my head, a branch slammed into my skull. Puck let out a caw of alarm, still in the form of a crow, while I rubbed my forehead and scrambled upright again.

A cage surrounded the pair of us, formed of tree branches. An illusion? No, it'd felt real enough when I'd hit my head on the branch above me. I reached outward and grabbed the cage bars, which felt solid too. The Morrigan's magic swept over my skin as a group of Aes Sidhe, led by Adria, approached us.

"Interesting," said Adria. "If I'd known you had *that* power at your disposal, I'd have kept a closer grip on you, human."

I bared my teeth at her. "I know what you're planning.

You're a fool to think freeing the Wild Hunt will end in anything other than complete disaster. Don't you know why they were jailed?"

Her mouth pulled into a taut line. "They were trying to avenge our Queen and were unjustly punished."

"They tried to summon a death god and came close to starting a war." My head throbbed where I'd hit it, but desperation pushed me onwards. "Didn't you know your Queen met her end at the hands of the same god?"

"Don't *lie*, mortal." Her words whipped at me, her eyes narrowing. "The Wild Hunt are our only hope for restoring our Court. I will not have you or the trickster stand in our way."

"Wait." Panic rose within me when she turned her back, indicating to her fellow Aes Sidhe. "You're not seriously leaving us in here?"

She flashed me a humourless smile. "I would like to see the extent of your remarkable abilities later, human, but we have a more pressing matter to attend to."

The Wild Hunt. "If you're planning a jailbreak, you're setting yourself up for a fall."

Or an eternity as an ice statue. Adria, however, ignored me, and continued to walk away from our cage. While some of her fellow Aes Sidhe wore disgruntled expressions as though they'd be happy to shoot a few more arrows at us, Adria was clearly their leader. They vanished among the trees, leaving Puck and me alone in the cage.

Puck shifted into human form, causing me to jerk back in surprise when his elbow caught me in the face. "Sorry."

"No worries." I looked around us at the thick web of

branches, which offered no obvious way out. "Can you turn into a flame and get us out?"

"I doubt they'd have made it that easy for us to escape." He paused. "Holly… Pepper left. He obeyed my order to go home and warn the others if the two of us were captured."

"You've got to be kidding me." That meant we were stranded in Faerie, with zero chance of warning anyone in the mortal realm even if we escaped our prison. "They won't arrive in time to stop the Aes Sidhe from attempting to free the Wild Hunt."

"They might." He shifted into a sitting position, unable to easily move with the pair of us crammed into the tight space. "Don't forget time tends to slip by faster in the mortal realm than it does here."

"They can't get into Winter without an invitation." As if in response to my words, a chill breeze swept over us. We were too close to the Courts for my liking, and for all I knew, someone from Winter had heard the disturbance. "Puck—you can get out of the cage if you shift into flames or leaves, can't you?"

"Maybe, but I'm not leaving you behind."

The coldness intensified. Had the wraith come back? Puck's grim silence implied he'd had the same thought. Though the wraith was nothing compared to the number of *living* Winter Sidhe who'd be more than happy to take out their anger on the pair of us. "Puck, seriously. We're trapped in Faerie. It's only a matter of time before the Winter Sidhe catch up to me. It wouldn't surprise me if they've been on the lookout since I stabbed Lord Lyle, and honestly, I don't blame them a bit."

"Bullshit," he said quietly. "You acted in self-defence. None of this is your fault."

His words struck the battered remains of my resolve. I averted my gaze, my eyes stinging. "Yes, it is. I'm not who you think I am, Puck, and to be honest, I'm surprised it took this long for the Sidhe to place a death sentence on my head."

Heat brushed my shoulder as he almost touched me, but not quite. "I have a pretty good idea who you are, Holly. I've seen you risk your neck a dozen times in defence of others. You were backed into a corner, and the Sidhe sentence one another to death for minor reasons on a frequent basis anyway."

"Stop it." I shot him a glare. He didn't need to make this any harder than it already was. "You spent the last few years underground. You haven't the faintest idea what went on in the interim. Like how I became Gatekeeper."

My feet stood poised on a cliff's edge, and when I jumped, there would be no surviving the fall. Yet if that's what it took to get him to save his own neck, I'd rip open my long-healed scars and expose the wounds for all to see.

"Then enlighten me," he said. "You can't claim you made your mother turn into a wraith to escape the curse. You tried to stop her."

"I hired a group of necromancers to keep her contained. None of them survived." I drew in a breath. "I as good as killed them."

"They knew the risks," he countered. "She killed them, not you."

"Have you been talking to Roseanne?" I scowled. "I downplayed the risks when I hired them, so yes, I indirectly caused their deaths. Besides, that's not the worst of it."

"Then what is?" This time he closed the distance between us, his hand resting on my shoulder. I wanted him to stay there forever. I wanted him to go away.

"I killed my mother." My words fell between us like stones. "I was the reason she became a wraith."

His hand fell from my shoulder. "You..."

"Got you there, didn't I?" A grim smile curled my mouth. "I didn't make her choose to become a wraith, but I'm the reason she died. It's no wonder the Morrigan's magic was able to latch onto me so easily, is it?"

"Holly..." His breath caught. "Someone's coming. From Winter."

Thought so. "Go on. Let me face the consequences myself."

Puck hesitated. "I'll drive him off."

"If it's Lord Lyle, then he deserves an explanation from me." I sat down on the floor of the cage. "Don't try to fight him."

Puck's warm presence disappeared from the cage. Several autumn leaves drifted to the ground, caught in the breeze which grew stronger with every passing second. The leaves slipped through the cage bars in the same instant that Lord Lyle walked into view. He *had* survived my assault. While he hadn't suffered any visible lasting damage, his eyes narrowed in anger when he caught sight of me. "Holly Lynn. Have you come to surrender to the Winter Queen?"

"Not quite." I glanced around for any signs of Puck, but he'd vanished into the surrounding forest. "The Aes Sidhe in the borderlands trapped me in here to stop me from warning you they're scheming against your Queen."

His jaw tightened. Then he swung his blade, so fast it blurred, slicing through the cage bars. For a heartbeat I expected him to deal a killing blow, but instead, he lowered the blade and beckoned to me with his free hand.

"Come with me," he said. "We're going to see my Queen."

18

There was no arguing, no talking my way out of this one. I might have unleashed the Morrigan's magic again—and from the way Lord Lyle kept a wary distance from me, he seemed prepared for the possibility—but if I did, then nobody would be left to warn the Unseelie Queen of the impending jailbreak.

When we reached the snowy lands of the Unseelie Court, panic seized me, along with wondering if I was better off facing death at the hands of the Aes Sidhe after all. At least Puck had escaped, but I didn't quite trust him not to try to intervene again. Assuming my revelation hadn't driven him away for good.

That was the intention. He has to survive this, even if I don't.

When we came within sight of the snowy mound containing the centre of the Winter Court, Lady Rive strode out to meet us. Her sharp gaze pinned me to the spot before she turned her attention to her fellow Sidhe. "You caught her?"

"She came back of her own accord," said Lord Lyle.

"And you're positive she acted alone?" Lady Rive looked doubtfully at me. "She doesn't look capable of dealing you such a mortal wound."

"She did," Lord Lyle said. "Her companions were not involved in the attack. She acted entirely alone."

Wait. Lord Lyle had told everyone that my friends and allies hadn't been involved? That seemed suspiciously generous, but the guy was honourable as far as Sidhe went, and we both knew that I alone deserved to face the wrath of his Queen.

I lifted my chin. "I acted in self-defence, but I came to speak to your Queen about something else entirely. I have a warning for the entire Winter Court."

"Quiet, human," snapped Lady Rive. "Come with us, and don't try to run."

Lord Lyle and Lady Rive flanked me the rest of the way to the entrance to the Unseelie Court. I hadn't asked Puck who he'd delivered the letter to, but nobody seemed to be rushing around preparing for a potential attack. It'd been a long shot as to whether the Unseelie Queen would take the warning seriously, whether or not she truly believed it'd come from her former adversary.

The two ogres at the tunnel entrance parted to let us through, but the cave seemed emptier than before. The usual Sidhe were absent, while the Unseelie Queen's throne lay bare of its usual occupant. *Where is she?*

Had she received my warning after all, or was she still trying to rid the Court of her unwanted ghostly visitor? It struck me briefly that if she had me executed, then *I* might end up haunting her as well. Which didn't seem much of an alternative to being stuck as a ghost in the mortal realm. Life might make a frequent habit of kicking me in the teeth, but I didn't want to die here in the freezing lands of Winter, even if I deserved it.

Footsteps sounded and all coherent thought fled when the Unseelie Queen strode out of a tunnel at the back of the room, her silver crown glittering on her head and her blade gleaming in her hands. Her vibrant eyes flickered up and down my body. "You dare to show your face here, mortal, after severely wounding a member of my Court and after stealing the Morrigan's magic and causing her death?"

I licked my lips, scrambling to find the words to forestall the inevitable. "She's not dead."

"You dare to argue with me?"

Magic slapped me head-on, sending me sprawling to the icy ground. When I lifted my head, tasting blood, I found to my horror that I couldn't move an inch. My hands had shifted to claws, but they'd frozen at my sides, so I couldn't lift them to retaliate even if I wanted to.

"I'm telling the truth." Inwardly, I cursed the tremor in my voice. "Lord Lyle tried to sentence me to death. I had no choice but to fight back, and I underestimated my own strength."

"Lord Lyle told me that he attempted to bring you to me in order to help return the Morrigan to her throne," she said. "Instead, you struck him down."

I stiffened. "He told me he intended to bring me to you, which would result in my death. He didn't mention restoring the Morrigan to her throne. If I knew how to do that, then I would try."

"Is that so, mortal?" Her blue eyes glittered, matching the blade in her hands. "Then you may be of use after all.

Since you currently possess the Morrigan's magic, I have little doubt that your death would enable her return."

"Then you're going to kill me." An odd sense of calm settled over me. On some level, I'd dreaded her wrath for so long that some measure of relief came with the knowledge that it'd soon be over.

"Not yet," she said. "I would not have your mortal spirit loose in the Court."

Ack. She'd had the same thought as me: that my ghost would be able to haunt her along with the other spirit she'd had so much trouble getting rid of.

Then what was the alternative? "Your Majesty, the ghost currently haunting your Court was sent by spies from the Aes Sidhe—"

"I have another plan for you." She cut straight through my words without acknowledging them. "Take her to the dungeon."

Her two security ogres stepped in behind me, hauling me into the air. While my body remained frozen, I couldn't fight back. I couldn't so much as move an inch while they carried me through one of the tunnel openings at the back of the room and down a dark corridor which led far below the depths of the earth.

I'd been in the jail a few times before. Sometimes as a witness, sometimes as punishment. My mother's actions had required some discipline, after all. The corridor was lit with lamps, bright enough for me to see the flutter of wings as something flew overhead—then the ogres flung me through the opening to a cell, and my limbs unfroze when I landed in a painful heap on the packed earth. The opening sealed itself behind me, cutting off the light.

My breath caught in my chest, and I struggled not to hyperventilate. *Not again. Not now.*

I sank into a sitting position, the cold ground beneath me the only sense of solidity while utter darkness surrounded me on all sides. The last few times I'd been locked up, I'd been able to call my Gatekeeper's magic to provide a faint light in the darkness. Not this time. The only magic I possessed made the shadows more pronounced.

The thought hit me that the Wild Hunt's warriors were imprisoned somewhere in here, but it was anyone's guess as to where they might be. Under tight security, I hoped.

I didn't know how long I sat there in the darkness. Minutes. Hours, maybe. Time in Faerie was fluid anyway, but here, no markers of the passage of the days existed. I fell into a fitful doze and woke to find my throat dry and my insides hollow with hunger, suggesting it was at least a few hours since I'd come here.

Had Puck managed to escape? If Pepper had returned with backup, then maybe. The puppy liked him enough to come to his rescue, I was sure. But me? I'd never been able to figure out why animals avoided me, but maybe they had some kind of sixth sense humans didn't have which enabled them to see the monster I'd been even before I'd wielded the claws of the Morrigan.

A light sparked in the gloom, and I forced myself into an upright position, looking around for the source. The light brightened, resolving into a transparent figure floating in front of the earthen wall comprising the front of my cell. *Is this the Unseelie Queen's ghost?* My eyes struggled to make out more than long curly hair, elfin features, and Winter-bright eyes.

"Hey there," I whispered. "I think you hit a dead end. You won't find anything in here."

The ghost studied my face. "You can see me."

"Of course I can," I said. "I'm guessing you can't see *me*, though, given how dark it is in here. Are you the ghost who's been bothering the Unseelie Queen?"

The ghost the Aes Sidhe had sent? I hadn't a clue what their reasoning had been, given that a ghost had no way of enacting a jailbreak, but the ghost vanished instead of answering me.

Then the Unseelie Queen appeared in her place, standing in my cell as if the earthen wall didn't exist at all. The blade at her waist dazzled my eyes, while her hands gripped a large piece of bark. The letter I'd written as the Morrigan. My heart dropped. *Crap. She didn't fall for the act.*

"Interesting." She held out the piece of bark, which I didn't take. "Does this look familiar to you, mortal?"

Lying wasn't an option, and besides, this was likely my last chance to warn her. "I didn't know how else to tell you they were coming. The Aes Sidhe sent that ghost. They want to break the Wild Hunt out of jail, and they're on their way here right now."

The Unseelie Queen looked down at me. Her menacing presence seemed to fill a space larger than the cell, and I had to resist the urge to back against the far wall to avoid her. "I should rip out your throat for mimicking the writing of someone whose death you brought about at your own hands."

"I didn't." I faltered. "She loaned me her magic

temporarily. It was supposed to disappear when I used it up. I don't know why it didn't, and I have no idea why she disappeared."

The Unseelie Queen reached out. I scooted away, but there was nowhere to run as she seized my wrist in her grip. My heart lurched, and it was impossible to repress the shadows flickering beneath my skin.

"Interesting." She studied my hand as it became a claw. "I never would have thought the Morrigan's powers would bond to a mortal so readily."

My head swam with dizziness, while I fought the urge to yank my arm out of her grip. "Why didn't they disappear after I used them to subdue the Wild Hunt?"

Instead of answering my question, she continued to examine my hand. Shadows crept farther up my arm despite my best efforts, while a scream built in the back of my throat as her grip on my wrist tightened. "Your Majesty—"

She released me—or to be more precise, she threw me against the wall. Breathless, I caught my balance, the shadows receding from my hands.

"Almost a full shift," she remarked. "I would guess that you possess the death goddess's talent for manipulating souls too…"

I frowned. Why would that matter to her? "I can— well, I can banish ghosts, but only with my cousin's help."

"That's why you came with her." She gave a nod as if I'd confirmed a theory of hers.

I didn't bother to correct her. My only route out of this cell was to prove I was more useful to her alive than dead. "I didn't know the ghost was sent by the Aes Sidhe at the time. She was there—just there, where you're standing. She came into my cell."

The blue light in her eyes brightened with anger. "Then you will banish her, mortal."

"I'm sorry?" I couldn't have heard her right.

"You will use the Morrigan's magic to rid me of this troublesome spirit."

Behind her, the earthen wall folded back until the corridor lay open to me, beckoning me towards freedom. My heart pounded. She wanted my help. I didn't know if I *could* banish the ghost, but if I had the sliver of a chance to regain her trust, I'd seize it. "I will. I am grateful, your Majesty—"

"It isn't a favour." She turned on her heel, and when I stumbled after her out of the cell, the corridor vanished too.

Bright lights dazzled me for an instant. I blinked a couple of times, noting that we now stood inside a living room decorated in silver and blue, with stained-glass windows at the back depicting ogres and trolls, lorelei and redcaps. We were inside the Unseelie Queen's private chambers. No wonder she'd been so eager to get rid of the ghost.

"Ah... your majesty, the ghost isn't here." I looked around the room, past shelves stacked with old tomes and comfortable-looking seats.

"Be patient, mortal." Her posture was tense, her tone irritable under its lilting melody.

Then, in a flicker of light, the ghost appeared hovering in front of a row of bookshelves. Without the darkness to hinder my vision, I could make out her features more easily. My gaze went to the Unseelie Queen, whose beautiful face remained frozen in anger. There was an uncanny resemblance between the pair of them. I saw it now, but I knew better than to pour gasoline on the Unseelie Queen's already volatile temper.

I faced the ghost instead. "Hey there."

"Gatekeeper," she said softly. "I thought you looked familiar to me."

You're one to talk. "You're making a nuisance of yourself, I hear."

The spirit gave a wicked smile. "I cannot believe my sister is desperate enough to persuade a *human* to come and get rid of me."

Sister? I blinked at the ghost, not quite daring to look at the angry Queen behind me. Where had the Aes Sidhe found the ghost of the Unseelie Queen's sister? To become a ghost, I assumed she must have died recently, given how most of the exiled dead became wraiths instead, but I couldn't begin to guess their history. Maybe I didn't want to know.

"Go on," snapped the Unseelie Queen. "Get rid of her."

"You won't get rid of me," the spirit said softly. "I told you I'd haunt you forever."

Despite myself, curiosity prickled at me. At a guess, she and the Unseelie Queen might have been rivals for the throne, and to win, one Sidhe had to kill all their competition... but that had been centuries ago, back when death hadn't been permanent. Unless, that is, the Unseelie Queen's sister had died somewhere she couldn't return from.

"Where'd you come from?" I called on the Morrigan's magic, which shadowed my hands. "The Vale?"

"Quiet!" The Unseelie Queen struck, sending a wave of

icy magic at both me and the ghost. I ducked, while the attack struck the wall hard enough to make the paintings rattle but did no damage to the spirit.

Getting the message, I ran towards the ghost, my hands shifting to claws. The ghost shrieked when my claw slid straight through her transparent form, latching onto her soul. "Your Majesty—I can throw her out, but I don't know how to banish her into Death."

The ghost shrieked. "Put me down!"

"The job is done," said the Unseelie Queen softly. "Goodbye, mortal."

The room vanished in a flash of white magic, to be replaced by a grey path stretching into the distance in both directions. Shock jolted my claws back to human hands, and the ghost floated away, still shrieking.

"No!" she howled.

I ignored the ghost, staring around in disbelief. The Unseelie Queen had tricked me into grabbing the ghost so she could get rid of both of us at once. Rather than risking the wrath of the Morrigan or my angry spirit returning to vex her, she'd thrown me into the Grey Vale: the one place I could meet my end and never be found.

I was wrong. Things could absolutely get worse.

The path I stood on was dappled with silver-grey leaves, while the trees were the same colour, giving the sense of being trapped between life and death. The realm was frozen in time, not so much a forest as an echo of a stretch of woodland which had been part of Faerie before they'd ripped it away in the process of exiling their gods. I doubted they'd intended it to become a haven for exiles, but either way, there was no way in or out for anyone who wasn't part of the Courts.

The ghost's continued howling snapped me out of my shock. I ran after her, more to keep something familiar in sight than anything else.

"Hey," I called. "Did you die here in the Vale? Is that why you turned into a ghost instead of being reborn?"

"Leave me alone, mortal!" she shouted, her voice echoing among the trees.

"The Aes Sidhe brought you back to Winter, didn't they?" I asked. "How did *they* get in here?"

More to the point, how had they possibly known the Unseelie Queen had had a sister who'd died in the Vale? The ghost, however, ignored my questions, drifting away among the trees until her howls faded to silence.

"Fuck," I whispered. The Unseelie Queen had dismissed my warning too. Had the Aes Sidhe already entered Winter to free the Wild Hunt? The Unseelie Queen wouldn't have been focused so intently on getting me to banish her ghost if they had, surely, but the jail was extensive enough that I didn't know whereabouts the traitors had been imprisoned.

Not that it mattered at this point. The Vale was even more of a dead end than the deepest dungeon in Winter, and the only reason the Unseelie Queen hadn't exiled the Wild Hunt was because their previous exile hadn't stopped them causing trouble in the mortal realm. Besides, I wasn't sure they'd been fully exiled, given that they'd been in possession of all their magic, including the ability to cross between realms.

Like the Ancients. The ones who'd survived exile had long departed the Vale, but it sure would help to have a talisman like Ivy's which contained part of their magic. She'd hinted at being able to walk between realms, but she wouldn't be able to come and rescue me if nobody knew I was here. Wraiths could slip through the gaps, because the barriers between Death and the Vale were narrow, but living humans didn't have that advantage.

Out of any other ideas, I began to walk down the leaf-strewn path. Given the uniform nature of the scenery, I might easily wander in circles until I collapsed from exhaustion and found myself vulnerable to the myriad beasts waiting to feast on trespassers. Only the Sidhe had control over the paths in the Vale, or anyone who wielded one of their talismans… though, come to think of it, the Morrigan was stronger than the average Sidhe.

Could her magic control the Vale's paths? It was worth trying, rather than waiting to see what kind of monster ate me first. I drew on the Morrigan's magic, shifting my hands to claws, and then cast my mind around to figure out what to ask the Vale. Like the rest of Faerie, I was willing to bet the Vale would interpret my words in any way it felt like, and there wasn't supposed to be any way out of here which didn't involve hitching a ride with someone who had the ability to cross realms. In other words, a Sidhe.

"Take me to the nearest route out of the Vale," I said aloud.

The echoes of my voice pursued me as I walked down the path, which otherwise remained as eerie and quiet as ever until I rounded a corner. An indistinct noise ahead of me drew me to a stop. I readied my claws when I heard the same sound again, which sounded like the growl of a wild animal. Or, knowing Faerie, some kind of monster.

Here goes nothing. I forced my legs to keep moving, taking another turning, and then spotted several horses roaming between the trees, all identical and graceful with sleek black coats. *Wild Hunt* horses.

Disbelief locked me to the spot for an instant. The Vale had answered my request, but it was Puck who had an affinity with animals, not me. I'd better hope the horses didn't remember the damage I'd inflicted on their owners, but this was my one shot at escaping the Vale before I joined the countless unfortunate souls who'd met their end here.

I trod closer to the nearest horse, but rustling came from the nearby undergrowth. Then a Sidhe strode into view, with long dark hair, clad in black-grey armour which covered his huge form—and, when he turned to glare at me, a patch covering his missing eye.

19

My heart leapt into my throat. The Wild Hunt had broken out of jail. It seemed they hadn't needed the ghost after all.

The Sidhe's remaining eye locked onto me, hate flickering in its depths. "What are you doing in the Vale, mortal?"

"I might ask you the same question." Dammit. I was inches away from being able to snag a horse and escape, but if this guy was walking free, it was a safe bet that his two buddies wouldn't be far behind. "How'd you manage to get out of your cell?"

His hand clenched on the hilt of his blade. "You put me in there. I should gut you right now, human, if you are who you seem to be."

Did he think I was an illusion conjured up by the Vale? I supposed most humans didn't wander in here on a regular basis. "You're lucky you weren't executed instead."

The Sidhe drew his blade in a smooth motion, and shadows flowed under my skin as the Morrigan's magic prepared to strike back. I'd nearly killed him by stabbing him in the eye with an iron blade when I hadn't had any magic to fight with, so I ought to be able to take him on. He'd survived the injury where another Sidhe might not have, but that didn't make him invincible.

I beat him once, and I can do it again. I refused to die here in the Vale, my ghost left to wander the endless paths for eternity. Or worse, to turn into a wraith the way my mother had.

The Sidhe swung his blade. I shifted my hand, my claw catching the keen tip of the sword. The blow made me stagger back, but he didn't move as blindingly fast as he had before. Still as graceful and speedy as any Sidhe, but last time even the half-Sidhe had had trouble keeping up with him.

The hint of bare skin under his armoured sleeves told me why. When we'd last fought, he'd been marked with blood magic symbols to boost his speed and stamina, but he hadn't had the chance to have them reapplied since his escape.

I pressed my advantage, getting a few solid hits in with my claws, but since his face was the only exposed part of him, most of my blows did little damage. Eyes watched us from the nearby trees. The Vale's beasts, drawn to our fight, waiting for one of us to lie bleeding out in the dirt.

"Did you and the Aes Sidhe have your escape plan figured out before or after you were locked away?" I asked him between blows. "Or was it all improvised?"

The warrior grunted and didn't answer, but now I thought back, I'd seen something small flying overhead when the ogres had brought me into the jail. Something like an Aes Sidhe who'd shifted into a bird, for instance.

Maybe they'd sent the ghost to distract the Unseelie Queen on purpose. The timing made no sense otherwise, but this dude must have hopped into the Vale the instant he'd walked out of prison.

I blocked a swipe from his blade, which nicked the skin of my wrist underneath the claws. Warm blood soaked my sleeve, but he'd given me an opening to grab his exposed arm. Yanking him forwards, I backhanded him across the face, right in his injured eye.

He fell back with a hiss of pain, but the sight of the horses retreating from our fight brought a rush of alarm. *No. I won't lose my chance.*

I ran towards the nearest horse and grabbed its reins, climbing onto its back. "Come on. Let's get out of here."

The horse didn't budge. I groped around in my mind for what I knew of faerie horses, which mostly consisted of them being fast and unpredictable but intelligent and possible to tame if you knew what you were doing. I doubted they appreciated being dragged between realms at the whims of a bunch of outcasts, but would they listen to me instead? One way to find out.

I leaned forwards and spoke into the horse's ear. "You remember me, right? I bested your rider once already. Want to get out of here? He has a price on his head, but you don't."

The horse leapt into action so fast that it would have slid out from underneath me if I hadn't tightened my grip and galloped wildly down the grey-silver path until we left the Sidhe in the dust.

"Whoa." I held on with a death grip as we veered around corner after corner. "Hang on. Take me to the mortal realm. You know the way, right?"

Dammit, the horse wasn't listening to me, and now I'd lost track of my location. The Vale appeared little more than a grey blur on either side of me, but the Morrigan's magic ought to still work even when I was at the whims of an out-of-control faerie horse.

Addressing the Vale, I shouted, "Take me to the nearest way out of this realm!"

The horse continued along the path, which began to grow transparent before my eyes, its coating of leaves turning from silver-grey to autumnal orange and gold and living trees replacing those frozen in time. Faerie. The real fae realm, not the washed-out and lifeless Vale.

"Holly!" Puck's voice called from nearby.

"Puck?" Startled, I slid backwards and tumbled off the horse into the bushes. The beast didn't slow, launching into a galloping trot into the borderlands, while I lay on my back, winded but alive. I sucked in a breath, pushing upright when I saw Puck approaching me.

His green eyes widened in disbelief. "Holly... where did you come from?"

"I think the question is, *why* are you still here?" He was supposed to leave as soon as the faerie puppy had come here with backup, but instead he stood amid the bushes, looking at me as though I'd risen from the grave before his eyes. No surprise, given that he'd likely seen Lord Lyle take me away. After...

Warmth singed my cheeks at the reminder of the last words I'd shouted at him... my last confession. I'd told him my worst secret in an attempt to drive him away, and having to face him again so soon after had not been part of my plan.

"I was helping the others drive the Aes Sidhe out of

their base," he said. "Then I heard hoofbeats and thought the Hunt was back."

"The—I'm sorry, what?" I disentangled myself from the bushes. "Who do you mean by 'the others'? Did anyone actually volunteer to come back to Faerie?"

"Yes, because that genius of a puppy stole one of the Aes Sidhe's arrows when he ran out of Faerie to warn them," he said. "River and Ilsa recognised the arrow right away and asked the council for permission to come here at once."

My heart skipped a beat. "Weren't they worried about getting caught by the Courts?"

Weren't you *worried?* Lord Lyle had placed the blame for his near-death firmly on my head, but I didn't see how the others could possibly know unless Puck had told them.

The sounds of fighting drifted from the direction of the borderlands, and I spotted Ivy leaping among the trees, her blade glowing. Nearby, a wraith bore down on the Lynn siblings and the puppy, but Ilsa countered the wraith's attack with a blast of magic from her talisman which caused it to explode into fragments.

"Ilsa," I called out, running to join them. "What in the world are you all doing here?"

"Looking for the Aes Sidhe," she replied. "They cleared out their hideout."

Damn. I'd wondered why I hadn't seen any signs of them in the forest. Had they gone to the Vale to join the Wild Hunt warriors they'd set free? Unless they'd gone to Winter instead, but even their illusory magic couldn't stand up to the Unseelie Queen. "Tell me they didn't go to the mortal realm."

"I *hope* not." Ilsa lowered her talisman. "Where did you come from?"

"I'd also like to know the answer to that question." Puck strode over to join us. "Where'd you get the horse, for that matter?"

"That was a Wild Hunt horse," Ivy said. "Did you steal it?"

"Yeah, you might say that." I drew in a breath. "The Unseelie Queen banished me to the Grey Vale, but I escaped by stealing a horse from a certain group of warriors the Aes Sidhe helped free from prison."

"Then we're too late." River joined our group, his expression taut with anger. "We got here as soon as we could, but the Aes Sidhe had already left their base."

"For the Vale," I guessed. "I didn't see them, but they must have gone there once they'd freed the Wild Hunt."

"The Unseelie Queen ignored our warning, then," Puck said. "As I thought."

I felt the weight of his gaze on me, and my body tensed. "She cared more about getting rid of the ghost haunting the Court, so she had me evict her guest before she banished both of us."

"Why banishment?" asked Hazel. "Why not kill you?"

"Hazel." Ilsa shot her a warning look, but it wasn't like she was wrong.

"She thought my angry ghost would come back to haunt her Court." I glanced around at the others, none of whom looked particularly thrilled to see me, but neither did they seem overtly hostile either. "Never mind her. The Wild Hunt and Aes Sidhe are likely plotting to target the mortal realm next, as if screwing with Death wasn't enough already."

"Damn," said Hazel. "Puck told us they're controlling the wraiths using blood magic?"

"Yeah, they are," I said. "Not sure how much control they have over the ones blocking the Gates of Death, but it's got to be them."

"How are we supposed to banish them if they're already dead?" Morgan wanted to know. "And already behind the gates?"

"No idea," Ivy said. "I hoped one of you might have a suggestion. Those wraiths must have been serious power-houses when they were alive."

"Who told you?" I looked among their group again. "I mean, how much time did I miss in the mortal realm?"

"I got the warning this morning." Ivy's brow wrinkled. "Don't make me calculate Faerie time zones. The day after you left, Roseanne came to tell me the Aes Sidhe had caught you and that you thought they were working with the Wild Hunt. Unfortunately, the rest of the council wouldn't take her word for it."

That figured. "I guess a death faerie and a puppy weren't convincing enough for them."

It must have been more than a day or two by now, given the hours I'd spent locked in the Unseelie Queen's dungeon.

"They'll have to listen to us now," Hazel said. "We can bring proof."

"Assuming they aren't already in the mortal realm," I added. "What're the odds that the Wild Hunt's about to try the exact same ritual again, this time with backup?"

"Pretty high, I'd say," Ilsa said. "We'd better leave before the half-faeries in the borderlands blame us for the disturbances."

"If anything, they should thank us," said Morgan. "Those Aes Sidhe were shitty neighbours, I'll bet."

"They also want us dead," I said. "For some reason, the Aes Sidhe blame the Gatekeepers for everything and want to kill all of us. I assume that means you as well, Ilsa."

"Everyone forgets me," Morgan muttered.

"You've never been Gatekeeper," Ilsa pointed out. "Don't complain about not having a target on your back."

At this point, I was pretty sure every single one of us was on the Aes Sidhe's shit list, but staying here wouldn't do the mortal realm any favours. Instead, we made our way towards the path linking the Courts. I found myself falling into step with Ivy. Despite being human, she didn't seem bothered by the bright colours of Faerie or the blatant alienness of it all. Had her Sight been a side effect of her talisman, or had she been born with it? Being able to see the fae wasn't innate to humans, but in theory, anyone could learn the skill if they spent enough time around faeries.

Ivy's gaze swept over me. "You did manage to banish the Unseelie Queen's ghost? Did you find out who it was?"

I doubted Ivy had any experience with Her Majesty, so I didn't see the harm in telling her. "Her sister. I think the Unseelie Queen killed her, and the Aes Sidhe sought out her lost spirit in the Vale in order to cause as much of a disturbance as possible."

Her brow arched. "Wow. That's dedication. You got rid of her, though? How?"

"Using the Morrigan's powers." I looked down at my hands. "Even the Unseelie Queen didn't tell me why I still have them. I'm not sure even *she* knows."

"Damn." Ivy was silent for a moment. "I know it's not

convenient, but you might need them if the Wild Hunt attempts their ritual again."

Didn't I know it. The one silver lining of our situation was that the Unseelie Queen and her fellow Sidhe had no idea I'd escaped the Vale, and if I returned to the mortal realm now, I'd be able to start afresh without fear of being visited by the Sidhe. The idea of living a peaceful life without them breathing down my neck was a tantalising one… were it not for the fact that I still had the Morrigan's magic and Death in the mortal realm remained majorly screwed up.

When we reached the path linking the Courts, the faerie puppy wasted no time in breaking into a run. In a flash, we landed on the street of Edinburgh near the half-faeries' territory. Silence spread throughout the streets, while I didn't see any unwanted ghosts wandering around. I also didn't see any Wild Hunt warriors or Aes Sidhe either.

"I think it's safe to say the enemy went to the Vale, then," said Ivy. "They'll be planning to jump us when our backs are turned, I don't doubt. So, who wants to come with me to warn the council?"

20

When nobody answered, Ivy raised a brow at me. She couldn't possibly expect me to say yes, surely. "No, thanks. I need to go and tell Roseanne we're back. I'm sure she'll be worried about us."

"The council will want to talk to you, Holly," said Ivy. "Sorry, but you're the reason for our impromptu trip to Faerie, and they wouldn't take Roseanne's word as good enough proof for us all to vanish at a critical time."

"I already got locked up by the Unseelie Queen," I pointed out. "I can't say I'm keen on the idea of throwing myself on the mercy of another supernatural authority."

"The mages don't make a habit of freezing people into ice statues," said Ivy. "Not as far as I know, anyway, and I spend enough time around them."

I raised a brow. "And will they react badly if they learn that I have the Morrigan's magic?"

"Ah..." She cleared her throat. "Some of them might, but most of Edinburgh's mages have never set eyes on the queen of the death fae. Besides, you don't have to tell them about her magic if you don't want to. The priority is warning them that the Wild Hunt is walking free and that they might attempt another ritual."

Yeah. They might. With the Aes Sidhe on their team this time around and the ongoing disruption in Death, they weren't to be underestimated. This time, we wouldn't be forced to deal with this alone, but someone needed to rally the other supernaturals.

I'd just never thought that someone might end up being me.

As far as the Council of Twelve knew, I hadn't broken any laws… not in the mortal realm, anyway. That was my one saving grace. "If I talk to them, I hope they'll be prepared to take action right away, because I doubt the Wild Hunt is planning to wait for us to be ready before trying to summon their death god again."

"Let them try." Hazel cracked her knuckles. "You'd think the Aes Sidhe would have seen their Queen get dragged into the abyss by that very same death god."

"I asked Adria the same question, and she didn't give me a straight answer." Strange, but then again, the Wild Hunt didn't plan to form an alliance with the god of death, but instead intended to slaughter him to rebuild their immortality source. "What we do know is that they want the Gatekeepers dead."

"Lucky us," said Ilsa. "Who else wants to come and speak to them? Morgan?"

"Yeah, right," he said. "You know the council forgets I exist most of the time."

"Join the club," said Hazel. "Ex-Gatekeepers aren't considered a good source of intel."

"You might have mentioned that before." I addressed Ivy more than the others, but when Puck's attention turned towards me, part of me wanted to run into a meeting with the council just to put off the inevitable moment when we'd have to discuss my outburst in the forest. "Why do you think they might listen to me, then?"

"You were in the city during the Wild Hunt's last attack," Ilsa said. "Not on holiday like certain people."

Hazel stuck her tongue out at her sister. "None of us expected the Wild Hunt to come back, did we?"

"You might have known the Aes Sidhe wouldn't let go of their loyalty to their Queen even after her death, though," I pointed out. "If we'd known they moved into the borderlands, we might have been able to stop this."

"Enough arguing," River said. "Look at the sky. It'll be dark soon, and we need to warn the council before nightfall."

Of which day, though? It felt like I'd spent longer than a few hours in Faerie. I was starving and exhausted and hardly in the mood for an interrogation, but what if the Wild Hunt had already started kidnapping people again? We hadn't any time to waste.

"I'll come." I hesitated, then addressed Puck. "Can you tell Roseanne where I am? And thank her for the warning?"

His mouth parted as though he intended to say something else, but he simply nodded. "Of course. I'll see you later."

At least he hadn't brushed me off, but I couldn't help feeling like I'd massively fucked up back there in Faerie, and I hadn't a clue how to fix it.

First, though, we needed to start fixing the mess the

Aes Sidhe's wraiths had made of the afterlife. Which began with warning the guild and the Council of Twelve.

Ivy led the way through the darkening streets. I moved in an exhausted haze, and it wasn't until we reached a pair of gates glimmering with security wards that I realised that we'd come to the home of Edinburgh's mage council. The gates blocked us from approaching the grand house with its whitewashed walls and balconied windows, but Ivy sauntered over to speak to the mage standing on security duty outside. He gestured at the puppy, and she shook her head to indicate Morgan wouldn't be bringing him inside the building.

As for the rest of us, I half thought we'd be turned away based solely on our muddy clothes and dishevelled state, but instead, the gates swung inward, revealing the impressive building in all its glory. My heartbeat quickened as we walked along a gravel path towards a set of stairs leading to the oak doors at the front of the mages' base.

Inside, a wide lobby greeted us, decorated with glinting chandeliers, walls panelled in dark wood, and a curving staircase with banisters carved with ornate dragons. I'd possibly never wished so hard for the temporary return of my glamour to hide my grimy clothes and dirt-covered shoes.

Apparently unconcerned with first impressions, Ivy strode up to a door on the right and knocked. Ilsa, River, and Hazel followed, and Ivy pushed open the door without bothering to wait for an answer.

The room on the other side contained a long table lined with chairs filled with smartly dressed individuals.

The meeting had clearly been in progress for a while, judging by the number of faces which turned in our direction when our bedraggled group walked into the room

I suppressed the urge to back straight out again, but Ivy didn't seem in the slightest bit bothered by all the attention. "Sorry to interrupt, but I thought you'd want to know what we found in Faerie."

My gaze travelled around the table, noting that surprisingly few of the people in the room appeared to be startled to see us. The mages, all of whom wore suits, looked the least impressed at the interruption, while I assumed the people dressed in more everyday clothing were witches. Ivy sat next to a dark-skinned woman who wore a number of bright bangles on her wrists to match her flowery shirt and who looked mildly alarmed at the sight of Ivy's dishevelled appearance. On her other side sat Jas, along with a stern grey-haired woman who wore a black cloak decorated with badges. Shit, that was Lady Montgomery, the leader of the necromancers and River's mother. She did not look thrilled at our entrance, and to make things worse, the only vacant seats were near to her and the other necromancers. Hazel and I shared a moment of solidarity in the mutual awkwardness—no doubt never to be repeated—as we found ourselves a couple of empty chairs at the side of the room and River pulled out a seat and sat beside Ilsa.

"As I was saying," a suited mage with neatly combed hair said in a posh English accent, "Ivy has been investigating a link between a group of rogues who formerly belonged to the Court of the Aes Sidhe and the Wild Hunt."

"The rogue Aes Sidhe broke the Hunt out of jail, Vance," Ivy said. "Not only that, they're causing the current issues in Death."

"According to whom?" Another mage, who sat in a prominent position at the head of the table, addressed Ivy in a Scottish accent.

"Holly." Ivy gestured in my direction, and my mouth went dry as everyone turned towards me again. "She's the one who initially went to spy on the Aes Sidhe and prove their guilt."

Dammit, Ivy. I glared daggers at her and then smoothed out my expression and put on the overly polite tone which I typically reserved for when I spoke to the Unseelie Queen.

"When I was spying on them," I said, "the Aes Sidhe admitted to using blood magic to control the wraiths, some of which I believe they sent into this realm to interfere with Death. They did the same to a ghost who they sent to the Winter Court in order to cause a diversion while they helped the Wild Hunt escape jail."

If they wanted to know how I'd seen wraiths blocking the Gates of Death, then River was welcome to tell them how he'd shown me the veil in person. The specifics didn't matter, not with the imminent threat of another attack from the Wild Hunt.

Lady Montgomery's gaze met mine, and I wondered if River had told *her.* If he had, then she probably knew I'd been sneaking in and out of the guild to meet with its members. Then again, so was Ivy, and everyone seemed to let her do whatever she liked, even the Council of Twelve. I guessed killing the Huntsman had earned her that right.

"I assume everyone here knows who the Wild Hunt is,"

added Ivy. "They returned to Edinburgh a few weeks ago in an attempt to conduct a ritual, but they ended up locked in jail in the Winter Court. Now they're free, there's a good chance they're about to come back for round two."

"Of what?" asked the Scottish Mage Lord who'd challenged her before. "What ritual do you speak of?"

"A ritual which requires them to sacrifice seven half-faeries to summon an Ancient," Ilsa said. "Last time, they only failed because one of their victims faked his death and we were able to hand them over to the Sidhe. This time, they'll be wise to any potential trickery, so if we want to prevent a repeat of the same incident, I think there should be more security stationed outside half-blood territory."

"Aren't there already candles in place?" the mage asked.

"Candles won't keep out the Wild Hunt," I said. "Even your wards might not."

Hazel shot me a grin as mutters broke out among the others at the table. The other Lynns' lack of respect for authority was rubbing off on me, apparently. Not that that mage hadn't deserved to be challenged. I didn't know if he was part of the Council of Twelve or one of Edinburgh's guild members, but the mages were typically members of society's elite, possessing the money and power that came with their titles. They kept to themselves, despite theoretically being in charge of the laws concerning all supernaturals, and ultimately, all magic-related decisions were up to them. Including whether to protect the citizens of the city against the return of the Wild Hunt.

"I doubt any of the Sidhe can breach our walls," he said dismissively.

"Don't be a fool, Lord Addison," said the English mage who Ivy had called Vance. "You remember the invasion, don't you? The Sidhe were able to take down the wards on highly secure buildings with ease, and exiles from the Hunt led the invasion in person."

"Then who are these Aes Sidhe?" Lord Addison's pronunciation was way off, but I got the gist of what he meant to say.

"The Aes Sidhe were exiled from Summer until their leader attempted a coup by murdering the King of the Summer Court a few months ago," Hazel said. "I sent you a report. Did you not read it?"

Ilsa shot her sister a worried look, while a murmur of discontent scattered throughout the room and the Mage Lord averted his gaze. "The Sidhe are not our priority. We aim to protect and serve the mortal realm, and no humans were threatened in that conflict—"

"Except yours truly," Hazel interjected. "And for the record, the Aes Sidhe who survived the battle took refuge in the borderlands of Faerie and have been experimenting with blood magic they learned from the Wild Hunt. Right, Holly?"

"They have," I said. "They're even able to control the dead. Don't underestimate them."

"What is their purpose, then?" asked Lord Addison. "If I'm to understand your claims, the Wild Hunt plans to summon an Ancient… for what reason?"

"To avenge their Queen," I said.

"Queen Etaina," said Hazel. "She was killed during the battle in Summer, along with the former Seelie Queen.

Oh, and they also want to use the Ancient's blood to replenish their immortality source, right, Holly?"

Is she supposed to say this in front of so many strangers? None looked overly surprised at the declaration, which contrasted the former secrecy of the Sidhe's greatest shame.

"They also want to kill the Gatekeepers," I said. "As vengeance for the fate of their Queen."

"And we're not a fan of that," added Hazel.

Vance cleared his throat. "You forget your predecessor was killed by an Ancient, Lord Addison. This is not a threat we can ignore."

"They want to summon the god of death," said Hazel. "I know not all of you were there at the battle of Summer, but trust me, he's not someone you want to show up at your house."

Ilsa rolled her eyes at her sister then addressed the others. "I've told you the Wild Hunt attempted to use *my* talisman to contact the god. They failed, so they're using rituals which I assume they learned from their former leader. The last one involved killing seven half-faeries. I don't know if they can resume the same ritual again or if they'll have to start from scratch, but the half-faerie community needs protection either way."

Everyone looked expectantly at the mages. With visible reluctance, Lord Addison said, "We will send some of our mages to patrol their territory, but given the volume of ghosts in the area, the necromancers will have to help."

"That won't be a problem," said Lady Montgomery. "I'm sure you'll do your fair share of the work."

Reading between the lines, she doubted the mages

would keep their word. No surprise, considering the necromancers were frequently saddled with all the responsibility.

The meeting came to a close in short order. While it surprised me that the Courts had never been mentioned save for the admission that the Wild Hunt had been freed from the Winter Court's jail, the Council of Twelve wouldn't have the slightest idea that I'd been kicked out of Winter twice over. The others wouldn't need to share that information either, not when Lord Lyle had covered for their involvement in my attack on him. Winter still wanted me dead, but if they thought I was trapped in the Vale, they might leave me alone for once.

As the others began to leave the meeting room, I joined them, fully intending to reprimand Ivy for putting me in the spotlight. When I walked out into the lobby, however, my gaze fell on a familiar bird sitting on the banister of the staircase. *Puck?*

He'd flown through the mages' security wards? He seemed in no hurry to leave, though I kept one eye on him as I walked out of the oak doors. Sensible of him not to draw attention, but why had he taken the risk to begin with?

I lagged behind the others, but it wasn't until I'd crossed the wards on the gates and rounded a corner away from the mages' guild that Puck swooped down to land beside me in human form.

I glanced sideways at him. "You know trespassing in the mages' guild is a serious crime?"

"For humans, not animals."

"Doubt they'd appreciate the distinction." I dropped my voice. "That's how the Aes Sidhe set the Wild Hunt free, you know. I'm ninety percent sure one of them shifted and sneaked into the dungeon in the form of an animal."

His amused expression vanished. "I should have guessed. I did wonder how they planned to use a ghost to break them out."

"It's done now." I kept on walking, my exhaustion beginning to return like a heavy weight settling on my shoulders. "I thought you were checking in with Roseanne. You didn't need to eavesdrop on the meeting, anyway."

"I was a little concerned that the mages might decide to throw blame in the wrong direction."

"Meaning at me." Meeting his eyes was harder than showing my face in front of the mage council looking like I'd been dragged through a hedge backwards, but I needed to know the truth. "Why? Did you think you could single-handedly take on the entire mage council?"

A heartbeat's pause. "I reckon I could give it a fair shot."

"You're mad." I shook my head. "I gave you *how* many chances to get away? You didn't even need to come back to Faerie."

"I did," he said. "It was my Court who instigated the jailbreak. They sent the wraiths, and they're the reason for the ghosts plaguing the city."

So he'd come back for them. Not for me. I shouldn't have been surprised, given how viciously I'd pushed him away, but the implication stung all the same. I forced my thoughts back to more important matters. "We haven't figured out how to solve the ghost problem yet, but the mages are sending extra security to half-blood territory to make sure the Wild Hunt doesn't try another ambush."

"How generous of them."

"I wouldn't get too excited." I unzipped my inside pocket in search of my phone. "It's in their own interests to stop a repeat of the ritual."

"You think they'll try again?"

"It almost worked the first time." Hawk, in fact, was the reason the ritual hadn't succeeded. "Did you check in with Hawk?"

"I did," he said. "Roseanne is with him right now, and I believe he's waiting for us both to join them for dinner."

I came to a halt. "Excuse me?"

"You recall what I said the last time about not hurting his feelings?"

I shook my head. "This isn't… I mean, did you not hear a word I said to you in the forest?"

"Yes." He spoke in a soft voice. "You were trying to convince me to leave so the Unseelie Court would take you and not me."

"I told you the truth." My voice cracked. "I told you what I did. Not a single word was a lie."

"If you're waiting for me to reprimand you, then you're going to be waiting a long time," he said. "I am in no position to judge anyone for the decisions they made for their own survival."

My eyes stung, and I blinked furiously. "You—when I stabbed Lord Lyle, you wouldn't look me in the eyes. You think I'm not that different from the Morrigan, don't you?"

"Neither is Roseanne, and she's relying on you to set an example," he said. "If I wasn't clear before, Lord Lyle put you in an impossible position and you responded in the only manner available to you. I was worried for you, not repelled by your actions."

"I don't..." The words tangled in my mouth, refusing to form coherent sentences. "I don't get it. I realise you grew up in Faerie, but—"

He held up a hand. "Exactly. Faerie makes monsters of us all. You and Roseanne have more in common than your family histories."

My mouth parted. "She told you?"

The Morrigan had forced her to kill her estranged human father, her last living family member, and it'd taken long enough for her to admit so to me. I hadn't known she and Puck had reached that level of trust.

"I believe she was trying to justify your choice to drive me away without knowing the specifics," he said. "Besides, why did you take Roseanne in?"

"What does that have to do with anything?" I'd taken her in because nobody else would. Yet if he was acting out of some misguided sense of pity, then he'd be disappointed. "I'm an adult who can take care of myself, not a teenage death fae without a family."

I *had* a family, if not one I'd trust with my life. Not that it was their fault, but even Puck's patience wasn't infinite.

"You think that the environment you grew up in has destroyed your chances at happiness," he said. "That you'll never deserve it."

"What do you know?" I tried not to snap at him, but he wasn't helping my attempts to keep a necessary barrier between us.

"More than you think," he said. "You haven't asked

how I came to be Queen Etaina's personal trickster, have you?"

"You didn't volunteer that information."

"No, I suppose not," he said. "The realm of the Aes Sidhe was a dull place to grow up, with little in the way of any connection with the outside world. By and large, my only companions were Sidhe, not half-bloods like me. Like in this realm, those of us who were half-human banded together for our own survival. The Queen paid us little attention until she became aware of my parentage."

"You mean Robin Goodfellow was one of the Aes Sidhe?"

"He never belonged to any Court," he said. "Even Summer had a hard job keeping him under control. I can only assume he had some dalliance or other with someone among the Aes Sidhe, who went on to have an affair with a human."

"You never met your human family?"

"No," he said. "Like many changelings, I was abandoned on the doorstep of the nearest entrance to Faerie, which in that case led to the Aes Sidhe. Anyway, I learned to shift at a young age, but it took until I was a teenager before word reached Etaina that I was capable of shifting into multiple forms, a feat even most Aes Sidhe aren't capable of despite their skill at illusions. At first, she thought I might be trained as a warrior, but then she decided I would be of more use as a spy."

"I thought you chose that path."

"Hardly a choice," he said. "The only reason any of us was allowed to leave the realm of the Aes Sidhe was if our duty compelled us to, and like many caged birds, I longed to fly away. And so I took the role of trickster, sowing discord among everyone the Queen requested. There isn't a group of fae on either side of the Ley Lines among which I don't have a sizeable number of enemies."

"You don't regret it, though, right?"

"I believe we aren't responsible for our circumstances," he said. "The choices that arise from those circumstances are ours, but we cannot change the past, and so the only way to move forwards is to accept that."

His words dug sharp nails into the bruised part of me which I'd left behind, standing beside my mother's corpse in the library of the Winter Gatekeeper's house. He hadn't asked me to share any more than I already had, and yet I found myself speaking anyway. "I might have made another choice."

"You never chose to become Gatekeeper."

No, I hadn't. "I chose... I mean, I chose to let my mother dictate my life. I might have turned out differently if she hadn't pulled me out of school and stopped me from talking to my cousins after I got my Gatekeeper's magic. After that, she only grew more and more obsessive."

"About what?" he asked.

I kept my gaze on the path ahead as we walked. "She was completely fixated on the Gatekeeper of Death. Before Ilsa, there hadn't been one for a few generations, and I think she wanted to use the magic of the Gatekeeper's talismans to break the curse on our family. I often found her poring over these old books in the library of our house."

Puck's silence invited me to carry on.

"Every Lynn has tried to break the curse at some point or other," I went on. "Nothing ever worked, but my mother used to lock herself up in her study for hours.

One day, the Sidhe came with a message for her while she was locked up, so I went to look for her. I had to kick the door in to get to her, and I found her surrounded by ritualistic instruments. She was trying a blood summoning."

"She was trying to summon an Ancient?"

"I don't know *what* she was trying to do," I said. "She seemed to think that if she laid her hands on enough power, she'd be able to challenge the Courts. The problem was, our house was situated directly on top of the Ley Line, so doing a ritual would have had knock-on effects, and she didn't appreciate me pointing that out."

"I imagine not," he said. "What happened then?"

"We got into a fight." I lowered my gaze. "She used her Gatekeeper's magic to subdue me before trying the ritual again. A blood summoning."

My throat went dry, my chest constricted, yet Puck's patient stare was enough to draw the final words out of me. "She grabbed her knife and said she'd teach me a lesson by using my blood in the ritual instead of hers. I fought back and—and she was stabbed. I didn't think I hurt her fatally, but she refused to let me get help. She made me watch her bleed out in her own ritual circle."

Puck swore under his breath. "That's sick."

"She turned into a wraith more or less there and then." I kept my gaze on my shoes, taking one mechanical step after another. "I had to listen to her taunting me for days while I tried to figure out how to keep her imprisoned in the house. She was even more dangerous when she was no longer human, but I didn't reveal her existence, even knowing she was planning to murder my cousins and attempt war on the Courts."

"I thought she put you under a vow so you couldn't tell them anything."

"Who told you—" I broke off. "*Ilsa*. How did that come up?"

"She inferred more about the circumstances in which we parted ways than I intended her to know," he said. "So did Roseanne."

I couldn't decide whether to be annoyed or relieved. Part of me waited for the other shoe to drop, and yet a weight had lifted from my chest all the same. "That's why Ilsa's siblings hate me so much."

"Then that's their problem, not yours," he said.

"I didn't help matters when I nearly got us all killed in Faerie."

"I've already told you my views on where the blame lies, haven't I?" he said. "Not with you. Now, I think it's about time we went back home before Hawk forcibly drags us there."

I snorted. "You aren't going to let this one go, are you?"

"No," he said. "This might be our last night of peace for a while. Besides, Roseanne wants to see you."

Yes, and I owed her, massively, for passing on the warning to the council. Like it or not, Puck was right when he said Roseanne had come to look up to me as an example. I hadn't exactly had any decent role models in that department myself, but if she'd shared her history with Puck for my sake, then I ought to at least consider letting him in.

A notion that was somehow scarier than any beast I'd faced in the past day.

"Fine," I said, to be rewarded with his brilliant trickster smile. "I'll come to dinner with you."

"It's a date."

"It's not a date if your annoying best friend and my teenage half-death fae housemate are there." I did my best to ignore the quiver his words ignited inside me. *Date.* As if such a thing was possible for someone like me. He knew the worst of me and hadn't walked away, yet I didn't quite dare let down my guard altogether.

Not yet.

I wouldn't call it a date, but it was a relief not to have to cook for myself and Roseanne after the day I'd already had. While I was pretty sure Hawk would have rather been on a date with Leyton than with Puck, Roseanne, and me, he was thrilled when Roseanne ate three platefuls of curry and rice and then tried to swipe my leftovers too.

"Honestly." I caught her wrist in mine. "I don't know where you put it all."

"I'm a death fae," she replied. "Be glad I don't eat souls instead."

"I'm a death fae too," I reminded her. "I'm not the one trebling my shopping bill."

Hawk and Puck both laughed, but Roseanne said, "You're not death fae. You're just disguised as one."

I shrugged, wishing I'd never brought up the subject. "Makes me sound like a spy, but I guess shapeshifting is one of the things I couldn't do with my Gatekeeper's powers."

It was only now I thought on it that I realised I'd never gone so long without noting the absence of my Gatekeeper's magic before. Another side effect of carrying the Morrigan's power, and not one I was looking forward to relinquishing.

"I think it's far superior to other magic," Puck said, "but I'm biased."

"Yes, you are," said Hawk. "What's your next move, then? Because if you're either planning to go back to the Grey Vale to seek out the Wild Hunt or wait for them to come here, neither of those sounds like a great option."

"We'd need the Sidhe's help to hunt them down in the Vale," I said. "I had to use the Morrigan's magic as a compass to get around."

"So that's how you did it." Puck gave a nod, as if I'd confirmed some unspoken theory of his. "And stole one of the Wild Hunt's horses."

"Wish I'd seen," Hawk said. "Is that twice you've managed to steal one of their horses?"

"Maybe they should keep a closer watch on them." I yawned. "I reckon the council will get the final say on our plan."

"They ought to go with your choice instead," said Puck. "You were the first to figure out the Aes Sidhe's involvement."

"And you believed her." Hawk grinned. "You'd agree with her plan if she suggested skinny-dipping in the Firth of Forth instead."

Roseanne snorted. Puck didn't look mortified at all, but when he met my eyes across the table, there was a kind of heat in there which brought to mind the memory of his hands transforming me from a bird into a human again and his body pressing against mine.

While Roseanne insisted on helping Hawk to clear away the plates, Puck remained sitting, his posture relaxed, his gaze inviting. As if waiting for me to ask a question.

Naturally, that was when my phone buzzed in my pocket. "That's Ilsa."

"The mages have sent people to watch half-blood territory?" Puck guessed.

"Yeah." I checked the message and returned my phone to my pocket. "About time."

"Would they be any good at keeping the Wild Hunt out, though?" Hawk winced when Roseanne hit him in the arm. "Ow. Why would you hit me when I was nice enough to feed you?"

"He has a point," I said to Roseanne. "No, they probably wouldn't. I got the impression that the faerie invasion proved the mages' wards can't keep the Sidhe out. Their magic is too rigid to fight off the unpredictability of the faeries in open combat. Most use iron instead."

"Interesting," said Puck. "Not surprising, though. The mages might be at the top of the magical world in this realm, but in Faerie, their magic hardly functions at all."

"Pity the same can't be said for the reverse." If the Unseelie Queen came here, she might be underpowered compared to when she was in her own Court, but she could still do some serious damage. Lucky for all of us that she and her fellow Sidhe had little interest in this realm.

The Vale outcasts, though, were all too interested... especially the former Wild Hunt and the Aes Sidhe.

"That's hardly fair, is it?" Hawk said. "Yet that's not enough for them. They want more."

"They want their immortality back," I corrected him. "Which is why we're in this mess. Even if the Wild Hunt does manage to summon and slaughter the god of death, though, that doesn't mean things will go back to the way they were before. The second the other Sidhe find out, they'll tear through anyone in their paths to get hold of that god's lifeblood. They might even destroy it, like the cauldron."

"Exactly," said Puck. "Though we can't dismiss the possibility that some of the other Sidhe will take the Aes Sidhe and the Wild Hunt's side once they realise gaining immortality was their goal and not conquering the Courts."

"Unless the Wild Hunt already screwed their chances of an alliance with Winter when they broke out of jail," I said. "Which is their own damn fault."

Then again, the Unseelie Queen had been set against them since Fionn's betrayal, and while the Sidhe hid their true natures from humans easily, they couldn't fool one another.

My phone buzzed again.

"Ilsa wants you to come?" Puck rose to his feet.

"Tell her you're busy," said Hawk. "You have to sleep at some point."

True. I'd been awake for the equivalent of far more than a day, but if the mages screwed up their security, we might wake up to a repeat of the Wild Hunt's ritual. "Someone needs to make sure the mages don't knock over the candles."

"Generous of them to send anyone at all," said Puck. "I'll come with you, then."

Hawk shot me a wink, which I ignored. When we left the office, Roseanne bounded ahead of us, leaving me to walk alongside Puck. While street lamps dotted the pavement, they cast long shadows which hid swathes of the road from view, and the alleyways remained shrouded in darkness. I had little doubt Roseanne could hold her own against most creatures of the night, but our proximity to the Ley Line made me edgy. How long would the Wild Hunt wait before striking? We might not even have a night before they returned.

"Holly." The serious note in Puck's voice drew my gaze to his face. "Adria specifically said the Aes Sidhe want the Gatekeepers dead. I don't think you should go back to the house tonight."

I frowned. "They don't know where I live. Besides, there'll be mages patrolling outside half-blood territory all night."

"You said yourself that there's little they'd be able to do to hold off the Wild Hunt," he said. "If the Aes Sidhe came alone, they might, but you don't have wards on your house the way the mages and necromancers do."

"What, you want me to sleep on the floor in the necromancers' lobby?" I shook my head at him. "I doubt they'd leave the Wild Hunt behind. They're not spectacular fighters, from what I've seen. Even that Adria."

"Perhaps not, but it's clear she's attached blame to your family for the Aes Sidhe's current predicament."

"Hazel." A flare of annoyance struck me. "Of all the Lynns, she's the most to blame for Etaina's death and the loss of the Aes Sidhe's home. I've never even *been* to their Court, for crying out loud."

"I know," said Puck. "I wasn't going to suggest staying at the guild. The mages have a hotel designated for the Council of Twelve's members."

"Er, no," I said. "Come on, do you think I can afford anything that's in the *mages'* budget? And if you're going to suggest I stay in your spare room instead, then I doubt Hawk would appreciate me putting a target on his back as well as yours."

"Is that it?" he asked. "Or is it me you're worried about?"

"Would it make you stop asking if I said yes?"

"Maybe."

A bright flash lit up the air, and the smile died on his mouth. I spun on my heel, looking for the source of the light, and spotted the gates to half-blood territory within sight.

"I don't see the candles."

Crap. Did someone knock them over again? I moved towards the gates, where Roseanne waited in the shadow of a street lamp. "The ghosts are back."

Sure enough, several bright spots shone behind the gates, while vibrant sparks of blue and green shot up to the sky from half-blood territory as the inhabitants reacted to their unexpected visitors. Had the candles only just been turned off? I opened the gate and squinted into the darkness of the wooded area bordering the territory, and several bright clouds detached themselves from the shadows. Wraiths. *It's happening already.*

It seemed we wouldn't get a reprieve before the Wild Hunt made their next move after all. As the wraiths moved in, Puck shifted to his bird form and flew to distract them, while shadows swept my hands and turned them to claws, banishing the chill of the wraiths' magic. More flashes of light pointed to Ivy, who ran towards us with her blade glowing against the darkness.

A sweeping cut from her sword sent a wave of icy magic at the nearest wraith, which disintegrated into nothingness. "Thought I saw some trouble over here."

"I thought the mages were supposed to send help," I said.

"They did," said Ivy. "Most of them can't do much against wraiths, especially with your candles out."

"The wraiths came here for a reason," Roseanne said, her face pale in the darkness. "*They're* here, aren't they? The Wild Hunt."

"I won't let them take you again," I promised. "We'd know if they were here, though. It's the Aes Sidhe who are commanding the wraiths."

Unfortunately, they had the Gatekeepers' names at the top of their hit list. And who'd shut off the candles? Half-faeries ran around their territory in a panic, while Ivy gave me an assessing look. "I'm told you saw wraiths creating an illusion to cover whatever is blocking the Gates of Death."

"I did." The wraiths in *this* realm were a more pressing problem, though when one of them glided over to us, Ivy dispatched it with an impatient wave of her sword. "So?"

"You have more experience with these Aes Sidhe than I do," she said. "I don't suppose you know how to break their glamour?"

"Not without going through the gates themselves, which is a whole other issue." The problems with Death seemed minor in comparison to the oncoming shitstorm at the hands of the Wild Hunt, but the Aes Sidhe were responsible for both. *Why* they'd blocked the Gates of Death, though, I couldn't begin to imagine.

Another wraith descended on us. I spun around and thrust my claws into the wraith's ghostly form. The wraith snarled and fought my grip, while Ivy finished it off. "Neat trick there. The Morrigan's magic… you know, I wonder if *she* might have been able to stop this."

I lowered my hands. "You don't think her magic might be able to get rid of the wraiths blocking the Gates of Death?"

"Most of us can't get that close to the gates without dying ourselves or risking the same," she said. "I wouldn't say it's out of the realm of possibility for you to be able to use her magic in that way, though."

I gave a firm shake of my head. "I don't have the spirit sight. River had to show me Death in order for me to be able to see the gates at all."

"I wonder." Ivy took a step closer to me, her face bathed in eerie blue light from her blade. "You're not a necromancer, but neither am I, technically. I wonder if you can travel on the spirit line?"

"I can't even *see* the spirit line." She couldn't possibly be implying I could walk between realms like the Ancients. Like Ivy herself. I looked past her for the others, but Puck had run off to help some of the other half-faeries fend off a wraith and only Roseanne remained nearby, watching Ivy and me with terror etched on her features. "Tell her she's being ridiculous, Roseanne."

"She won't listen."

"You've got that right." Ivy's gaze flicked over me. "I'm

not supposed to do this without you being in a candle circle, but if it works, it shouldn't kill you."

"Wait, what?" Roseanne yelped. "What do you mean?"

"I'd quite like to know that myself." As Ivy reached out her hands towards me, shadowy claws rose in response. "Ivy?"

Her hands passed *through* my shoulders, yanking me backwards into oblivion. I flipped over, feeling oddly weightless, and startled at the sight of my own body standing below me. She'd pulled me out of my body as easily as drawing a breath.

"Ow." My head spun with vertigo, except I didn't *have* a head. Not a physical one, anyway. The thought made me even dizzier, especially when I tried to look for Roseanne and saw nothing but greyness masking the world below.

Ivy hovered in front of me, her transparent face apologetic. "Sorry. Frank taught me to do that, so I figured it wouldn't hurt if I tried."

"Who the hell is Frank?" I spun around, alarmed to have lost sight of my body altogether. Not to mention Roseanne. Instead, I found myself drifting, unable to tell whether I was moving forwards or backwards.

"Whoa," said Ivy. "Don't go floating off. I might not be able to find you if you end up in the Vale."

"We're near the Vale?"

I drew myself to a halt, with difficulty. The grey smoke surrounding us was uniform, and by far the weirdest part about the afterlife was the fact that I had no grasp on its size. It felt as small as a room and as large as a planet simultaneously, with nothing but the faint outlines of other ghosts as landmarks. Except for a bright line stretching across the emptiness nearby. *The Ley Line.*

As I watched, the line became clearer, a glowing current of energy travelling endlessly in each direction. Beyond, I glimpsed hints of grey smoke resolving into patterns which resembled trees. Ivy was right. Not only could I see the Line, but I could see the Grey Vale too.

"Now what?" I dragged my gaze away from the Line's hypnotic flow of energy. "I see the Vale, but I don't see the gates."

"They're not exactly a fixed point," she said. "They'll show up, though."

"That's… bizarre."

"Hardly more than Faerie is."

"Good point." Death evidently had its own brand of logic, just like Faerie did, with the added complication of being smoky and indistinct, temporary and blurred. "What do you expect me to do? Because I'm told the gates try to draw in any nearby spirits."

"Oh, they do," she said. "You'll have to be careful not to end up being sucked through to the other side, though with Death being as weird as it is at the moment, that might not be a permanent state."

"Death is pretty fucking permanent, Ivy." When she pointed behind me, though, I swung in that direction. A long shadowy blur crested the horizon, growing in size the longer I stared at it. "There they are."

The expanse of the gates looked even more impossibly large from this angle, covering the entirety of my vision and seeming to extend for an eternity to left and right. I found myself moving closer, trying to see through the gap between the twin gates where a steady current of glowing spirits floated into nothingness.

"Wait," Ivy said. "I told you not to drift off. You might not be able to find your way back."

"You brought me here." The flow of transparent figures had already drawn me into their midst, heading towards the gates and towards the wall of flickering darkness on the other side. Was there supposed to be a wall of greyish blackness between the gates, or was it an illusion, conjured by the Aes Sidhe? To see it properly, I'd need to get closer.

At the thought, a tugging sensation gripped me, like a strong current determined to drag me to the abyss. Alarm blared through my nerve endings as the gates loomed even closer until I could almost see the place from which my mother's wraith had emerged in a cloud of shadow and bright-blue Winter magic.

I recoiled, panicking, desperately trying to lock my attention on anything solid. Except there wasn't anything, not even Ivy—only an endless stream of ghosts. I might have drifted for miles for all I knew. Death made Faerie's sense of timelessness and lack of consistency look like nothing.

Then, out of nowhere, Ilsa's transparent figure appeared and grabbed my arm. "There you are."

"Hey!" The weird paradox of her seizing me and yet not being able to physically touch me set my head spinning again, but the sight of my cousin's familiar face jarred me from my trance. In Death, the glowing mark of the Gatekeeper on her forehead stood out like a brand.

"Ivy sent me to get you." Without another word, she pulled me downwards. The greyness faded, revealing the street of Edinburgh, and a solid mass crashed into me. It took several painful seconds to connect the weird solidness with the shock of having a body again, and for a panicked moment, I thought the Unseelie Queen had frozen me into a block of ice. My hands were numb, my feet unwilling to move, and I struggled for a few long minutes before I managed to struggle upright.

"Shit." I groaned. "I don't envy you necromancers."

"You get used to it." Ilsa blinked back into her body beside me, seemingly unruffled by her trip to the other side. "I didn't know you could disconnect from your body without a candle circle as an anchor. That was risky."

"Ivy thought it would work, but she didn't give me much warning," I said. "She wanted to show me the gates. And *I'd* like to show her my fist when I see her again."

"*Ivy.*" Ilsa hissed out a breath. "She should know better, but she's as bad as Hazel for making rash decisions. Keep walking and sensation will come back into your feet eventually."

"Reassuring," I said through chattering teeth. "If I'd accessed the Morrigan's magic, I might have been able to get through. There's definitely an illusion of some sort blocking the gates."

"Never mind the gates," she said. "We have a situation here."

I walked on, the numbness gradually fading from my limbs. "Will you be able to redo the circle around half-blood territory?"

"Not until the wraiths are all gone," she said. "The others are helping to deal with them."

"Holly!" Roseanne ran over to us and threw her arms around me, while I gave a grunt of surprise. "I thought you were dead. I thought Ivy *killed* you."

"I don't need to tell you not to do that again, do I?"

asked Ilsa. "Holly, you know I was on the verge of death when I went to the other side myself? If I hadn't been Gatekeeper, I wouldn't have been able to come back."

I didn't need to be told twice. I'd nearly lost myself in the process of trying to see behind the gates, and then where would we be? There was no guarantee the Morrigan would return to Faerie even after my death, but the fate of our elusive death goddess was the least of our current issues. "Got it. Give Ivy the lecture, not me."

Roseanne let go of me. "I think Puck's with the others."

"Meaning whom?"

Ilsa answered by approaching a group of people standing near the gate to half-blood territory, including Hazel, Morgan, and Puck. The faerie puppy ran in excitable circles around them, while Puck spotted me first. "Holly. I wondered where you'd got to."

"I was with Ivy." I'd decide whether to give the details of my literal near-death experience later, when we didn't have an audience. "Are the wraiths all gone?"

"I think so." Hazel strode over to join us. "Slight problem? I think they were sent here as a diversion."

"How'd you figure that one out?" I peered around half-blood territory, but I didn't see any signs of the Wild Hunt or the Aes Sidhe. Granted, they were good at hiding themselves, but where would they be if not here?

"The Ley Line." Ivy ran towards us. "It's not good news."

I suppressed the impulse to backhand her for nearly getting me killed. "How much of an understatement is that?"

"You tell me." She pointed behind her at the spot where the Ley Line cut through the road. Perhaps as a side effect of being in Death, I could see the faint shimmering light more clearly than I had previously... and a dark shape lying in the road.

A body.

Puck ran over to the body, reaching it first. "This is a half-faerie... but not someone I recognise from this realm."

Horror crashed over me. "They went after the half-faeries living in the borderlands instead."

22

We had no time to waste, so I ordered Roseanne to hide out in the house and then went to the Ley Line with the others. As much as I wanted to wring Ivy's neck over her stunt in Death, that would have to come later. For all we knew, the Aes Sidhe and the Wild Hunt had already got hold of their seven victims, since they'd waited for us to declare their hideout abandoned before heading straight back to the borderlands again.

Morgan directed the faerie puppy to take us into Faerie, and in a flash, we landed on the path between the Courts. Ivy and Hazel took the lead, walking into the tangled paths of the borderlands, while the rest of us followed more cautiously. Thick trees bordered us on either side, while fog drifted in as we walked farther and farther, our footsteps crunching on fallen branches and leaves. At first, nothing appeared to have changed.

Then Hazel came to a halt near a body which lay

sprawling in the bushes, several arrows in his back as though they'd caught him while fleeing.

"He's not Sidhe," River said in a low voice. "He's half-fae."

"I should have known," Ilsa murmured. "They tricked us into thinking they were coming for the half-Sidhe in the mortal realm."

"Instead, they went after their own neighbours." I should have guessed too. Why would they come back to the mortal realm when an entire territory of half-Sidhe stood on their doorstep?

Hazel's gaze lingered on the body, her expression unusually grim, before she walked on. Soon enough, we found three more half-fae bodies lying in the undergrowth, and while I couldn't tell if they were from Summer or Winter, it was pretty obvious someone on a horse had ridden them down while they'd been fleeing the borderlands. Yet they hadn't been sacrificed. How many needless deaths had the Wild Hunt caused?

When we reached the trampled remains of a fence made out of interwoven thorns, Hazel swore at the top of her lungs. "These people had already been through hell. All they wanted was to be left alone, not sacrificed in some twisted ritual."

"Quiet," Ilsa said to her sister. "The Hunt might still be here."

"I fucking hope they are." Hazel climbed over the wrecked fence, and the rest of us followed.

Ahead of us lay a palace with snow-white walls adorned with thick curtains of ivy which flanked a pair of oak doors. I hung back, not wanting to trespass in case the palace's inhabitants mistook us for the enemy, but River joined Hazel, and they both knocked on the doors.

The twin oak doors opened to reveal several half-Sidhe gathering in the entryway, wielding swords, bows, and spears.

"Hang on," Hazel said. "It's me. Hazel Lynn. You know, the former Summer Gatekeeper. Can I talk to Lord Hornbeam?"

"We're not here to attack you," said River. "We came to help."

"You're too late," said the lilting voice of a female half-Sidhe. "They're gone. Didn't stop them from taking some of us with them, though."

"Shit." I turned to Ilsa. "They're going to do the ritual elsewhere. Somewhere they won't be interrupted."

"I'll search the rest of the borderlands." Puck shifted into a bird and took flight into the canopy while River and Hazel exchanged a few more words with the half-faeries in the palace doorway. I didn't know any of them personally, so I wouldn't know which had been taken as hostages, but I was willing to bet they were all Summer half-Sidhe who possessed healing magic.

The palace doors closed, prompting Hazel and River to rejoin the rest of us.

"They didn't want to invite us in?" Morgan asked.

"They were attacked by people they trusted," said Hazel. "I wouldn't take any chances either. Anyway, the Wild Hunt captured some of the half-faeries, but they didn't know whereabouts they took them."

"Puck is looking around the borderlands." I wouldn't have thought they'd stay this close to their old hideout, but the Courts weren't an option, and the Vale was a magic-free zone. "I guess they might be on the path between the Courts again."

Out of any other options, we retraced our steps through the borderlands until we came to the deserted path. Shortly after, Puck returned, shifting back to human form. "They aren't in the borderlands."

"They didn't go back to Winter, did they?" Ilsa asked. "Or Summer?"

My head snapped up. "The Death Kingdom. Nobody would think to look for them there."

Worse, with the Morrigan gone, nobody would be left to stand in their way. Most of the death faeries didn't care if they had a leader or not, and the other Sidhe avoided that part of Winter. Which made it the perfect location for a deadly ritual.

"I bet that's where they are," said Ilsa. "Lead the way, Holly."

I did so, making my way into the wilderness around the edges of Winter's territory and hoping Faerie didn't send me on any detours. The Wild Hunt might not have gone far into the territory, but I knew they'd had enough of a head start on us that the odds of us catching up before the ritual was underway were shrinking by the second.

As we drew farther into the Death Kingdom, the sound of voices came from somewhere up ahead. We quickened our pace and halted at the opening to a clearing bordered by leafless trees and several red-leafed, spiky bushes. Amid the bushes stood a number of Aes Sidhe warriors, while several sleek fae horses roamed nearby.

Their riders, meanwhile, occupied the centre of the

clearing, where seven bodies lay in a careless heap, slick with blood and gore. I doubted any of them had faked their deaths like Hawk, since they'd had no warning. My stomach lurched. Swirling, glowing marks covered their bodies and mingled with the blood staining the ground, while the three Wild Hunt warriors crouched over them, daubing more marks onto the frigid earth.

Hazel swore under her breath. "Tell me they didn't."

"They did." They'd had their seven victims.

Seven souls. Seven sacrifices.

The glyphs ignited. Then a gaping slash in the world yawned open behind the bodies, growing bigger by the second. The god of death was rising, and it was too late for us to do anything but stand and watch as the Wild Hunt waited for the beast to appear from the depths of the void.

The redheaded female Aes Sidhe spotted us first, her head swinging in our direction. "You."

As if in response to an unheard signal, the other Aes Sidhe moved to surround our group. While they only had a slight advantage in numbers, the Wild Hunt had us beaten by sheer brute force *without* whatever was hiding in the dimension they'd opened up behind them.

"If I were you, I'd close that portal," Ilsa warned them. "Didn't I already tell you what that beast you're trying to summon did to your Queen?"

"That was *your* fault, Gatekeeper." Adria's mouth pulled taut, her companions closing in around us. "You as good as killed our Queen with your own hands."

"Wrong Gatekeeper," Hazel said. "Were you even paying attention during the battle? Or did you sleep in?"

Ilsa's expression flickered with panic as the Aes Sidhe

turned their attention towards Hazel instead, but then her gaze locked on the gaping slash in the air. She opened her mouth and spoke a single, clear word. The word wasn't in English, yet the meaning rose in the back of my mind as the sound of the Invocation rattled around my skull. I'd heard it before: *close.*

Yet despite Ilsa's command, the gaping hole in the universe remained open, unchanging.

"One voice isn't enough, Gatekeeper," growled one of the Wild Hunt members.

"Try two, then." Ivy sauntered over and spoke the same word in unison with Ilsa.

Close.

Again, the word rattled around the air and left a trickle of power in its wake, yet the opening the ritual had ripped open didn't so much as stir. *Damn.* It wasn't like we had a flock of Sidhe from both Courts waiting to help us this time around, and I had zero idea if the Morrigan's magic would enable me to speak Invocations without consequence the same way Ilsa and Ivy's talismans did. Now did not strike me as the right time to do a trial run. Besides, three voices might not be any better than two. We needed the Sidhe... and we had to draw them here before the god of death made an appearance.

I took a step back, and my arm brushed against Puck's. He turned to me, an apology in his gaze, and I whispered, "Think you can fetch backup?"

"I can try." He shifted into a bird and took to the sky.

In the same instant, the Aes Sidhe snapped into action. A storm of arrows whipped into the air, and my heart leapt into my throat to see Puck's wings beating to avoid them. Then the sound of a dozen blades being drawn drew my eyes back to earth.

An Aes Sidhe swung his weapon at me. I dodged, the Morrigan's magic wreathing my body in shadows, and struck him with my claw. As the warrior fell back, Ilsa blasted him off his feet with a current of magic from her talisman. River fought another, sword clashing with sword, easily keeping pace with the Aes Sidhe. Morgan and Hazel wielded iron blades, which gave them an edge despite their opponents' superior speed and stamina, since a wound inflicted by iron would sap their opponents' magic. Even the puppy joined in the fray, nipping at ankles and doing his best to unbalance anyone who got close.

Meanwhile, redcaps popped up from the bushes, eager to join in with the bloodshed and to feast on the spoils of war, while death fae swarmed in, not caring whose side they fought on as long as they got to feed on life and death energy in equal measures. I cut down an Aes Sidhe warrior, finding myself next to Ilsa again.

"We've got to stop that ritual," she hissed in my ear.

"I'm aware of that." The Morrigan's wings stretched behind my shoulders, and in a brief lull in the fighting, I launched myself into the air and flew directly at the spot where the Wild Hunt guarded their ritual.

The one-eyed warrior saw me coming and blocked my path with a whirling strike. I caught the blow on my claw, the impact jarring my arm. From his blurring speed and sheer strength, he and the others must have reapplied their blood magic with the help of their Aes Sidhe allies.

"Let's finish this," I said to the warrior. "Just you and me."

He bared his teeth and brought the blade down, while I blocked and struck back. My claws raked across his face, blood spraying out. I reeled back, startled at his lack of response. Then I saw what commanded his attention.

In the gaping dark hole he and the others had opened on the ritual site, something was moving. A shadowy form stirred, too indistinct to be recognisable, until all three Wild Hunt warriors stopped watching the battle and focused on the portal.

"You called me?" A booming voice cut straight through the clamour of the fighting and brought everyone to an abrupt halt. The words weren't English, weren't any language I knew, and yet I understood them as surely as if their meaning had been projected directly into my mind.

"We did," said one of the warriors. "We were once the Wild Hunt, and we are here to request the aid of the one known as the god of death."

Somehow, not being able to see the speaker made it more frightening when the voice said, *"And what will you offer me in return?"*

"I have come to offer you the Gatekeepers," said the Wild Hunt warrior.

"Hey!" I grimaced as the one-eyed soldier grabbed my arm and dragged me towards the gap in the universe.

Elsewhere, two other warriors moved in a blur, dragging Ilsa and Hazel over to my side. Both were trembling with outright horror, the latter stunned to silence for possibly the first time in her life, yet I didn't blame her a bit. She had no magic to defend herself with, but frankly, I wasn't sure even the Morrigan's power could stand up to an actual god.

The presence spoke again. *"They are not the Gate-keepers."*

"I told you," I snarled at the guy who held me. "We're not your sacrificial lambs."

"They are no longer the Summer and Winter Gate-keepers, true, but they are the reason you were denied your sacrifice," said one of the Wild Hunt soldiers.

"Thomas Lynn is the one I wanted, and eventually, I had my wish."

My blood turned to water. Somehow, the god rejecting us seemed more terrifying than the alternative, though I suspected we were nothing more than bait. The Wild Hunt wanted to kill the death god, after all, and they'd offered us to him in order to lure him out of whatever dimension he inhabited.

"Then will you not make a new deal with us?" The one-eyed warrior approached the gap in the world, still gripping my arm hard enough to bruise. "This one possesses the magic of the goddess of death."

"I see no need for deals with mortals. I am more than the god of death: I am the Scourge."

The shadows *moved,* and a shimmering shape detached itself from the gap in the world. Its translucent, rippling form was vaguely humanoid but blurred around the edges like a person glimpsed through a glass window. The Wild Hunt soldier let go of me at once, turning his blade on the newcomer instead—except the creature was no longer there. Nor was the opening in the air, which had vanished as soon as the god—the Scourge—had left its home.

The humanoid figure reappeared, flickering around the edges not unlike a Sidhe encased in full glamour, and then wings stretched out from its back. Before the Wild

Hunt's warriors could do more than turn in the god's direction, it launched into flight in a manner that reminded me disconcertingly of the Morrigan. Was it some kind of distant relative or ancestor of hers?

Like that matters, Holly. The Wild Hunt warriors erupted into action, leaping onto their horses and giving chase after the fleeing beast, while the clearing dissolved into confusion and noise. Some of the Aes Sidhe ran after their allies, others attempted to fight, while the few death fae who'd lingered on the battlefield retreated into the bushes. While I knew how fast those horses could move, the sound of pounding hooves seemed to grow louder, not quieter.

Wait. Those weren't the Wild Hunt's horses.

Puck's crow form soared down from the sky, accompanied by none other than Lord Lyle leading a small group of Winter Sidhe. His blade slashed out, catching one of the Aes Sidhe in the chest, while Lady Rive rode in to finish him off.

I ran over to meet them. "They summoned the death god already. It's on the loose in Faerie and the Wild Hunt's chasing it down."

Lord Lyle swore in the fae tongue and wheeled his horse around—but one of the Aes Sidhe's arrows struck him in the side, and he flew gracelessly off his horse and into the bushes.

Lady Rive let out a scream of pure rage and rode at the person who'd fired the arrow—Adria, who wore a defiant expression on her face. While she engaged the Aes Sidhe in battle, I ran over to Lord Lyle, whose side was already soaked through with blood. He tried to struggle to his feet, only to fall back into the undergrowth. His eyes were wide, fearful. Like all Sidhe, he feared death above all else.

A flickering in the corners of my vision showed me the bright spark of his soul leaving his body. Like Puck, back in the first battle with the Aes Sidhe.

Instinct took over. Without stopping to think, I hooked my claw into his soul and pushed it back into his body. Shadows swept in, smothering the wound, and I kept feeding power into his side. Healing him.

Lord Lyle's eyes blinked open. "Mortal…?"

"You're welcome." I lurched to my feet, already regretting my moment of weakness. Especially when I saw that the other Sidhe had gone in pursuit of the fleeing Aes Sidhe and the Wild Hunt, leaving us alone in the forest.

Puck flew up to me and shifted to human again. "They're gone. I'm pretty sure they just fled through the Ley Line."

My heart gave a jolt of dread.

The god of death, the Scourge, had escaped from Faerie.

23

I stared at Puck. "Then where'd the Wild Hunt go?"

"The Sidhe were chasing them down the last I saw." His hair was in disarray and his face streaked with dirt and blood, but he didn't look to have suffered any injuries. "I didn't manage to bring many of them here."

"I'm impressed you found anyone at all." I looked for Lord Lyle, who'd mounted his horse again. Without so much as a word of gratitude, he rode away among the trees.

"Hang on!" I hurried after him, but I had zero chance of keeping pace with a faerie horse. I slowed to let Puck catch up, since he was still in his human form. "How'd you talk him into helping?"

"Not much talking was involved," he said. "I was in my crow form, and I thought it wise not to give them a bigger target in case they decided to strike me down. Luckily, Lord Lyle recognised me from before and realised I was trying to give him a warning."

"Unluckily, we're all too late." I kept walking downhill. "I do appreciate it, though. We'd be worse off without any of the Sidhe even trying to contain this catastrophe."

Farther down the slope, we encountered Ivy, whose blade gleamed with fresh blood and who was surrounded by the corpses of a dozen redcaps.

"Bloody scavengers," she said. "Looks like the god of death gave the Wild Hunt the slip."

"He called himself the Scourge." I sidestepped the fallen redcaps and continued downhill. "Where'd everyone go?"

"No idea, but the Sidhe are pissed off," she said. "Everyone else ran that way."

"They'd better not be going back to the borderlands." I continued downhill towards the path which lay between the Courts, where no signs remained of the Wild Hunt except for a lot of trampled undergrowth. The Sidhe stood more of a chance than the rest of us of catching up to them on horseback, but the rest of the Aes Sidhe had vanished among the trees as well. Where were they hiding?

I spotted Ilsa nearby and ran to catch up to her. "Did they all chase after the death god? Including the Aes Sidhe?"

"Looked that way," Ilsa said breathlessly. "So much for their revenge on the Gatekeepers."

"So much for convincing the death god to cooperate." I scanned the area on either side of the path for any sign of illusory traps, but nothing leapt out at me. "You don't think the so-called Scourge would attack the Courts?"

"Might do, considering it was the Sidhe who banished the gods to begin with."

My mouth went dry. "Not the Sidhe who rule the Courts at the moment. Most of them hadn't even been born back then, right?"

"You think he'd care?"

I cursed under my breath and paced to the other end of the path between the Courts, close enough to Summer to feel a warm breeze emanating from that direction. No signs of the Aes Sidhe, or the Wild Hunt, either. The trampled undergrowth came to an abrupt halt just off the path as if they'd vanished into thin air.

"Did they hop through the Ley Line?" I spun around to face Ilsa, who wore a grim expression. "They did, didn't they?"

Question was, had they gone to the Vale or to the mortal realm?

"We can't get through without the puppy," Ilsa said. "And I'm not leaving the others behind."

"I'll find them." Puck launched into flight as a bird before either of us could reply, leaving Ilsa and me alone on the path.

"The Sidhe were chasing the Wild Hunt," Ilsa said. "I don't see them catching up to that god of theirs until they've shaken off their pursuers."

"Not like we can follow them if they went to the Vale," I replied.

If they'd gone to the mortal realm, though, it would spell disaster for everyone unlucky enough to stand in their way.

"The Sidhe can," Ivy said. "Ah—there's your friend."

Puck returned to the path, leading Morgan and a dishevelled faerie puppy behind him. The puppy greeted

Ilsa with a joyful bark and utterly ignored me, while Puck's bird form vanished among the trees again.

"Useful trick, that," said Ilsa, petting the puppy. "Morgan, did you see where Hazel and River went?"

"Dunno," said Morgan. "This place is a maze, and those Aes Sidhe ran like hell the instant the Wild Hunt disappeared."

"Cowards." Ilsa tensed when rustling came from the undergrowth at the edge of the path again, and then she relaxed when Hazel emerged from a tangle of fallen branches. "Hazel, are you okay?"

"Sure." She watched as Puck swooped down to land at my side. "I ran back to check on the borderlands, but the Aes Sidhe seem to have ditched their hideout."

"There you are." River ran up to join us, relief flooding his face at the sight of Ilsa. "They didn't go back to the borderlands. So where—?"

"There." Puck shifted to human form and pointed towards some trampled earth at the edge of the path. "The Wild Hunt and the Aes Sidhe chased after the god, and the Sidhe chased *them,* but if they didn't go to the Vale..."

"They went to the mortal realm." Ivy strode into view. "This is out of our hands now."

"Damn right," said Morgan. "C'mon, Pepper."

Dread coiled within me, intensifying when Pepper the faerie dog barked, once, and then lurched forwards, dragging Morgan along with him.

The path around us warped and changed, grey fog filtering in and the ground reforming underneath our feet. It took a moment for me to realise we'd landed in Edinburgh, near the half-faeries' territory, because the level of impenetrable fog masking the street around us rivalled the first layer of Death.

"Whoa," said Hazel. "Is everyone seeing what I am?"

"Looks like Death," said Ilsa. "Did the Wild Hunt do this?"

"Or the god of death?" I squinted through the fog, hardly able to see the fence bordering the half-faeries' territory nearby. "We don't know what kind of powers *that* creature has."

Which made the odds of us catching up to him worryingly low. The Sidhe had managed to banish him the last two times because the god had never managed to escape the realm he'd originally been in, but he'd come straight here along with whatever deadly magic he possessed.

Had this been part of their plan? Given the death god's abrupt escape, I guessed not, but I wouldn't be able to see if the Aes Sidhe or the Wild Hunt were anywhere nearby unless they walked directly into me. Worse, if the Scourge remained here, then he might well cause damage on the same scale as the faerie invasion.

"Whatever it is, I'm guessing the necromancers are having a bad day," said Ivy. "I'll see if it looks any better from the other side."

"I'll check Death too," said Ilsa. "Can one of you check in half-blood territory?"

I took a hesitant step in that direction, but the trees were barely visible through a layer of thick grey-whiteness. "I can't see the candles..."

"Candles wouldn't be much use against whatever caused this," said Morgan. "This is creeping me the fuck out."

You and me both. Despite the smoke swirling around

me, I couldn't see much more than the shadows at my fingertips and an odd shimmering effect in the air. The Ley Line? Since we stood directly on top of the boundary between realms, it ought to be easier for me to see through to the spirit realm, especially with the grey fog seeping through into this realm as well, but no such luck. I stared at the smoke hard enough to go cross-eyed, but even after my earlier impromptu separation from my body, my spirit sight remained as inert as ever. When Puck caught my sleeve in his grip, I startled.

"Sorry," he said. "It was the only way to get your attention. What are you doing?"

"Trying to see into Death," I said. "I didn't have time to tell you before we went into Faerie, but Ivy showed me the other side of the gates, and there's definitely some kind of illusion blocking them. Maybe this—whatever it is—is an escalation of that."

He sucked in a breath. "She showed you… how?"

"By yanking me out of my body."

"By doing *what*?" Puck swung his head around as if trying to spot Ivy, but she might have been standing right behind us and we wouldn't have seen her. "She might have killed you."

"If not for the Morrigan's magic." I shifted my hands to claws, but even the shadowy magic encasing my body was barely visible to my own eyes. "Look, the Morrigan… she's not quite an Ancient, but she's more than a Sidhe, and Ilsa and Ivy can both use the magic inside their talismans to cross between realms and leave their bodies behind."

"That doesn't give a guarantee that you'd be able to do the same." He muttered a curse under his breath in the faerie tongue. "The power she loaned you was conditional, besides."

"Puck, I think we both know she's not coming back," I murmured. "Whatever she intended, I have full access to her magic now, and she specifically gave it to me to beat the Wild Hunt."

"The Wild Hunt isn't hiding in Death," he insisted.

"Something is," I said. "It's connected. I came close, but—I don't understand why I can travel out of my body and yet I don't have the spirit sight. Even Roseanne can see ghosts, and she doesn't have all the Morrigan's powers..."

"Did you try a full shift?" he asked.

"Did I what?" I tried to look at his face, but all I could see was the faint greenish glow of magic in his eyes. "Why would that matter?"

"Well, if I shifted most of my body into a bird and not my eyes, I wouldn't be able to see like one of them."

"Thanks for the mental image." Was that the problem? I'd come close to fully shifting into the Morrigan's weird bird-human hybrid form, but even in Death, I'd looked through my own eyes, not the Morrigan's. Was it that simple? Would it be different if I used her magic when I crossed over? "Okay, give me a second."

My hands shifted into the Morrigan's, my wings extending behind my shoulder blades. I let the shadows continue to flow over my skin, and this time, I didn't try to rein them in. My posture shifted, my claws touching the ground, my wings growing, and while my face remained humanoid, my vision began to shift.

Then everything sharpened. Bright spots began to appear in my line of sight. Ghosts. I hadn't left my body—

yet—but my Morrigan's eyes had turned on the spirit sight. Puck was right.

And I could see the Vale, too, its grey paths winding through the middle of the gleaming Ley Line, close enough that a single step might take me directly into Faerie. *Careful.* I wouldn't be able to count on stealing a faerie horse again if I got stuck there, and besides, it was the mortal realm that needed my attention. I turned away from the Ley Line and studied the glowing shapes nearby. They weren't ghosts, but spirits… of *living* people. My friends. A shimmering figure resolved into the form of Ivy. "Holly? That *is* you, right?"

"Yeah," I said. "I found my spirit sight."

"You look exactly like the Morrigan," she said. "If I hadn't seen you do it before, I'd be worried the old bird herself had come back."

"Things would be different if she had." It was weird speaking to Ivy outside of her body, especially when I could feel the Morrigan's feathery wings and claws even when I couldn't see myself beneath the smothering fog. "Can you see what's going on over there? In Death?"

"No," she said. "I never thought of the Morrigan having the spirit sight before, but I think she can cross between realms too. When she's not in chains, anyway."

"No wonder the Unseelie Queen chained her up," I remarked. "*Is* this weird fog due to the Scourge? Or is it more trickery on behalf of the Wild Hunt and the Aes Sidhe?"

"Wish I knew," she said. "The god of death, though… if he's anything like the others, he'll be able to travel via the spirit realm as well as walking between realms."

I was starting to wish I'd asked Ilsa for more details

when she'd mentioned the gods had the ability to cross between realms, but I'd hardly expected we'd end up facing a genuine Ancient anytime soon. "He can travel through the *spirit realm?* How the hell are we supposed to find him, then?"

"Only way I can think of is to do a summoning," she said. "To summon him back, we'd need his name, but if any of the Sidhe know it, none of them have volunteered that information."

Meaning: we needed the Wild Hunt's help if we wanted to find the Scourge, but if they were in the Vale… well, the Morrigan's magic could travel through the realms. I opened my mouth to make that suggestion, but Ivy spun around on the spot when several shouts rang out and dark shapes moved within the fog, glimmering with bright-green magic and wielding blades and bows.

Aes Sidhe.

"Ivy, get back into your body!" I warned, raising my claws. "Get Ilsa too."

I focused on my spirit sight again in an attempt to pinpoint Ilsa, but the sudden ambush had scattered our group, and the darkness and fog didn't help me identify which of the vibrant lights belonged to my friends. I blinked a couple of times, abruptly understanding why necromancers didn't keep their spirit sight switched on all the time. I drew some of the shadowy magic back below my skin, willing my eyes to see like a human's again.

Unfortunately, without the spirit sight, the lack of visibility in the fog returned. Ivy's glowing blade helped me pinpoint the others, but before I reached her, Adria struck. I caught her blade in my claw, the momentum sending me staggering backwards. I heard Puck shouting my name somewhere amid the chaos, but I didn't dare take my eyes off the enraged Sidhe in front of me.

"You," Adria spat. "Murderer."

"Wrong Gatekeeper. Again." I released her blade in an attempt to unbalance her, but she lunged again with agile grace and launched into a series of attacks which put me on the defensive. "Did you give up on finding the god you set loose? The Scourge?"

"We had no control over the beast," said Adria.

"That's why I told you not to summon it." I grimaced when her blade snagged my arm and would have broken the skin if there hadn't been thick layers of feathers in the way.

"This is your fault, mortal." She dodged when I swiped at her with my clawed hand, narrowly missing her face.

"*My* fault?" I echoed. "For what? I wasn't even the person who broke the Gatekeeper's curse."

That honour went to Hazel, who was presumably fighting another Aes Sidhe elsewhere in the fog. I was more concerned about Ilsa, who'd been in the spirit realm when the fighting started, but Adria refused to let up, forcing me to meet her blow for blow.

"Thanks to Thomas Lynn and your family, our Queen is dead," she said. "Our only option was to serve the Wild Hunt."

"Your Queen is the one who made a deal with the Scourge in the first place and got burned for it. Don't blame it on the one guy who resisted."

I'd never particularly *liked* Thomas Lynn—though it wasn't like I'd known him well, except via the stories of his escape from Faerie and the impact of his accidental bargain on the rest of his descendants—but I was through with these dickheads blaming all their woes on my family.

Her fighting grew wilder, more desperate and less coordinated. Through the fog, I saw another Aes Sidhe warrior fighting with Puck, both of them changing forms too quick to tell one from the other. I took the advantage, fighting with both clawed hands, and in one swipe, I knocked her weapon from her grip.

Adria's eyes flew wide as my other claw pierced her chest. Blood spurted out, but when I withdrew my hand, more than crimson blood stained the claws. Her soul flew out of her body in my grip, mouth stretched open in a scream.

"Let me go!"

"Too late." As I held onto her struggling spirit, the shadows swept over my vision again, and my spirit sight showed me the towering form of the Gates of Death hovering behind her. The world beyond tugged on her soul, attempting to drag it through to the other side, but I held fast. "What did you do to the Gates of Death? You sent wraiths there by using blood magic to command them to block the world beyond, didn't you?"

Adria's struggles grew weaker, her transparent form drawn closer to the gates with each passing second. "I didn't need to try hard, mortal. My fellow warriors were more than happy to punish those who saw to the death of their Queen."

"The wraiths used to be the Aes Sidhe who were killed in the battle." That must be how she and the others had found them so easily. They'd persuaded the wraiths of their deceased fellow warriors to enact revenge on

Earth… and by extension, the Gatekeepers. "Why did you send them here? The mortal realm did nothing to you."

"Mortals brought about our end." She detached herself from my claw with one smooth motion, drawn towards the gates, and then she was gone.

My wings beat behind my shoulders as I kept my gaze on the shadowy form of the Gates of Death, but they didn't disappear even when Adria's spirit vanished from sight. Yet this time, I felt no tug urging my own spirit through to the place from which none could return. Instead, when I beat my wings, they drew me closer to the gates.

Despite the mass of spirits drifting towards the gap between the endless gates, the weird flickering persisted. I drew closer, no longer able to see the mortal realm at all, but I was solid as ever, my wings beating fast. The Morrigan *could* travel between realms. Including, it seemed, into Death itself.

The mass of spirits noticed me and drifted away with cries of alarm, no doubt terrified to see a giant, solid bird in their midst. Ahead, the gates beckoned, and the blurred illusion barring them.

Time to see what lay beyond.

Closer and closer I flew, my claws reaching out to penetrate the illusion. A brief echo of the tugging sensation seized me, but the Morrigan's magic kept me hovering on the threshold between the two endless towering gates. If I were to fix the damage, would I have to fly straight through to the other side? The illusion drew closer, formed of a mass of flickering lights, and then became a more distinct shape. A blurred humanoid form which addressed me in a high, cold voice. "You are not the harbinger."

What? The figure didn't look like a wraith, but neither did it resemble a ghost. Unless this was what ghosts became if they spent too long on the other side of the gates.

I found my voice. "What are you? Why are you barring the Gates of Death?"

"You're human," said the voice. "Yet you wear the skin of the harbinger."

"Did the Aes Sidhe send you?" I asked. "To block the gates? You're not a wraith."

"I am no echo, mortal," the voice said softly. With each word, the figure became less distinct, somehow, barely recognisable as humanoid and yet familiar to me all the same.

Raw fear hit me. "You... you're an Ancient. You escaped when the Wild Hunt's first ritual failed, didn't you?"

"I have no need to serve the Sidhe, mortal." The godlike being's form flickered around the edges, wings appearing at its back more like a blurred reflection of the Morrigan. "This realm is a haven of souls to feast upon... and I will devour yours with pleasure."

My clawed hands came up in defence as panic rippled through my nerves. The spirit wasn't a wraith and wasn't Aes Sidhe, either. Could it even be banished? Given the lack of effect from the Gates of Death, I'd guess not, but it was hard to think when the god reared up, wings becoming more distinct, and raised a claw that mirrored my own.

I caught the blow in my hand, wincing as chills raced

through my entire body at the god's touch. "You look a little like her. The Morrigan. Are you a relation?"

Was the Morrigan a less-powerful descendant of this particular branch of death gods? I hadn't *exactly* assumed the Sidhe had managed to kill every last one of the Ancients, but it was anyone's guess as to how many more lurked within that sinister dimension the Wild Hunt had opened.

The godlike creature snarled, freeing itself, and lashed out at me again. We fought like mirror images, which was in effect what we were. Banishment was out. Killing something which didn't possess a solid form was too. Which left...

Ducking the god's claws, I gave a swipe which travelled straight through its transparent form, hooking my claws deep into its spirit. A screech escaped the beast, which writhed against my grip. "Release me, mortal."

"I don't think so." The beast was part spirit, part corporeal, at a guess, which made it vulnerable to the same magic as anything else with a soul. Her words echoed through my mind. *This realm is a haven of souls to feast upon... and I will devour yours with pleasure.*

It gave me no pleasure whatsoever, but my instincts seemed to know what to do. I lifted my clawed hand, along with the semi-transparent spirit hooked onto it, and sank my pointed beak into it. I tasted nothing, but the spirit vanished in a flash of silvery light.

The glowing light travelled through me, momentarily turning my feathery arms transparent, while I hovered in a daze until I became aware that a commotion filled the background.

The ghosts, temporarily pushed back from the gates

during my fight with the god, had begun to move through to the other side again. Hastily, I beat my wings in flight to get out of their way. The illusion had vanished along with the god, leaving the path to the gates clear. Anything on the other side would be sucked into the world beyond… if they didn't run into the Scourge, that is. The true god of death. The Morrigan's ancestor, or distant relative. Just like the one I'd—

I reeled, suddenly, and if I'd been in my human form, I might have thrown up. I'd consumed the soul of a god. I could only hope *that* wouldn't have lasting consequences.

"Holly!" shouted a voice.

I spun around. Amid the glowing lights, two familiar faces appeared in front of me. Ilsa and Ivy.

"Holly," said Ilsa. "Did you do that?"

"I cleared the way through the gates." The croaking voice of the Morrigan came from my throat. "You won't believe what—"

Ivy cut through my words. "Oh, *there's* Frank. I was beginning to wonder if he'd gone for good."

A ghost drifted past our group from the direction of the gates, his movements more purposeful than the typical spirit. "Ivy Lane?"

"That's me," she said. "The Council has been looking for you for days. We'd have filled your spot at the table, but you don't take up much space, being dead."

"As respectful as ever, I see," said the ghost. Then his gaze landed on me. "And who is this?"

"Holly Lynn," I said. "You're one of the necromancer guardians. Have you been stuck behind the gates the whole time?"

"I am Lord Frank Sydney," he said. "Necromancer

guardian and a founding member of the Council of Twelve. And yes… we have been trapped on the other side of the gates thanks to that abomination. How did you get rid of it?"

"Long story." Even Ivy and Ilsa might raise their eyebrows at the idea of me eating someone's soul, even if it'd been the Morrigan's magic which had been responsible.

"I expect it is," he said. "You, though… *what* are you? Fae?"

"That's a long story too," Ivy said. "I won't lie, I thought you'd moved on."

"Not with this big a mess to clean up," Frank said. "The others will be on their way out soon, I expect."

"Good," Ilsa said. "Let's get out of here."

In a blink, she and Ivy vanished, presumably back to their bodies. I, meanwhile, flew in the opposite direction to the flood of ghosts, only to find Lord Frank Sydney keeping pace with me.

"Yes?" I asked.

"You resemble a certain fae who is supposed to be incarcerated," he said.

"I'm not the Morrigan," I told him, assuming he was the sort who refused to let up until he had answers. "I borrowed her magic and haven't managed to get rid of it yet."

"That allays some of my fears," he said. "You're human, aren't you?"

"Mostly," I said, not wanting to think too deeply on that one yet. "Can the ghosts move on now?"

"They should be able to," he said. "Here we are."

Relief flooded me at the familiar sight of Edinburgh's

streets, where the grey smoke was already fading and revealing the Aes Sidhe stragglers being rounded up by the half-faeries.

As for Roseanne, she ran over to me as I descended to land near half-blood territory.

"Holly?" She squinted at my face. "Is that you?"

"Yeah." I forced the shadows to sink back under my skin until my human form returned, breathless and shaking. "It's over."

"You went into Death," she said. "Didn't you? You fixed it."

"An Ancient was blocking the gates," I said. "Some kind of offspring of the god of death, I think."

"Damn." Her eyes rounded. "How did you stop it?"

"I ate its soul."

Roseanne blinked at me. "Oh. That's good. I think."

"I hope it is." I looked around, my gaze landing on Puck. Instinct told me to keep that part quiet, but was it truly that much worse than everything I'd told him already? "C'mon. Let's help round up those Aes Sidhe."

24

Two days passed, and Edinburgh remained ghost-free… or free from more than the regular number of ghosts, anyway. The guild was no longer on high alert, while half-blood territory no longer needed candles to keep out unwanted spirits or extra security to fend off potential attackers.

Yet two facts remained undeniably true: the Wild Hunt was still at large, and so was the Scourge. The notion of an all-powerful Ancient being loose in this realm wasn't an appealing one, but if the Scourge had gone into Faerie instead, he might well have started a war with the Courts. As a result, the Council of Twelve stayed in the city while I counted down the hours until they inevitably invited me to a private interrogation where they'd force me to admit I'd devoured a death god's soul. I'd got away with giving them a vague explanation of my confrontation with the monster beyond the gates, but sooner or later they'd realise that something in my story didn't add up.

I'd been waiting two days for the knock on the door

when it finally came. I was on my feet in seconds, peering through the gap in the curtains to see the outline of none other than Lord Lyle standing outside. Somehow, in the aftermath of clearing up the city, it'd slipped my mind that the Sidhe wanted a piece of me too. I hadn't expected to hear from him for a while, but until I got rid of the Morrigan's magic, I'd be tied to Faerie by necessity.

I opened the door. "What is it, Lord Lyle?"

"My Queen requests your presence," he said.

"No, thanks," I said, abandoning all thoughts of diplomacy this time around. "She tried to kill me. She exiled me to the Vale to die."

"She exiled you because you attempted to have *me* killed," he clarified. "And you took the Morrigan's magic."

"I also got rid of the ghost haunting the Winter Court." Maybe that's why she wanted to see me: to clear up the loose ends and ensure I didn't spread tales around about her sister's ghost. "Look, no offence, but the Winter Court is not my priority. Unless you've got news on whether you've been able to track down the Wild Hunt or the escaped death god yet? Or the Aes Sidhe?"

"The Summer Court took the surviving Aes Sidhe to be tried for the murders they committed in half-blood territory," he said. "As for the Wild Hunt, it's my belief that they have hidden themselves in the Vale."

"Is anyone actively looking for them?"

"Yes, of course," he said. "The Unseelie Queen has been sending regular patrols, but I am not part of them, due to the debt between the two of us."

"Debt?" *Oh.* I'd saved his life, which in Sidhe terms, meant he owed me a favour in return. No wonder he'd stopped trying to drag me to Faerie by force. "Does that mean she won't lay a finger on me next time I'm in her Court?"

"You raised me from death," he said. "That skill would be valuable to the Winter Court, as my Queen knows well."

Oh. *Of course* that was the real reason she'd sent him here. The Unseelie Queen wouldn't let a potential resource go so easily. "Why did she never ask the Morrigan to do the same, then?"

"Because the Morrigan cannot be trusted."

"Maybe I can't, either."

I was pushing my luck by defying his offer, but if I was the closest thing to their old immortality source that existed, the Sidhe wouldn't dare to harm me. I knew I'd pay the price for insolence later when I did part ways with the Morrigan's magic, but I couldn't suppress my triumph at finally having a reliable way to keep them off my back.

"You misunderstand what I ask," he said. "My Queen would like you to work with the Sidhe in our current search for the survivors of the Wild Hunt, and if any are injured to the brink of death, to heal them when appropriate."

The bloody cheek of it. "What part of 'no' did you fail to understand? If you need me that badly, you can beg the Morrigan for help when she comes back. Whenever *that* is. I'm not a permanent solution, either. I'm still mortal."

Or I hoped I was, anyway. I might have the Morrigan's magic for now, but when it left, I'd rather not be locked into another vow with the Unseelie Court.

"This is not a permanent situation," he said. "Once we've found the exiles and punished them, we will set you free."

"Nice try, but you forget about the death god they summoned," I said. "Frankly, that's more of a concern than the Wild Hunt. Do you even know which realm it's in?"

His jaw twitched, but I didn't miss the flash of concern in his eyes. "The Vale, I believe. The Wild Hunt is stalking the god too."

"To slaughter it and remake the source of immortality." He'd probably guessed as much already. "You know how ridiculous that is? You all live for thousands of years and never age, but immortality was clearly never a natural process for you in the first place. Besides, if you stopped trying to kill one another all the time, you wouldn't need to fear death half as much."

He drew himself up to his full height, avoiding my eyes. "My Queen will decide what the best course of action is to take."

"Considering she failed to notice Fionn was a traitor who took the place of the real Huntsman, I'm not entirely convinced."

This time, he met my eyes, anger flaring within them. "You overstep, human."

"No, she's right," Ivy interjected, striding over to join us. "Let it go. This immortality crap has taken far more lives than it's saved, even when you had a functional cauldron. Banish the god and be done with it."

"You need the god's name from them to summon it back," I said to Lord Lyle. "I don't suppose your Queen knows what it is?"

"That is not for me to know."

"Then tell her that if she gives me that information, I *might* consider helping her."

Another bargain was the last thing I wanted, but we needed to be rid of the Scourge, and the Wild Hunt too. If the Sidhe had had no luck finding their target by themselves, then maybe my allies would be able to help.

Instead of answering, Lord Lyle beckoned to his horse, who'd been lingering near the gates. He then mounted it and departed in two quick gallops, leaving Ivy and me blinking after him.

"That means yes," Ivy said. "But he won't admit it. Did you say the Unseelie Queen wants you back?"

"To act as a portable immortality source," I clarified. "Turns out I can reattach souls to bodies and heal wounds, and Lord Lyle couldn't keep his mouth shut."

It was my own damn fault for healing him in the first place, but I'd needed at least one of the Sidhe to have my back. Even if he was as self-centred as the rest of them.

"The side effects of having the Morrigan's magic make me glad I never tried to take it," Ivy remarked. "Including the soul-eating part."

"I never told you that. Did Roseanne...?"

"No, I guessed," she said. "The presence blocking the gates disappeared. I figured you couldn't have banished it, because it was already resisting the gates' effects. It was too strong to be sent away, even by the Gatekeeper."

"It was some kind of relation of the god of death." I dropped my voice. "And the Morrigan, I think. Don't ask me how distant a relation *she* is."

"I always wondered if she was part Ancient," said Ivy. "Ah... here's your friend."

My gaze snapped up. Puck walked through the gates, his expression notably brightening at the sight of me. "I saw Lord Lyle. I take it he came to grovel to you?"

"He wants me to work for the Unseelie Court," I said. "I said no, but we'll see what he comes up with next."

"Persistent, isn't he?" he said. "He didn't try to haul you off with him this time. I wondered if he might."

"Nah, I saved his life, so I guess he's in my debt."

"He won't like that." Ivy turned on her heel and headed towards the gates again. "See you later."

When she'd left, I turned back to Puck. "What're you doing here?"

"Thought I'd drop by in case anyone tried to ambush you again." His gaze went to my house, where the curtains on Roseanne's room had pulled back for the first time ever and she was pointedly gesturing at the pair of us. Puck grinned. "Nice to see she's settling in."

"She really is." Roseanne was getting much better at ignoring the disdainful comments of the half-Sidhe who disliked her, but it was difficult for them to decry the Morrigan as a harbinger of doom when Ivy had been telling everyone who would listen that I'd used the Morrigan's magic to end the fight and bring an end to the trouble in Death. They didn't know *all* the details, but I wasn't complaining about Roseanne's life being that tiny bit easier. "Bet Hawk's happy now the ghosts have gone."

"I think he's disappointed not to have an excuse to go and visit Leyton, to be honest."

"Does he need one?" I glanced sideways at him. "You didn't come here because Lord Lyle did, unless you were already hanging around in the form of a bird or a pile of leaves. Right?"

"You got me." A smile slid across his mouth. "I was checking up on the aftermath of the trouble the ghosts caused, and I spotted your Sidhe visitor. I thought it wise to see if he intended to haul you into Faerie again."

"So you could follow me." I shook my head at him, despite the quiver in my chest which rose at the sight of his intent stare. "Why? My past is a hot mess."

"Doesn't matter."

"My future is looking questionable, too, considering I can shift into a soul-eating monster."

"That's not a deal-breaker either," he said. "Holly…"

My phone buzzed with a message. Puck frowned, but when it buzzed twice, I resignedly pulled out my phone and stared at the screen for a moment.

I know how to find the Scourge -Janet Lynn.

Puck's quizzical gaze met mine. "Is that your cousin?"

"Someone called Janet Lynn just texted me." I closed the message. "I don't have the slightest idea who she is, but she claims to be able to find the Scourge."

"Weird." He glanced over his shoulder. "We have company."

So we did. Ilsa, Morgan, and Hazel walked towards half-blood territory. Resigned to another interruption, I headed over to join them. "Have any of you got a message from someone called Janet Lynn?"

"You got it too?" Ilsa held up her phone. "We all did. Same message."

"It's got to be a joke," Hazel said. "There's nobody in our family called Janet. Our mum's called Flora."

"Does your mother know we're hunting the god of death?" I asked.

"No…" Ilsa glanced at her siblings. "Unless either of you told her."

"Don't look at me," said Morgan. "Who else knows?"

"Nobody should know outside of the council," Ilsa said. "Unless you count the Sidhe, but they don't have mobile phones in Faerie."

"Can you imagine the Sidhe sending text messages?" Hazel snorted. "Nope, this is someone's idea of a prank."

"Probably." Yet the name snagged on something in my subconscious. *Janet Lynn.* "We'd know if we had other relatives, right?"

"There aren't many of us left," Hazel said. "Mum's an only child, and so was your mother, right, Holly?"

"Right." I *really* didn't want to discuss my own family. I'd never even met my father, but since my parents hadn't married, he wouldn't have had the surname 'Lynn.' Mum hadn't said much about him except that he'd been from Scotland too.

"Then who is it?" Morgan asked. "Does anyone know how to find the god?"

"No," said Ilsa. "I'm guessing he went to the Vale, but… well, the Sidhe would need his actual name in order to banish him."

"I mentioned that when Lord Lyle came and attempted to haul me back to Winter." I caught an alarmed glance from Puck. "He said he doesn't know the Scourge's name, but he was cagey about whether the Unseelie Queen did. Anyway, I'm not under the impression the Sidhe are in a hurry to deal with the problem."

"We don't even know who this Janet person is," said Hazel. "Ah… there's Ivy. Maybe *she* knows."

Ivy walked up behind the others. "Don't mind me. I saw you all gathered over here and figured you were scheming."

"We all got a message from someone calling themselves Janet Lynn," said Ilsa. "Does the name ring a bell?"

"Why would—"

Ivy cut off my question. "I'm supposedly a distant descendent of your family line that lucked out of the Gatekeeper's curse. Thomas Lynn's wife, whoever she was. Her side of the family… I don't think they were magical. And no, I have no idea who Janet is."

"Some of them might have survived," said Ilsa. "Our family used to be way more extensive than it is, but now it's just us and Mum… and Dad, too, but he's not a Lynn."

"You?" I studied Ivy's face, but I didn't see any resemblance to my own family members, distant or otherwise. Then again, the other side of Thomas's family had split with the Gatekeepers centuries ago.

"So I've been told," said Ivy. "I don't have a clue if there are any other survivors, least of all with the same surname as you."

"Then who is it?" Hazel asked.

"That's the question, isn't it?" I reread the message. *I know how to find the Scourge.* "Whoever it is, I think we're going to need her help."

ABOUT THE AUTHOR

Emma is the New York Times and USA Today Bestselling author of the Changeling Chronicles urban fantasy series.

Emma spent her childhood creating imaginary worlds to compensate for a disappointingly average reality, so it was probably inevitable that she ended up writing fantasy novels. When she's not immersed in her own fictional universes, Emma can be found with her head in a book or wandering around the world in search of adventure.

Find out more about Emma's books at
www.emmaladams.com.

www.ingramcontent.com/pod-product-compliance
Lightning Source LLC
Chambersburg PA
CBHW050759190726
48285CB00005B/1726